FIRST SKIRMISH

"Hello, the house!" John shouted, his voice carrying clearly in the cold air.

"What do you want, Barrone?"

"To talk. How about it?"

"Talk about what?"

"Your staying alive."

"We're alive."

"Don't be a fool. You can't get out. You're trapped. We can bring that house down around you anytime we like."

"You say! We got people comin' to help us. You're the ones is gonna die."

"You're doing great, John," Jenny said, working with something that looked a lot like Silly Putty. "Keep it up."

John ignored her sarcasm. "I'll make a deal with you!" John shouted. "You give up your labs and dope dealing and you all can walk out of here."

"Ride out," Jenny corrected. "On their stupid-looking motorcycles."

"You go to hell, Barrone!"

"Told you," Jenny said.

John ignored her. "This is the last offer you're getting," he called. "Take it or die. The choice is yours."

A wild chorus of shouts and profanity was the bikers' answer.

John sat down and looked at Jenny.

She smiled at him. "Now we go to work, Boss."

BOOK YOUR PLACE ON OUR WEBSITE
AND MAKE THE
READING CONNECTION!

We've created a customized website just for our very special readers, where you can get the inside scoop on everything that's going on with Zebra, Pinnacle and Kensington books.

When you come online, you'll have the exciting opportunity to:

- View covers of upcoming books
- Read sample chapters
- Learn about our future publishing schedule (listed by publication month *and author*)
- Find out when your favorite authors will be visiting a city near you
- Search for and order backlist books from our online catalog
- Check out author bios and background information
- Send e-mail to your favorite authors
- Meet the Kensington staff online
- Join us in weekly chats with authors, readers and other guests
- Get writing guidelines
- AND MUCH MORE!

Visit our website at
http://www.pinnaclebooks.com

CODE NAME: SURVIVAL

WILLIAM W. JOHNSTONE

PINNACLE BOOKS
KENSINGTON PUBLISHING CORP.

http://www.pinnaclebooks.com

PINNACLE BOOKS are published by

Kensington Publishing Corp.
850 Third Avenue
New York, NY 10022

First Printing: October, 2000
10 9 8 7 6 5 4 3 2 1

Printed in the United States of America

Well, if I called the wrong number, why did you answer the phone?

James Thurber

ONE

Lincoln, Nebraska

"So how long do we hang around here?" Jenny asked after listening to the verbal change in orders.

John Barrone, the leader of the team, shrugged his shoulders. "Until Control gives us new orders?"

"What happened to the assignment in the Northwest?" Al Durstman, the former FBI agent, asked.

"They didn't say. Only that we sit tight and wait for new orders."

"I don't mind it a bit," Don Yee said. "The steaks are great here."

"You're a bottomless pit, as my mother used to say," John replied with a smile.

"I'll never deny it," Don said.

The team had left New York City immediately after the final shoot-out with the terrorists in a side-street bar. All the experts agreed that it would not be the last terrorist attack on a U.S. city. But there was not much authorities could do to prevent terrorists from attacking, not without stepping all over the rights of law-abiding citizens, certainly not if the terrorists were prepared to die for their "cause."

The team was made up of men and women from

various government and civilian law enforcement and intelligence agencies. They had been checked out very carefully concerning their views on just about everything, especially how best to deal with violent, hardcore criminals.

All the team members agreed that in many cases the legal punishment, if any, was not adequate for the crimes committed.

So they now were working for the law, but operating far outside the law.

The team had unlimited funds, unlimited equipment; one phone call could get them anything they wanted to do the job, usually within hours.

Now they were waiting for a job.

"All the damn crime in this country, you would think an assignment would be easy," Jenny groused.

Jenny Barnes had spent eight years with the FBI. She was an explosives expert. Blond hair, blue eyes, and very cute. A gymnast in college. Jenny could, at times, cut loose with a string of profanity that would make a Marine D.I. blush.

"Why don't we go out to a local redneck bar and start a fight," Don Yee suggested, trying to keep a straight face. "That would certainly liven up the evening."

Don was a martial-arts expert who once took out three very large men who were needling him about his size (five feet six inches tall).

John gave Don a very stern look.

"Just kidding, Boss," Don said.

Don was a ten-year veteran of the CIA.

"My dad was a redneck, you midget Oriental asshole," Jenny said to her teammate, adding an uplifted middle finger to her statement.

Don grinned at her, returning the rigid digit.

John sighed as Jenny and Don both laughed at the exchange.

John Barrone was fifty years old, the oldest member of the team, retired from the CIA after a long and distinguished career. He was from old New England stock—Boston upper crust—and could be a bit on the stuffy side . . . although Jenny could usually break through that veneer very quickly.

The team had a row of connecting rooms at a motel just off the Interstate. The weather had turned rotten, with cold temperatures and a hard rain.

"Maybe they'll send us to Paris," Linda Marsh said. "I've never been there and I've heard it's just beautiful."

Tall, shapely and beautiful, Linda was a nine-year veteran of the Los Angeles P.D. She had left as a detective sergeant. She was thirty years old.

"I don't care where they send us as long as it isn't back to New York City," Mike Rojas said just as he was leaving the motel room. "I think we've all taken a big enough bite out of the Big Apple."

Mike was a former enforcement officer with the IRS, a job he had come to hate. He was born and reared in South Texas and was thirty years old.

"I sure agree with that," Al Durstman said.

"I hate Hawaii," Lana Brewer said. "But I do love seasons. Maybe Maine."

Lana was in her midthirties, a former member of the Bureau of Alcohol, Tobacco, and Firearms.

"Maine!" Chris Farmer blurted out. "Good God. They have two seasons up there: July and winter."

Chris was twenty-seven years old and the youngest member of the team. He was six feet four inches tall and 220 pounds. A former sniper with the FBI.

"I'll just settle for someplace warm and dry," Bob Garrett said.

Robert "Bob" Garrett had come to the team from NSA, the National Security Agency. He was in his mid-forties.

"I'll second that," Paul Brewer said. "At least the dry part."

Paul was African-American. Forty years old and a former member of the Border Patrol.

All of the team members were either single or divorced. Several had children, but no immediate family member knew what they really did for a living. Very few people in the world were privy to that knowledge.

Control had set John up in a security business that was real and functional, right down to the business cards each team member carried. And each carried a federal firearms permit, authorizing them to carry concealed weapons, all types. How Control had managed that was a mystery to John, but he knew not to ask questions. In addition, each had been given an I.D. card, with picture, issued by the National Security Agency. And it was real and valid. Even Bob had no idea how Control had managed to do that.

"Some people very highly placed in government are involved in this," the former NSA man had opined.

"You bet they are," John had agreed. "And I don't want to know who."

The team now waited in Lincoln, resting, reading, talking, playing cards, watching TV. Killing time.

On the afternoon of the third day, the phone rang in John's room. The message was very short. John hung up the receiver and stood for a moment, a puzzled look on his face.

"What's up?" Jenny asked, standing in the doorway that connected the two rooms.

"I think we've just received word on our next assignment," John replied.

"You think?"

John smiled. "You know how the Mossad gets their assignments, Jenny?"

"No."

"The Prime Minister walks into a room, points to a spot on a map, and says, 'We have a problem there.' Or words to that effect. Then the PM leaves the room."

"Cuts down on paperwork, I suppose."

"Indeed it does. And lets everyone except the agents off the hook."

"And that's the sort of message you just received?"

"Yes. Get the others in here, will you, Jenny?"

The team gathered in John's room, several rubbing sleep from their eyes. Don Yee looked at Al and said with a smile, "Ancient Chinese philosopher say one should only rub one's eyes with one's elbows, Al."

"Ancient Chinese philosopher is probably right," Al replied. "But since you grew up on cheeseburgers and John Wayne movies, be quiet."

Don rubbed his stomach. "Speaking of cheeseburgers . . ."

"Later," John said. "I think we have our assignment."

"You think?" Lana asked.

"I just got a strange message from Control. So get packed up. We're pulling out."

"Where are we going?" Paul asked.

"I'm not sure," John said with a grin. "I think that is being left up to me."

"Oh, good," Linda said, returning the smile. "I knew it would be Paris."

"However, we'll stop in New Mexico on the way," John said.

"New Mexico?" Bob said. "What the hell is in New Mexico?"

"Outlaw bikers and drugs. Get packed up. We're out of here."

TWO

The team pulled out within the hour, in new Ford, four-wheel drive SUVs. The big Expeditions were the team's favorite vehicles, and that information had been passed along to Control—whoever Control was and wherever he, or they, might be located. Somewhere around Washington, D.C., John guessed.

The team stopped shortly after dark and spent the night at a motel in Kansas. There, John called in to further clarify the team's orders.

"Outlaw bikers have long dabbled in drugs, John," Control told him. "You'll soon know all the names. But this group of bikers doesn't even have a name."

"Are they that new?"

"Meaning have they just been formed?"

"Yes."

"The information we've got, so far, is that they're breakaways from a dozen or so biker gangs. They brought with them all the information the host gangs had concerning buyers and distributors and so forth."

"I'm surprised the other gangs didn't start a war."

"Oh, they did. A very quiet and very violent one that attracted no attention from the press. But they gave it up very quickly."

"Why?"

"Some very prominent businesspeople in the South-west are backing the breakaway bikers. Those same people own the local radio stations, television stations, and newspapers. You'll be receiving a full report via computer."

"I see. Money talks."

"It swears, as the saying goes."

"Suppose, just for the sake of argument, the monied people get in our way while we're busting up this dope ring?"

"That would prove to be very foolish and very tragic . . . for them."

"I understand."

"I hope so." Control broke the connection.

John looked at the humming receiver for a few seconds, then slowly hung up. "Thanks so much, you insufferable jerk."

"You and Control really have a love/hate relationship, don't you?" Jenny said. She had plopped down on the side of the bed while John was talking.

"Control can be very irritating at times."

"So what's the skinny?"

"We break up a dope ring."

"What kind of dope?"

"Control didn't say. He said we would receive further information via computer."

"What part of New Mexico are we heading for?"

John shrugged. "I don't know. He didn't say."

"You get the impression Control is putting this together as we speak?"

John nodded. "It would certainly appear so."

"I would like to point out that outlaw bikers are not known for their kind and gentle ways."

"That, Jenny, my dear, is what is called a classic understatement."

"So let's call in for some supplies. Maybe a minigun,

a PUFF, some rocket launchers, perhaps a couple of platoons of Marines . . ."

"Get serious, kiddo."

"We ditched most of our heavier weapons back in New Jersey, remember?"

"We'll be supplied before we reach our objective, you can be assured of that."

"You ever worked a case involving outlaw bikers, John?" Paul asked, walking in from the adjoining room.

John waved him to a chair. "I have no experience with bikers of any kind."

"Mean bunch of bastards and bitches," Paul said, settling down in the chair.

"The women can be as mean as the men, or meaner," Jenny said. "And before you misunderstand"—she held up a hand—"we're talking about your real outlaw bikers here, not your weekend riders who like to dress up in leather and ride around."

"We had a lot of trouble with outlaw bikers on the border," Paul observed. "And there's not much backup in them. Hurt one, and you've got the whole bunch to fight."

"A lot of info coming in on 'puter," Don said, sticking his head in the room.

"Print it out," John told him. "A copy for us all. I want everyone to be familiar with what we're getting into."

"Will do, Boss."

Linda had walked into the room and caught part of the conversation. "I don't have any use at all for outlaw bikers. I've tangled with them on several occasions."

"Obviously, you won," Jenny remarked.

"I wouldn't have if I hadn't had a shotgun in my hands. And they knew I'd use it."

"How did they know that?" Paul asked.

John already knew the answer from reading Linda's dossier.

"Because I blew the legs out from under one biker a few years back," Linda said flatly. "Then I stuck the muzzle into his partner's mouth, breaking off several teeth in the process, and asked him if wanted his fucking head blown off."

"Did he?" Jenny asked.

"He respectfully declined."

"But that wasn't the end of it, was it?"

The former LAPD sergeant shook her head. "No. The biker gangs have so many contacts in so many different areas, the friends of the one I killed and the one I arrested—who, by the way, was released on a goddamn technicality—somehow got my phone number and the threats began. It was a nightmare that lasted for several years. I cannot adequately describe the events. They threatened my boyfriend until we broke up over it. He finally moved out of state. They threatened my parents and my relatives. My mother suffered a breakdown. Then they killed my dog, Sally: my loving companion for ten years. It was horrible." She paused for a moment to take several deep breaths and calm herself. "I swore that someday I'd kill every one of those goddamn bikers responsible for the misery and pain they caused, and as I stand here today in front of witnesses, I swear before God, I will find them and I will kill every goddamn one of them." She spun around and walked out of the room.

No one said anything for several seconds after Linda left the room. Finally, John cleared his throat.

"Well, we now know how Linda feels about outlaw bikers."

"Without a doubt," Jenny said. "And I feel the same way."

"You have a story about outlaw bikers?" Paul asked.

"Yeah. But I'll save it for later. Suffice it to say, I have absolutely no use for any of them." She rose from the side of the bed. "I think I'll go see about Linda."

"Let's each get a copy of the printouts and start learning something about outlaw bikers," John suggested.

"I know this much about the true outlaw biker," Paul stated.

"Oh?"

"I don't like them," the former Border Patrol officer said. "And society would be better off if they were all dead."

"I'll keep that in mind," John said.

"Perhaps you should."

"According to this, the biker labs for making the dope are all over parts of three states," Al said, looking up from reading the report.

"Methamphetamine. Speed," Linda put in. "And that date-rape crap too."

"They're shipping it all over the United States," Chris said. "And some of it is bad."

"A number of kids have been hospitalized and some have died after taking these drugs," Bob said. "Yet the labs keep pumping out deadly product."

"The reason they're still in business, and growing, is the bikers seem to have intimidated a lot of otherwise good people into silence and inaction," Lana said.

"I understand how that works." Linda spat out the words as if they were leaving a bad taste on her tongue. "I've seen it firsthand."

John slipped out of the room, leaving the team members to talk among themselves. He stepped outside to stand for a moment in the cold winter air.

John had worked the international scene for most of his CIA career and knew very little about outlaw motorcycle gangs, but he knew he was about to find out more than he wanted to know about them. What he did not understand was how and why the local authorities allowed them to flourish.

He turned as the door opened and Jenny stepped out to stand beside him. "I'm glad you put on a coat. It's chilly out here," he said.

"Feels good. At least for a few minutes. John?"

"Yes?"

"You don't know much about outlaw bikers, do you?"

"I'm afraid not, Jenny."

"Vicious bunch of people. Cruel."

"After listening to the team talk, I'm beginning to believe they're capable of anything."

"They are. And they've done it too. I've seen pictures of some of their victims. I felt like puking."

"This bunch seems to be into everything that's illegal. Rape, kidnapping, murder, extortion, and more."

"This gang is the absolute dregs of society. We'll be tangling with the worst of the worst."

"Interesting way of putting it."

Linda pushed open the door and stepped outside. "Talking about the outlaw bikers?"

"Yes," Jenny said.

"Rotten assholes," Linda hissed.

"A lot of hate in you, Linda."

Before Linda could respond, Jenny spoke up. "John, you'll understand much better after we've talked with some of their victims. That is, if they'll talk to us. And that is one big if. Most of them will just slam the phone down or shut the door in our faces."

"It's difficult for me to believe the authorities would allow this type of gang thing to go on. Even more difficult for me to accept is why the citizens haven't done anything about it."

"Fear," Linda said. "The citizens really aren't allowed to protect themselves, their loved ones, their property. It's no myth that criminals have more rights than the law-abiding."

"That is the very reason we exist," John said.

"We're going to earn our money on this op, John," Jenny told him.

"And I have another suggestion," Linda said. "No one works alone."

"All right," John replied. "We'll partner up. If that's what the others want."

"Those who have worked with gang units will want to," Linda said, a grimness in her voice.

"You and me, John," Jenny was quick to say.

"All right."

"The rest of us will work it out," Linda said. "I'll bring it up right now." She pulled open the door and stepped into the corridor. The door hissed shut.

"She's edgy about this assignment," John remarked.

"She has plenty of reasons to be edgy. She's seen firsthand what these scum are capable of doing."

"I'm sorry to say I haven't."

"And you don't think they're as bad as we say?"

"You paint a terrible picture, Jenny."

Jenny smiled in the cold wind. "Don't ever turn your back on any of these bastards or bitches, John. Don't let them know your parents or any brothers and sisters are still alive or where your kids live."

"I'll know more about them when all of the report comes in."

"Yes, you will," Jenny said. "And you'll know even more the first time we make contact with them. If you can stand the smell, that is." She turned and went back inside the motel.

"It appears I have a lot to learn about what is taking place in the United States," John muttered to the cold wind.

The side door pushed open and Don Yee stepped out. "More coming in on the outlaw bikers, Boss. It's bigger and nastier than Control first thought."

"All right, Don. Tell me, what do you think we need in the way of supplies for this op?"

Don smiled. "How about a battalion of Marines?"

THREE

The team split up as soon as they approached the New Mexico border. They would gradually work their way south, gathering intelligence along the way. They would stay in touch by cell phone and computer. At the state border, they picked up several crates of supplies from a truck at a rest area.

Jenny and Al rode with John. Don Yee, Linda, and Paul rode in the second car. Bob, Mike, Chris, and Lana were in the third unit.

John and those riding with him would head straight down through the center of the state. The second team would take the western part of the state, the third team the eastern part. The first linkup would be in Albuquerque, unless plans changed.

In the extreme northern part of the state, John stopped in a small town just off Highway 285. "Mrs. Carlos Sanchez lives here. Her daughter was missing for almost a year. She turned up a few months ago and refused to tell police where she'd been."

Al was in the backseat of the SUV, reading the report on Maria Sanchez. "A few months shy of her fifteenth birthday when she vanished. She's just celebrated her sixteenth." He looked at her picture for a few seconds. "What a beautiful girl."

"That was taken just before she disappeared," Jenny

said. "Look at the recent picture attached to the inside of the back folder."

"Jesus Christ!" Al said. "Looks like she's aged ten years."

"A California private investigator who was working on the case was killed last year," John said. "His body was found just north and west of Yuma. Just across the state line."

"Beaten to death," Jenny said.

"Yeah," Al replied. "I'm reading about that. Stomped to death. Typical outlaw biker method."

"Where do we start?" Jenny asked.

"We're licensed security experts and investigators," John said. "Our cover is rock solid. We talk first to the sheriff of the county and see what he's got."

"And if he's willing to share it with a bunch of outsiders," Al said.

"We'll know in a few minutes," John replied. "There's the courthouse." He pulled into the parking lot and found a parking space.

"Pretty town," Jenny said.

John cut the engine. "Let's go to work, people."

Sheriff Morales looked at the business cards and each person's I.D. Then he tossed everything on his desk, sighed, and leaned back in his chair. "Let me guess, folks. You're here about the Sanchez girl, right?"

"That's it, Sheriff," John said.

"Officially, the case is still open. Unofficially, it's closed."

"Why closed?" Jenny asked.

Morales smiled. "Have you talked with the girl or her family?"

"Not yet."

"I can't stop you from investigating. That's your

right. So you'll know when you talk with them . . . if they'll talk to you, that is. But the odds are pretty good they'll slam the door in your face."

"Scared?" John said.

"Terrified is a better word."

"And the people who frightened them into silence?"

"Long gone from here." Morales leaned forward and put his elbows on the desk. He met John's eyes. "There are no dope labs around here, people. None. There were at one time, I'll sure admit that. But we busted them up and sent those sorry bastards and their whores packing. I can't say the same for the surrounding areas—and that includes remote parts of this county—and I'm sorry to have to tell you that. But this area is clean."

"No outlaw bikers?" Jenny asked.

Morales shook his head. "None. At least not in this immediate area. We rousted them. Every time they broke the law." He smiled. "And it was all done legally. They moved out."

"To the surrounding communities."

"Unfortunately, yes.

"You must have really put the heat on them," Al remarked.

"We did," Morales said flatly. "And we did it hard and often. But as I said, for the most part, legally."

John smiled. "I like that 'for the most part.' "

The sheriff returned the smile. "They decided not to file any harassment suits."

John stood up and held out his hand to the sheriff. "Thanks for your cooperation, Sheriff. Believe me when I say it's much appreciated."

Morales rose from his chair, hesitated for a heartbeat, and took John's hand. "No problem, Mr. Barrone. Glad to help out. And I wish you luck. I've been sheriff here for a long time. I've met a lot of P.I.'s, but I have to say that you people just don't fit the bill. I don't really know what you are. And to tell you the truth, I don't much care, as long as you're not some damn civil rights lawyers coming in here to make trouble for me and my people."

John laughed at that. "I assure you, we're not here to make any trouble for you."

Morales stared at John for a few seconds. His dark eyes were unreadable. "I guess I'll just have to take your word for that. You checked into a motel yet?"

"No. Not yet."

The sheriff named a motel. "It's a nice one. Serves good food too."

"We'll try it. Thanks for your help, Sheriff."

The motel was very nice. Not the largest one in town, but very comfortable and the staff was friendly.

"Let's go see the Sanchez girl," John said, after they had dumped their luggage in their rooms.

"I picked up a map of the town," Al said. "The Sanchez family lives right on the edge."

"Let's go.

"Get out of here and leave us alone," Mrs. Sanchez said. She slammed the door in John's face.

John politely knocked on the front door again. "Mrs. Sanchez?" he called. "We're not here to cause trouble for you. We've spoken with Sheriff Morales. We told him we were coming out to see you."

"I got nothing to say to you!"

"We're staying out at the Rio Motel, Mrs. Sanchez. In case you change your mind."

"I won't!"

"As you wish, Mrs. Sanchez."

"Damn it, Mama!" another voice yelled from inside the house. "It's my life!"

"Wait a minute," John said to Jenny and Al. "We might get to see the girl after all."

"It's me and your papa's life too!" the mother yelled.

The front door was abruptly jerked open and Maria faced the three team members. "Come on in," the young lady said. "Whoever you are."

"Independent investigators, miss," John told her. "And thank you."

Seated in the neat living room, Mrs. Sanchez glared at the three for a moment, then shrugged her shoulders. "Well, you're here, for better or worse. Probably worse. You want some coffee?"

"If it would be no trouble, that would be nice, Mrs. Sanchez," John said.

"No trouble making the coffee. The trouble comes when Maria tells you her story. I'll be right back." She walked out of the room.

"So what do you want to know?" Maria asked, sitting down in front of the small fireplace.

"Where were you during your disappearance?" Jenny asked.

"All over the place," Maria replied. "Los Angeles, Seattle, San Francisco."

"Doing what?" Al asked.

"Gettin' fucked mostly," Maria answered nonchalantly. "In ways none of you could ever imagine."

"By whom?" John asked, doing his best to hide his surprise at the girl's crude language.

"Bikers, at first. Then I was sold out as a whore to anyone who had the money. Usually to older men who had a hangup about assholes."

John blinked a couple of times. Cleared his throat. "You want to explain that, Maria?"

"What's to explain? They screwed me up the ass. Sometimes I took on five guys at a time."

"Five guys!" Jenny blurted out.

"Yeah. It was for money. A whole room full of people, men and women, would pay to see it. Two men, usually bikers, would double-team me. You know, one in the regular way, the other in the back door, while I was suckin' a third one off and jackin' off the other two."

John rose, walked over to a window, and stared out, doing his best to regain his shaken composure. He turned to face Maria. "Are you telling the truth, Maria?"

"How could I make up something like that?" she challenged him.

"Good question," John muttered.

"And why would I?" Maria added.

"Another good point," John said.

"Were you drugged, Maria?" Al asked.

"At first, yeah. For a couple of months. When I would get my head on straight—I mean, when the drugs would begin to wear off—I'd try to get away. They'd beat me. You can only take so much of that. Then they threatened to kill me if I tried to escape again." She sighed and shrugged. "I figured what the hell. I was alive. I would wait and maybe get a better chance to get free. When it came, I took it."

"But you won't identify your kidnappers or testify against then," John said.

"No way. I've seen what these people can and will do. I've seen their victims and I know how much power these dudes have. As long as I keep my mouth shut, me and Mama and Daddy will stay alive."

"But you agreed to talk to us now," Jenny said.

"But I didn't tell you anything you can use in court," Maria said with a smile.

"You said you saw some of their victims. What did you mean?" John asked.

"I saw them, and then I never saw them again. I heard the bikers talkin', that's all."

"These victims, they're dead?" Al asked.

"Dead and cold as a hammer, man. Buried where they'll never be found."

"In the desert?" Jenny asked.

"Everywhere, lady. Some of them was cut up in a dozen pieces with a chain saw. I *saw* that personally . . . just once. That was enough. They made me watch it. I was sick for a couple of days. Believe me, I got the message."

Mrs. Sanchez came in with the coffee, and for a moment there was silence in the living room as the team members creamed and sugared their coffee.

John took a sip and said, "You won't testify but you're telling us all this now. How do you know we're not wearing a wire, Maria?"

"I don't. But my folks are plannin' a move out of this area. Never mind when or where. It's soon. So I know they'll be all right."

"How about you?"

"I don't matter no more."

"Why?" John pressed.

"I'm dying of AIDS, man. There ain't any hope for me. No big deal. I've accepted it; I've done my cryin'."

"I'm sorry, Maria."

"So am I."

"Feel like answering a few more questions?"

"Sure. As long as it's off the record."

"It is. I promise you that."

"All right. I'll take your word for it. It's time, I guess, for me to say something."

"But not to Sheriff Morales?" Jenny asked.

"No. He's too straight-arrow. He's law and order right down the line."

"You think he's a good man?" Al asked.

"Oh, yeah. Always has been. So are his kids. I went to school with them from the first grade on. But he sees things in black and white only, if you know what I mean. You couldn't buy Sheriff Morales with a million dollars."

John nodded his head in understanding. He had gotten the same impression about Morales. He was straight to a fault. "It isn't just bikers involved in this, is it?"

"Naw. There's all sorts of people mixed up in this mess. Money people. Big shots, I guess you'd call them. Millions of dollars to be made in dope. And you should have seen the people who came out to see me gettin' screwed by those heavy-hung guys. You could tell some of them were rich folks. But your bikers, now, most bikers are pretty decent people. They just have a different way of life, that's all. Your true outlaw biker, that's another story."

"The group that grabbed you . . . why did they kidnap you?" Jenny asked.

Maria shrugged her shoulders. "Who knows? I never did know the answer to that."

"For kicks?" Al asked.

"That's as good as anything, I suppose." She looked at each team member. "Who are you people really? You're not cops. I can tell that."

"Independent investigators, Maria," John told her. "We have no legal standing."

"You're not from the state?"

"No."

"Or from the government?"

"No."

"That's wild, man. Anything else?"

"Yes. Where are the people who grabbed you?"

Maria smiled. "All over. They got it covered from here to California."

"In this county?" Jenny asked.

"Naw . . . not much goin' on here. Sheriff Morales won't put up with it. I told you, he's tough."

"The people who grabbed you, they have no club name?"

"I never heard one. I don't think they do. They come from all over. And I mean that. Some was from as far away as New Jersey."

"A mixed bag," Al said.

"Yeah. A bag of shit."

Mrs. Sanchez shook her head at her daughter's language. "She didn't used to talk like that. She came home with a foul mouth. She used to be such a good girl. Worked hard at our church. Now she won't even go."

Maria's expression didn't change, showing a total indifference to what her mother thought about her.

"But a few of the bikers associated with those who grabbed you are in this county?" John said, pressing on.

"I've said all I'm going to say," Maria answered, standing up. "Probably said too much, but hey, what the hell? I don't have that much to lose now." She walked out of the room without so much as a backward glance.

"She's got a lot of demons to fight," Jenny said. "And that tough act is just that, an act, I believe."

"You think so?" Mrs. Sanchez asked.

"Yes. A lot of it."

"I wasn't at first, but now I'm glad she told you all that she did," Mrs. Sanchez said. "But I wouldn't have let her tell Sheriff Morales."

"Why is that, ma'am?" Al asked.

"Could he protect us night and day forever? No." The woman shook her head. "No, he couldn't. But I will tell you this, knowing that you are not from the police. My husband is a Vietnam veteran. A Marine. Two tours over there, in combat. If those outlaw biker criminals come back, we have guns in this house and we will use them."

"I'm sure you will, ma'am," John said. "Just be sure your life is being threatened when you do." He stood up. "Thank you for your time and thank Maria for being honest with us. We won't tell Sheriff Morales about this conversation."

"If he asks you, tell him everything Maria told you," she surprised them all by saying. "Don't try to lie to that man. You can't. He has the gift."

"The gift?" Jenny asked.

"Yes." She smiled. "Not really. But he's hard to lie to."

"I would imagine so," John said. "I certainly got that impression. Well, thank you, Mrs. Sanchez. We'll be around for a few days. We're staying out at the Rio Motel if you need to get in touch with us."

"You told me already. Thank you. I will call you if I think of anything or if I need your help."

"Do that, ma'am. If the bikers come around bothering you, please call us."

"Believe me, I will."

John drove around for about an hour after leaving the Sanchez house. The county was dotted with small towns, none with more than a few thousand in population, most of them no more than a few miles apart.

"Look up there," Al said. He was sitting in the front seat, Jenny in the back.

"Well, now," John said. "Look at the bikes."

"And not a rice-burner in the bunch," Jenny said as John slowed down and they all got a better look.

"By that rather racist remark I assume you are referring to Japanese-made motorcycles?" John asked.

"Right. That's how a lot of Harley riders refer to them."

"How quaint," John said drily.

"You guys want a beer?" Jenny asked.

"In there?" Al asked. "In that joint?"

"Sure, I'm dry," Jenny said.

"Oh, why not?" John said, turning into the parking lot.

"Lord help us all," Al muttered.

FOUR

The honky-tonk went silent when the trio entered, except for the blaring of the jukebox. A dozen or so men and a half dozen women, all dressed in jeans and leather, stopped what they were doing to stare at John, Jenny, and Al.

"What a lovely-looking crowd," Al muttered.

Jenny led them to a table next to a wall and the three sat down.

The crowd continued to stare at them in silence.

After receiving a nearly imperceptible nod from the man behind the bar, a woman finally walked over to the trio and said, "You folks need something?"

"A beer for me," Jenny said.

"Whiskey and water," Al said.

John smiled faintly. "Vodka martini on the rocks, with olives."

The woman looked at him, then called, "Hey, Sonny, we got a real class act here. Man wants a vodka martini, on the rocks with olives."

"Well, la-dee-da," a man sitting a few tables away said. "Don't he think he's something?"

It was exactly what John felt would happen, which was why he'd ordered the martini. He met the speaker's eyes and said, "You have a problem with that?"

"I might have," the man said. "You think you too good to drink beer like the rest of us?"

"As far as I'm concerned they can pour it all back into the horse who pissed it out."

Jenny arched an eyebrow. This wasn't like the very proper and usually cautious team leader.

Al's right hand suddenly disappeared from sight. He unbuttoned his coat, making his pistol in a shoulder holster easier to grab.

"You sayin' I drink piss?" the biker asked.

"I'm saying I don't care for a beer at this time," John told him. "I'm also saying that what I drink is none of your damned business."

Whoa! Jenny thought. John was definitely stepping out of character.

"I'm makin' it my business," the biker replied.

"Obviously," John said. "But the reason for that escapes me."

"You folks don't belong in here," Sonny, the bartender, called. "Why don't you just leave?"

"It's a public bar, isn't it?" John asked.

"Yeah, it is."

"Have we created any sort of disturbance that would warrant you asking that we leave?"

"No. But one is damn sure coming."

"Be that as it may, we won't be the ones to instigate it."

"Talks kinda hoity-toity too," another man said from the end of the room.

"A resident from the country of cretin has spoken," John said.

"The country of what?" another biker asked.

"Cretin," yet another biker said. "Means stupid."

Boots hit the floor hard. The biker whom John had

referred to as a cretin stood up. "You callin' me stupid, asshole?"

"There is an old saying about if the shoe fits," John replied.

"You just bought yourself a whole lot of whup-ass, mister," the biker told him.

Sonny reacted to the ringing of the phone, picked up the receiver, and listened for a couple of seconds. He hung up and said, "Griz, cool it."

"Who says so?" the biker called Griz said.

"Benny."

Griz looked at the bartender for a few seconds, then sat down. "All right."

"Somebody's been watching our every move," Jenny whispered.

John and Al nodded their agreement.

"How about those drinks, Sonny?" John called.

"Comin' right up, mister."

The big, bearded biker called Griz walked over to the bar and talked with Sonny for a few seconds, then walked out the door. Half a dozen other bikers and three of their women followed him out.

The jukebox became silent after the last selection played. Mercifully quiet, John thought.

All but two of the other bikers and all their women walked out of the saloon, and within seconds the outside air was ripped with the sounds of motorcycles cranking up. Then it became quiet as the bikers roared away into the early afternoon.

The waitress brought the drinks and carefully set them on the table, took the bill from John, then backed away quickly.

"Keep the change," John told her.

"Thanks." She walked back to the bar.

"Strong drinks," Al muttered after taking a sip. "Has an odd taste."

"Don't drink it," John warned softly.

Al pushed his drink away. Jenny looked at her mug of draft beer and pushed it away.

John shifted his gaze to the bartender. Sonny refused to meet his eyes. After a moment, John motioned to the waitress. She wandered over.

"Bring us three bottles of beer," John said. "Unopened."

"Unopened?" she questioned.

"Yes."

"Okay."

She was back in a minute and sat three bottles of unopened beer on the table. John gave her a twenty dollar bill.

"I'll bring your change," she said.

"Keep it."

"A twenty for three beers?"

"Yes."

"Hey, thanks, man."

Jenny dug in her purse and came out with a complicated knife that looked as though it could do everything, including calculus. She opened the bottles of beer.

"That's a neat knife," the waitress said.

"Comes in handy," Jenny replied.

"I bet. Looks like you'd have to have a college degree to work it. You folks just passin' through?"

"Yes," John told her. "You lived around here all your life?"

"Naw. I come in last year from California with my old man. He lost it on a curve a few months later and was killed. I started workin' here."

"You enjoy working here?" Jenny asked.

"Beats a jab in the ass with a sharp stick, I guess."

"All the bikers that just left live around here?" Jenny asked.

"Naw. Well . . . some of them. Most live up in the hills."

"Big club," Al said.

"I guess."

"What's the name of the club?" John asked.

"It don't got a name. Them guys come from all over."

"Carrie," the bartender called. "Got glasses to wash."

"Okay, Sonny." She wandered off.

"Not exactly a candidate for intellectual of the year," Jenny observed.

John smiled. "No. But she's talkative. That's something we need to remember."

Jenny took a swig of beer. "Well, the beer's good. But I'm not familiar with this brand."

John pushed his bottle toward her. "You can have this one too."

"Mine too," Al said.

"No thanks, guys. This one will do. Any more and I'll have to head for the ladies' room, and I got a feeling the one in this joint might not be suitable for human usage."

"Let's get out of here," John suggested. "I think we've all seen enough."

"With great relief," Al said. "I thought for a minute we might have to shoot our way out. And that might upset Sheriff Morales."

Standing outside the juke joint, breathing in the cold air and enjoying the fresh scent, for the joint had smelled rather gamy, John said, "Speaking of the sheriff, I want Control to run a comprehensive background check on him. I have a few questions about Sheriff Morales."

"Oh?" Jenny arched an eyebrow. "Well now, let me guess, John. Morales's statements about those responsible for Maria's kidnapping being long gone from here, there being no dope labs anywhere except the remote parts of his county, and there being no outlaw bikers around here?"

"Bingo, kiddo!"

"If those weren't outlaw bikers in that stinking joint, I never saw any," Al said. "And unfortunately, I have dealt with a few from time to time during my years with the Bureau."

"And did you notice anything else?" John asked, his eyes moving from Al to Jenny and back.

"They were all ugly," Jenny said. "And a lot of the women weren't wearing bras."

"They were sort of sagging," Al said, smiling. "I did notice that."

"No club insignia on their jackets," John said. "Yet they all left together, as one unit."

"And who is Benny?" Jenny asked. "Obviously he's the head honcho."

"We'll find out what we can about Benny and that ape called Griz," John said.

"How about the barmaid?" Al asked. "Carrie probably knows a lot more than she realizes."

"Yes. We can work on her. She might be able to tell us something. And we'll find out who owns the license for this joint. We've got a starting place, so let's get on it."

"Sonny is watching us," Al said after a quick glance toward the front windows of the bar.

"Let's head back to town," John replied. "We can make some calls on the way."

Several motorcycles rumbled by, the riders and their women behind them giving the trio some hard looks. One of the women gave the rigid digit.

Jenny returned the gesture.

John sighed.

"Fuck you!" one of the men yelled, giving the trio another middle finger.

The riders made a quick U-turn in the road and returned, rolling into the parking lot. They cut their engines and glared at John and Al and Jenny.

"Me and my boys is about a half minute away from puttin' a king-sized ass-whuppin' on this cunt and you pricks," one extremely ugly biker said.

"That would be a very stupid thing for you and your boys to try," John told him.

"There won't be no tryin' to it, old man," another biker said, looking at John's gray hair. "You dudes got to learn not to come sneakin' around stickin' your noses in things that don't concern you."

"And what might those *things* be?" John asked.

"You know."

Al looked at John. "Now we get to play children's guessing games."

"Not for long," John replied. "I'm in no mood for idiotic games."

"Yeah," Jenny said. "Me neither. Besides, it's getting cold out here."

"It's damn sure hot in hell, bitch!" one of the outlaw women said.

"Oh, my Lord," Jenny said. "That observation positively reeks of originality. Do you mind if I use that in conversation sometime?"

"You 'bout a smart-assed bitch, ain't you?" the woman said right back.

"Who, me?" Jenny replied with mock surprise.

"Why . . . heavens, no! How could you possibly think that? Why . . . I'm deeply offended by that remark."

The motorcycle mama stepped closer to Jenny and balled her hands into fists. "I think, bitch, I'll just jack your jaw all out of shape."

"And while she's doing that," her main man said to John, "I'm gonna be kickin' your uppity ass all over this parkin' lot."

Before the situation could reach the physical point, a sheriff's department car roared into the driveway and slid to a halt in a cloud of dust. Sheriff Morales stepped out.

"Good afternoon, Sheriff," John said to the county's top law enforcement officer. "How nice of you to stop by."

"Mr. Barrone," Morales said. "What's the problem here?"

"No problem at all. We were just having a conversation."

"Is that right?" He looked at the bikers. "Who in the hell are you people?"

"Back off, Sheriff," one of the bikers said. "We ain't done nothin.' "

Morales stepped closer until his nose was about three inches away from the biker's. "Don't tell me to back off, you bastard! I asked you a question and by God I expect an answer. You understand that?"

"I hear you."

"Good. Now what is your name?"

"Jimmy Cisco."

"And your business here?"

"Visiting friends."

"What friends?"

"Buddies of mine."

"That doesn't tell me a thing. What's your buddy's name?"

"Benny Ballinger."

"Benny doesn't live around here. He left several months ago."

"He come back."

Morales stepped back a few feet, a strange expression on his face. "Where's he staying?"

"Vista Road."

"Is that right?"

"Yeah. Can we go? We ain't done nothin'."

Morales looked at John. "You want to file a complaint?"

"No. No harm done here."

Morales looked at Cisco. "Take off. But if I ever catch you or your bunch bothering decent people again, I'll run your asses into a cell faster than you can blink. Understood?"

"Yeah." Cisco and his bunch cranked up and roared off.

When the roaring had faded away, John asked, "You know this Ballinger person?"

"Unfortunately, yes. He's a world of trouble. I ran him out of the county months ago."

"We almost had trouble in the joint with a bunch of bikers. Then the bartender answered the phone, listened, and said this Benny person wanted the bikers to back off. The ringleader here was someone called Griz."

"Pete Ford. Nicknamed Griz. How the hell did Benny know you were here and why would he be interested?"

"Obviously, we're being watched. Someone saw us going to the Sanchez house."

"Do any good over there?"

"Yes. She gave up everything but names."

"She did? Maria?"

"Yes."

"Well, I'll be damned. You want to tell me about it?"

"Mrs. Sanchez said to tell you if you asked. She said not to lie to you. You had the gift."

Morales shook his head. "Old country superstition. They die hard. Let's get out of this damned cold. Meet you back at the motel restaurant?"

"Suits me." John smiled and pointed to the juke joint. "Or we could go back into the saloon and have a drink."

"If you do, you'll do it alone. Meet you back at the motel."

FIVE

"Well, I'll be damned," Morales said softly. "She told you folks all that. How much of it do you believe?"

They were sitting in a far corner of the dining area, away from any other customers.

"All of it," John said.

"She was very convincing," Jenny added. "And very matter-of-fact."

The sheriff looked at Al. "You bought it all, Mr. Durstman?"

"Call me Al, please. Yes, I did."

The sheriff signaled the waitress for a coffee refill all the way around. When she had come and gone, he said, "The girl talking so openly to you folks makes me look incompetent." It was said without rancor.

"Not at all," John told him. "Maria's been back several months and had lots of time to think about what happened. She talked to us because, she said, you're too law and order."

Morales stared at John for a couple of heartbeats. "Too law and order?"

"That's what she said. Her mother said the same thing. In so many words."

The sheriff slowly nodded as he stirred his coffee. "Yeah, no point in my trying to act surprised. I've heard that before. I guess maybe sometimes I am too law and order."

"She also said you couldn't protect them constantly," Jenny told him.

"That's certainly a valid point," Morales agreed.

"They are also, according to Mrs. Sanchez, well armed and will use those weapons if it comes down to that," John added.

"I knew they were armed. Nearly everybody in this area has at least one weapon around the house." He smiled. "And about half of them have a pistol in their car or truck . . . many of them on their person."

"With or without carry permits," Al added.

The sheriff nodded his head. "Yeah."

"So now what?" John asked.

"I try to find out what the bikers are up to."

"Why would the bikers set up here?" Jenny asked.

"The terrain, for one thing," Morales replied. "This is pretty rugged country around here, and the snow is late this year. We normally get around two hundred inches of snow a year."

"Great skiing, I'll bet," Jenny said.

"You know it." Morales glanced at John. "You have a funny look on your face, John. What's the matter?"

"The terrain might be great for concealment around here, but the chances of getting snowed in with thousands of dollars of illicit drugs on hand and no way to get them out is pretty high too. And we've got a hard winter looking at us very soon."

"So you think . . . what?"

"I think they might have congregated here to gather forces and move out. And maybe to silence Maria and her family."

"But she really didn't tell you anything." Morales paused. "However, the outlaw bikers don't know that.

Yeah, I see what you mean. I can order patrols to increase their passes through that part of town and roust the hell out of known bikers who show up over there. That's about the best I can do."

"That'll have to do. Advise your people that we'll be prowling around that area as well. Give them our vehicle description and number if you will, please."

"No problem. I figured you would be. I'll do that now. See you guys. Take it easy."

After Morales had left, Al asked, "What's our next move?"

"We get in touch with the other teams and find out if they've discovered anything. Which I doubt. We were just incredibly lucky to have stumbled into this." John glanced at his watch. "It's too early for dinner . . . at least for me. I'm going to unpack my gear and relax for a time."

"Sounds good to me too," Al said. "I'm going to make a drink and take off my shoes and relax for a few minutes."

"I'm going to unpack my stuff," Jenny said. "Then get on the horn and call the others."

"Great. Meet you all back here at seven for dinner?" John asked.

"Sounds good," Al said, pushing back his chair and standing up.

Their adjoining rooms were on the outside tier, facing the parking area. John unpacked his things and hung up his jackets and trousers, stowing his shirts and socks and underwear in the bureau drawers. Then he fixed a martini from his small travel bar and sat down to watch the news. It was local news from a station in the north-central part of the state. The newscaster was lamenting the lack of snow for this time of the year and talking about how it would hurt the economy if the unusually warm weather continued.

John sipped his drink and paid little attention to the news until the topic turned to drugs.

A date-rape drug had hit the market and was being widely circulated all over the state. In addition, a strong new type of "upper" had just surfaced, and it was making the rounds. The methamphetamine was so strong it was causing some serious health problems among the users, many of them kids—liver and kidney problems. Several young people there in the north part of the state had died from using the drug, and many more had been hospitalized, a couple of them in a small town just outside of Sheriff Morales's territory. Down south a few miles.

"They don't want anything to do with Morales," John muttered. "He's too tough for them."

But that wouldn't prevent some of them from living in this area and cooking the crap in another county.

John found the phone book and looked up rental-car agencies, finding one that rented rugged off-road vehicles. He gave them a call and, yes, they did have several for rent. Yes, they all had racks for spare gas cans. And yes, they were all ready to go. They could be personally delivered to the motel if that was what Mr. Barrone wished. John reserved three of them and gave them his name, where he was staying, and his credit card number.

Then he made a list of some other items they would buy in the morning: heavy winter hiking boots and clothing, a dozen different types of emergency gear, citizens-band radios with the strongest signal available, food, water, and camping gear, compasses, and several other articles necessary for survival in the rugged country. And several good detailed maps of this area and the areas surrounding it.

John leaned back in his chair, sipping his drink and reviewing the list, adding a couple more articles. Then he glanced at the clock/radio on the nightstand. It was time to meet up with his team members and have dinner. He tapped on Al's door. No response. Knocking on Jenny's connecting door got the same results. They had already left for the dining room.

John slipped into his jacket and stepped out of the room. It was full dark and the lights, widely spaced along the walkway, were dim. John was alone on the long covered walkway. There was no one else walking to or from a room.

One of those long extended-cab pickup trucks rounded the corner of the motel, traveling slowly and almost silently, with only its parking lights on. John mentally noted the vehicle, but he could sense no cause for undue alarm. He walked on.

John again cut his eyes toward the truck just as the driver's-side window was lowered. In the dim glow of interior lights he could see the outline of the driver. The man wore a drooping Fu Manchu–type mustache. John caught a glimpse of light glinting off metal, and immediately went down to one knee behind a car parked in front of a room, his right hand snaking under his coat and jacket and coming out with his .45 autoloader.

The truck stopped. "Okay, asshole," a voice called from the truck. "There'll be another time."

"Time for what?" John replied, crouching behind the cover of the parked car.

"You know."

John sighed. More juvenile guessing games. "Why don't you tell me?"

There was silence for a few seconds. "You and your private investigator buddies back off, asshole. If you know what's good for you."

"Back off of what?" John pressed.

"You about a dumb son of a bitch, dude."

"Enlighten me, oh, wise one."

"And a smart-assed son of a bitch too." Another voice had been added to the conversation.

John looked up and down the long walkway. No one else had made an appearance.

"Let's kick some dude ass." A third voice had entered the conversation.

"Come on, boys." John spoke just loud enough to be heard. "Before your ass overloads your mouth."

"He ain't no Fed," the driver said. "They don't talk like that."

"You and your friends want to step out of the truck and talk about this?" John asked.

"If we come out of this truck it'll be to kick your ass," the driver said.

"Then come on and do it," John challenged.

"Another time, nosy."

"I'm not hard to find. But next time try it in the daylight. If not, I might get the idea you're all nothing but a pack of cowards."

"That does it," the man on the passenger side blurted out. "I'm gonna put some whip-ass on this gray-headed old bastard."

"Yeah, Chink," the man in the rear compartment said. "Let's break his goddamn legs."

"Shut up," Chink said.

Chink is the driver, John thought.

"Another time, dude," Chink called. "We'll be seein' you around. Bet on it."

"I'm no frightened little teenage girl you can kidnap and terrorize, Chink," John replied. "Were I you, I'd give that a lot of thought."

There was a moment of silence from the pickup truck. "I knowed that was why you meddlin' bastards was here. Look here, that deal's over and done with, dude," Chink said. "Let it rest, why don't you?"

"I choose not to."

"Your funeral."

"We all have to die of something. And you know Maria's dying. That's why you allowed her to escape."

Another moment of silence from the truck. "You're a smart one, I'll give you that much."

John said nothing.

"Yeah, we know she's got the queer disease."

"So you let her escape."

"Somebody did."

John remained crouched behind the car, wondering how long this conversation was going to continue.

Chink answered that immediately. "All right, we'll see you, Pops. We'll be around, watching you. Keep your nose out of our business if you want to stay healthy."

The truck slowly rolled on. John tried to get the license number, but the plate had been smeared with mud and the numbers were difficult to read. John holstered his .45 and walked on to the dining area.

"Not very smart of them," Al said after John had told them what had happened.

"We'll run this Chink person when we call in with the other names." Then he told them about the rental vehicles and showed the list of items they would buy the next morning.

"Are we going camping?" Jenny asked.

"Not unless we're forced to. But I don't want to get caught out in rough country without provisions."

"Or get caught out there when a blizzard comes," Al said.

"That too."

"So we're going to split up?" Jenny asked.

"We won't ever be more than a mile or so away from each other. I hope. But that isn't the reason I rented three of these vehicles. If one breaks down, we won't be afoot in rugged country."

Al looked toward the dining room entrance. "Sheriff Morales just walked in. He spotted us."

Morales didn't take the time to sit down at the table. He looked down at the trio and said, "Maria Sanchez was grabbed by some guys in a pickup truck. Right out of her front yard. Her father's on the prowl and he's armed."

SIX

After John told Sheriff Morales about his encounter with the men in the pickup truck, and told him one of the men had been called Chink, Morales told the team to get a good night's sleep and to stay clear of everything concerning Maria's disappearance. Then he walked out of the dining room without saying another word.

"I am now getting the impression that Sheriff Morales would like us to leave," Jenny remarked.

"Either that or he's suddenly got a lot of pressure put on him," Al opined.

"But pressure from which side?" John said.

"You still have the thought that Morales might be dirty?" Jenny asked.

John shook his head. "Not dirty in that he's taking a payoff."

"Then what do you mean?" Al asked.

"Morales is married with a wife and three kids. All three of them still in school. The oldest is seventeen and a senior in high school. The youngest is ten. Their safety just might be a big question mark in his mind."

"You think he's been contacted by someone connected with the bikers?" Jenny asked.

John shrugged. "It's certainly a possibility we have

to consider. Now that he's very abruptly turned somewhat chilly toward us." John picked up the menu. "Let's eat and then get some rest. We've got a busy day ahead and it's going to start early."

"What time will the rented . . . whatever they are, be here?" Jenny asked.

"They're Jeeps. Those sporty types. They'll be delivered about seven o'clock."

"Oh, good," Jenny said. "Those things are cute. I used to have an old Army-surplus Jeep when I was in high school. Dad bought it and rebuilt the engine and transmission. I had a ball in that thing."

"I just bet you were a holy terror roaring around. How many times did you wreck it?" Al asked.

"Right on both counts." Jenny grinned. "Oh . . . a couple of times."

"Are you going to tell the sheriff we're going prowling around his county?" Al asked.

"No. But I'll wager he'll know within an hour after we take delivery of the Jeeps. I doubt that very much escapes his attention. Jenny, did you contact the others?"

"Yes. Nothing going on in their sectors so far. I told them what we had found and we'd keep them advised."

"Good. The three of us are all we need for the time being. Any more might make Morales really nervous."

"I want the porterhouse," Jenny said, picking up the menu. "The big one, with baked potato, sour cream, and lots of butter."

"Growing girl," Al said with a smile.

"But in which direction?" John said.

Jenny frowned at that and again looked at the menu. "Well . . . maybe the small filet . . . oh, the hell with it. I'm hungry!"

* * *

The three Jeeps were delivered promptly at seven the next morning. One light tan, one green, the third cherry red. John signed for them and was handed the keys.

"I want the red one," Jenny said.

"It's all yours," John told her. "Al?"

"Doesn't matter to me."

"All right. I'll take the green one. Now let's go shopping for some gear."

They were on the road two hours later, with two-way radios, emergency rations, spare gas cans filled up, and heavy winter clothing. The day was cold, but the sky was clear. The weather forecasters were saying no snow for at least several more days.

They stopped at a small store on the edge of town and bought bread, lunch meat, soft drinks, and small ice chests to keep the perishables cold. They filled up thermos bottles with hot coffee, then drove out past the honky-tonk where the bikers gathered. It was still closed. It was just past nine in the morning; a bit too early for swigging beer, at least for most people.

"We'll head up the road for about a mile," John radioed. "I'll pull off just past the first intersection, with it in view, then Jenny will take the next one, then you, Al."

"Ten-four."

"Do we pull off into the timber?" Jenny asked.

"If at all possible. But in that red Jeep of yours, I don't know how much good that will do."

"Smart-ass," she radioed.

It was a long wait for the team. They kept the motors running and the heaters blowing against the cold. Almost two hours passed before Al radioed in.

"A couple of cars just pulled out of the intersection. Some real hard-looking guys."

"Let's see what they do."

A moment later Jenny radioed, "They just passed me, Boss." A couple of seconds later: "Nope. They spotted me. Stopping and pulling over."

"Get out of there, Jenny," John said. "This could turn dangerous."

"Too late. They've got me boxed in. They're just sitting in the vehicles pointing and looking at me. They're making no hostile moves."

"Two more vehicles, a short-bed pickup truck and a car, stopping at the intersection," Al radioed. "Just sitting there, looking at me."

"They've made us," John radioed.

"You think someone at the rental agency is on the biker's payroll?" Jenny questioned.

"Probably." He glanced down the highway toward town. Two cars were approaching. The cars slowed as they drew nearer, then pulled over to the shoulder and stopped about fifty yards away from John's location. John lifted his binoculars and got a close-up look at the occupants. "I've got two carloads of guys staring at me," he radioed. "But that's all they're doing . . . so far. No weapons showing."

"What now?" Al asked.

"We stare right back," John said. "Neither side is breaking any laws."

"Ten-four."

"I spoke too soon," John radioed. "One car pulled up alongside me. The man on the passenger side is showing me his hands. Telling me he's unarmed, I suppose. Heads up, now, people. I'll see what's on his mind." John slipped his .45 out of leather and held it out of sight.

"Mr. Barrone," the man said, walking up to John. "Enjoying the view?"

"Not really. Too many ugly faces spoiling the scenery."

"That's really funny. Ha ha. I'll have to remember that."

"What do you want?"

"The question is, Mr. Barrone, what do you want? The deal with the Sanchez girl is over, so why don't you and your people go away?"

"Over? Are you joking? The girl was kidnapped, raped, beaten, and forced into perverted sex acts. The people responsible have not been brought to justice."

"But she's back home with her parents. Everything's all right now."

"She's dying."

"Yeah? I heard that. That's too bad."

"And she isn't back with her parents."

"What do you mean?"

"She was kidnapped yesterday, as if you didn't know."

"Kidnapped? Hey, man, I don't know nothin' about that. And that's the truth. I been up in my cabin all night. Just left. I ain't seen no TV or listened to no radio news. I swear that."

John looked at the man for a moment. He thought he detected a ring of truth in the man's voice. Maybe. "Been too busy cooking up a new batch of drugs to listen to the news?"

The man smiled at that. "I told the boys that was the real reason you people come in here. They thought it was purely the Sanchez girl."

"Her disappearance hasn't been on the news. But that doesn't answer my question."

"It's the only answer you're gonna get."

"How did you know my name?"

"Magic."

John chuckled as the cold outside air blew through the open window. "Where did you park your motorcycle?"

The big man laughed. "You shift gears faster than I do, Barrone. My Hog? It's parked in a shed until the weather warms up."

"You know my name. What's yours?"

"Benny."

"Let me give you a bit of advice, Benny. Stop making illegal drugs and get a regular job."

"And if I don't?"

"I might have to put you out of business."

"Just like that?"

"Just like that."

The big biker stood in silence for several seconds, looking at John. Then he smiled. "You figure it would be that easy, huh?"

"It wouldn't be difficult."

"I could haul your ass out of that right now and stomp it, Barrone."

"No, you couldn't."

"You figure you're hoss enough to stop me?"

"This .45 I've got in my hand damn sure is. And if you doubt that, try me."

"You might be bluffing."

"You want to bet your life on it?"

Benny was thoughtful for a moment, then grinned. "Naw, I don't think so. You're just too damn cool. That tells me, among other things, that you're not a state or federal officer."

"Oh? Why is that?"

"They're all dumb as shit and obvious as a boil on your nose, that's why. Naw . . . you're something else, Mr. Barrone. I don't know, but I betcha I find out."

"I hope you won't object too much if I don't wish you good luck."

Benny laughed aloud. "Chink said you were a cool one. I got to agree with him on that. Look, I really don't know nothin' about the Sanchez girl's disappearance. You can believe that or not, but I'm tellin' you the truth. I didn't even know she was gone again."

"Did you have anything to do with her disappearance the first time?"

"What did she have to say about that?"

"Nothing, Benny. She gave us no names."

"Then why would anyone grab her?"

"You tell me."

" 'Fraid I don't know."

"Why did this ape called Chink threaten me last night?"

"Well, he shouldn't have done that. He was out of line for sure."

"So I have your assurance it won't happen again?"

Benny shrugged. "I don't know. You folks keep stickin' your noses in places where they shouldn't oughta be . . . no tellin' what's liable to happen."

"It's a free country, Benny."

"No, it isn't. That's crap and you know it. Maybe at one time it was, but not no more. You been warned, Mr. Barrone. Take heed." He turned and walked away, back to his vehicle.

John raised the window and watched the vehicles drive off, heading in the direction of town. He lifted the handy/talkie and keyed the mike.

"I'm clear here. How about you people?"

"No trouble here," Jenny was the first to reply. "They're driving off."

"Same here," Al responded.

"Let's follow, see where they go."

The caravan of car-bound bikers drove straight to the honky-tonk run by Sonny. John and his team drove on past and pulled into the parking area of a convenience store several miles down the road.

"Now what?" Al asked.

That question was answered by a sheriff's department car pulling in. The deputy got out and walked up to the trio.

"Sheriff Morales wants to see you folks," the deputy said. "Now."

"What's the problem, Deputy?" John asked.

"The Sanchez girl was found about an hour ago. Dead."

SEVEN

John had to fight back waves of nausea when he was shown the pictures of Maria Sanchez.

"Oh, my God," Jenny said, looking over John's shoulder.

Al glanced at the pictures and walked out of the office.

"Grim, isn't it?" Sheriff Morales said.

"I would say so." John's reply was tight-lipped "She died awfully hard."

Maria was naked, tied to a wooden straight-backed chair. She had been tortured hideously.

"Was she raped?" John asked.

"We don't think so. The M.E. will have to determine that."

"Have you located her father?"

"Yes. Thank God we found him before he could kill any bikers."

"Is he in custody?"

"For the time being. Until he calms down and can talk to a priest. I don't want any charges filed against him."

"I won't ask you for any more particulars about Maria's death. You wouldn't tell me, and besides, as civilians, it's none of our business."

"Thank you for that, John. But speaking of your

business . . ." Morales paused, stared at John, and drummed his fingertips on the desk top.

"Yes?"

"What the hell is your occupation anyway?" He held up a hand. "And don't tell me about some security business. I checked on that, from the information on your business card, and came up with damn little."

John smiled. "It's legitimate, Sheriff."

"Oh, I know that. Your company has all the proper licenses, taxes are paid and local, state, and federal forms all filed. You, or somebody, has gone to great lengths to make it look one hundred percent on the up and up. But frankly, I don't buy it for one second. Too many gaps, John."

John knew then for a fact that Sheriff Morales was a very thorough man, and a very inquisitive one. He said nothing.

"Somebody very recently busted up a terrorist ring in New York City," said Morales.

"I read about that, Sheriff."

"I'm sure you did."

Al stepped back into the office, a cup of coffee in his hand. He took a seat and listened.

Jenny was inspecting her nails.

Morales sighed and shook his head. "Okay, okay. The wall of silence just came down. Maria is dead now, John. We'll pick up the pieces of this case and continue from here. No reason for you and your people to stick around, right?"

"We like the scenery."

"Horseshit!"

"Beautiful country."

"Don't get in my way, John," Sheriff Morales warned. "I like you, but I won't tolerate interference."

"Oh, we won't interfere with your investigation into Maria's death, Sheriff."

"All right." Morales shook his head as he lifted a hand. "I've told you and shown you all I can. And you've been warned. Now, I've got work to do. You folks know your way out. Have a nice day."

Standing in the parking area, Jenny said, "He's not going to take much pushing, John."

"We came here to do a job, and we're going to do it."

"Morales could make things a bit rough," Al said. "This is not New York City where we can blend into the crowds."

"Those responsible for the hours of torture and the killing of Maria Sanchez are going to pay for it. This state has a death penalty, but I don't know if it's ever been used here since the Supreme Court okayed it years back. If it has, it's been only a few times."

"So?" Jenny asked, stepping closer, her collar turned up against the cold wind.

"So we're going to bump up the execution rate a bit."

"When do we start?" Al asked.

"We start laying the groundwork right now."

The news of Maria Sanchez's torture/murder leaked out. While it was not front-page news statewide, it did make the evening TV news, and a section of the local area paper. The reporter obviously had a source in the DA's office, for the article had a few facts that Sheriff Morales had not told John and his people.

"Definitely biker work," John said after carefully reading the report. "Motorcycle tire tracks were all over the place."

"And the prelim report from the M.E. showed no signs of sexual assault," Jenny said.

"The girl has, had AIDS," Al said. "The bikers knew it. They wouldn't risk contracting that deadly disease."

"Want to take a ride out to the biker honky-tonk?" John asked with a smile.

"Are you serious?" Al asked.

"Yes. But first let me get a couple of surprises out of my war bag."

Jenny and Al watched John as he rummaged around in a large suitcase. Jenny smiled and said, "This just might be fun."

John slipped into his topcoat while Al and Jenny checked their pistols. "You don't want to take any presents with you?" he asked.

"I think you have enough for the three of us," Al said.

The three of them stepped out into the cold early evening air.

There were several dozen motorcycles and a few cars and trucks parked around the honky-tonk. A live band was performing inside, the sounds of what John assumed was some sort of music roaring out into the night, contaminating the cold air.

"What the hell is that?" John asked.

"Heavy metal, sort of," Jenny replied.

"Whatever happened to the Platters and Bobby Vinton and Peggy Lee?" John asked.

"Yo, dude," Jenny said with a smile. "You're about three or four decades behind time."

"I will forever be grateful for that," John said. "Come on, let's enter the lion's den."

The noise was nearly deafening as the three agents

opened the front door, and a very startled biker took the trio's money for admission into the honky-tonk. He glanced at two big bikers standing nearby, probably bouncers for the evening's crowd. They shrugged and nodded their heads. The band abruptly stopped playing with an electronically magnified cymbal crash.

"Do we wait to be seated?" John asked with a straight face.

Jenny hid a giggle.

"Park your asses anywhere you can find a place," one of the bouncers said.

"Thank you," John said. "What's your name?"

"Huh?"

"Your name. You do have one, don't you?"

"Everybody has a name, you asshole!"

"So what is yours?"

"Pisspot."

"I beg your pardon?"

"Are you deaf? *Pisspot!*"

"Wonderful," John muttered.

The three threaded their way through the crowd, which was very reluctant to let them pass, and took a table next to a wall and close to a door that John hoped was unlocked and would lead them outside. If it wasn't unlocked, he had something in his pocket that would open it.

"This is the damnedest mass of near-humanity I have ever seen," Al said.

"Or want to see again," Jenny added. "At least up close."

"I imagine we'll be seeing them up close many more times before we're through here," John said.

One of the waitresses was Carrie, and she spotted them as they walked to the table. She pushed her way through the crowd, sat down at the table, and said in a low voice, "You people shouldn't be here. Get out now, if you can."

"Why shouldn't we be here, Carrie?" Jenny asked.

"Don't play stupid with me, lady!" Carrie said sharply, her voice still just above a whisper. "I know about the Sanchez girl and what happened to her. Everybody here in this club knows you people are investigating the case. Now it's gonna get worse, you can bet on it."

"Hey, Carrie!" someone called. "Get your ass over here. We need some beer."

"What a polite way of calling in an order," John said. "Who is that?"

"That's Ax. Him and Ox ride together."

"Ax and Ox?" John asked.

"Yeah. That's Big Train and his woman, Hot Pants, with them."

"Big Train?" Al said.

"Yeah. You'll see why he's called that if he stands up. He's six-six and three hundred pounds." Carrie stood up. "Get out of here, people, and don't come back."

"Why are you warning us?" Al asked.

Carrie hesitated. " 'Cause I think you folks are allright people. I'll bring you three beers in a minute. Unopened, like you told me before. Then you get gone from here."

"Carrie, goddamnit!" Ox or Ax or Big Train roared.

She slipped away into the crowd.

"I have my doubts about us getting out of here," Jenny said. "Not without a lot of trouble."

"I'm counting on it," John replied.

"Counting on us having trouble?" Al asked.

"Yes. That ape at the front door just locked it. After

about half a dozen bikers slipped out. We probably won't have a vehicle when we get outside."

" 'Bout forty or fifty bikes out there," Jenny said with a smile.

John looked at her and slowly shook his head. "I would hate to think I had to straddle one of those things again."

"I thought you said you'd never ridden a motorcycle?"

"I lied."

"Shame on you, John," Al said with a grin.

"Throttle jammed on me one night," John said with an embarrassed smile. "I must have been running a hundred and twenty miles an hour before I realized all I had to do was turn off the ignition." John laughed at himself. "I was one scared fifteen-year-old. I swore I'd never get on another motorcycle, and I haven't."

Carrie brought three unopened bottles of long-neck beer, placing them on the table. She took the money from John and whispered, "Get ready, folks. I'm sorry about this. I slipped outside and unlocked the door behind you. That's all I can do. I'm being watched." She walked away.

"Don't open the beer," John said. "They make great clubs."

"And we're probably going to be using them for just that in a few seconds," Jenny said, glancing over the crowd. "Three apes are heading this way."

"Let them start it," John whispered.

"I'm quite sure they will," Al said very drily.

The three bikers, dressed in jeans and boots and black leather jackets, walked to the table and glared at the trio. "Whup-ass time," one said.

"Really?" John said, looking up at the very large,

unshaven, and extremely ugly biker. "Now why would you want to do something as inhospitable as that?"

"Huh?" the second biker asked.

" 'Cause you got a damn smart mouth and a big nose you keep stickin' in business that ain't none of your concern," the third biker said.

"That's very rude of us, isn't it?"

"Damn right it is. And now you gonna learn a hard lesson."

"Jump right in and start the dance then," John said softly.

"Huh?" the second biker, who appeared to be rather slow on the uptake, repeated.

"Let the festivities and merriment begin," Jenny said. "Bring on the matadors and turn out the bulls."

"What the hell is she talkin' 'bout?" the dullard asked.

"Damned if I know," the third one said. "How 'bout you, Greaseball?"

"Shit!" Greaseball said. "I'm gonna tear your fuckin' head off, old man." He reached down with one big hand and grabbed John by the front of his topcoat.

Bad mistake. John grabbed the ape by the thumb, bent it back, and twisted. Hard.

"Owww!" Greaseball yelled. "Turn loose of my thumb, you asshole!"

Jenny jumped up and smacked Greaseball in the center of the forehead with her full beer bottle. Greaseball sighed, his eyes rolled back, and he released his grip on John and slowly sank to the floor.

"You bitch, you hit Greaseball!" Number Three said.

Al stood up and popped Number Three in the face with his beer bottle. Number Three staggered back as the beer spewed, and sat down hard on a tabletop. "Shit!" he said, and fell off the table.

"This ain't workin' out," Slow Brain said.

"Try this," John said, and hit the ape on the forehead with his beer bottle.

The beer sprayed and the biker went down hard and stayed down.

"Get those bastards!" someone in the crowd yelled.

"Don't kill 'em," another biker yelled. "Griz and Chink want 'em alive so's they can finish 'em."

"Open the door behind you, Jenny," John told her. "And you and Al step outside."

"What about you?"

"I'll be right behind you. Believe me." John reached into his topcoat pocket and came out with a grenade. He held it up and pulled the pin, holding the spoon down. The grenade was held down at his side, and could not be seen in the dim light of the honky-tonk.

"Hold it!" John yelled, and the advancing mass of leather and chains halted.

Behind him, John heard Jenny whisper, "Door's open."

Someone cut off the jukebox and the club became silent.

"What you got in your hand, man?" a biker shouted. "You pulled out a gun?"

"Not yet," John told him. "But it might come to that."

"None of this would be happenin' if you'd kept your goddamn nose out of things that don't concern you," a woman yelled.

"You right, Big Tit," a biker called. "Now shut your damned mouth."

"Big Tit?" Jenny whispered. "Does she only have one?"

"Don't you tell me to shut up, Hook!" Big Tit yelled.

Greaseball staggered and lurched to his feet, blood dripping from a gash on his forehead. His eyes focused and he cursed John. "You one dead motherfucker! I'm gonna stomp your guts out and stretch 'em out so's the birds can eat 'em."

"I don't think so," John told him, and lifted his right hand.

"That's a goddamned grenade!" a biker hollered.

"Holy shit!" another yelled.

"Nobody move!" John yelled. "Or I toss this little bomb."

"Son of a bitch damn sure has my attention," a biker said. "What do you want us to do, mister?"

"Stand still until we get clear."

"I'm gonna find you all and kill you," a biker promised. "Count on it."

John stepped out the door and into the cold night. "Night, night, boys and girls."

He slammed the door shut.

EIGHT

"The Expedition is out of commission," Al said. "The tires are flat and the windows have been knocked out."

"Is that all?" John asked, slipping the pin back into the grenade, securing the spoon.

"No," Jenny said. "Someone poured yellow paint all over it. Inside and out."

"The natives are getting restless," Al said, pointing toward the honky-tonk and the sounds of yelling and cussing and wild threats coming from inside the building.

"Well, we have two choices as I see it," John said calmly. "We can walk back to the motel, or we can ride."

"Ride in what?" Al asked. "All the cars and trucks that were parked in the lot are gone."

"Not in," John corrected. "On."

"Are you serious?" Al questioned. "Ride a motorcycle into town?"

"You have a better idea?" John asked.

Al muttered something under his breath about hara-kiri.

Jenny had already straddled one of the bikes and kicked it into life. She was smiling and twisting the handlebar throttle, gunning the engine.

"Hey!" The shout came from inside the beer joint. "Them bastards is stealin' our bikes."

John swung onto a Harley and fumbled around, finally kicking it into life.

"Shit!" Al said. "Is there a Honda around here anywhere? I have ridden one of those. A long time ago. Back in my teenage years."

"Not a chance," Jenny yelled over the sound of the grumbling engines. "No self-respecting outlaw would get anywhere near a rice-burner. Pick one and get on, Al, and let's get the hell out of here."

Al managed to crank a chopped Harley and keep it upright. "I'm ready," he shouted. "I think."

The front door of the honky-tonk burst open and the bikers jammed each other up in the doorway.

"Let's go," John said, and sprayed gravel all over the front of the building as he spun around.

"Great wheely, John!" Jenny yelled.

John couldn't hear her over the loud grumbling ripping sound from out of the tailpipes. Jenny made the highway with ease and backed off the throttle, slowing down considerably, waiting for John and Al. They both almost lost it when they left the gravel parking and hit the pavement, but managed to straighten up and keep control.

"Shit!" Al hollered. "These things are hot!"

John didn't reply; he was having trouble finding the switch that turned on the lights. He finally fumbled around and got the headlight on, just about two seconds before he would have run into Jenny.

"Any pursuit?" Jenny hollered after she leaned her Hog out of the way.

"I haven't looked around to check," John shouted.

"It's cold on these damn things!" Al yelled, pulling up alongside them.

"I agree. I'm freezing. But we'll be in town in a few minutes," John called. "It won't be long now."

There was no pursuit from any of the bikers, and that puzzled John. But he didn't dwell on the lack of any chase for very long. They left the motorcycles about a half mile from the motel and walked the rest of the way, then gathered in John's room to warm up and have a couple of drinks from John's travel bar.

"You think the outlaws will report their motorcycles being stolen?" Al asked.

"I don't know. They might. Depends on how mad and how reckless they are. But I'll bet you we've seen the last of our Expedition."

"I was going to mention that," Jenny said. "It's probably on its way to a chop shop right now."

"I didn't think of that," Al said. "The cold must have numbed my brain."

"As soon as we warm up and finish our drinks—at least our first one," he added with a smile, "check the computer and see if there's any reply from Control to our questions."

"Will do," Jenny said. "I have to visit the rest room, so I'll turn the 'puter on now."

John and Al freshened their drinks and stretched and relaxed for a couple of minutes. Al suddenly chuckled, and John glanced at him. "You think of something funny, Al? Please share it. I could use a laugh."

"Us," Al said. "Wobbling around on those motorcycles. I'm not ashamed to admit I didn't think we were going to make it back here alive."

John smiled as the absurdity of what they had just done hit home. "Yes. I'd have to say we were the Two Stooges. Jenny was riding along like a pro."

"A pro what?" Jenny asked, appearing in the doorway that connected the rooms. "You guys talking about me again?"

"Where'd you learn to ride a motorcycle, Jenny?" Al asked.

"When I was a kid. One of the guys who worked with my dad restored old motorcycles. Harleys and Indians. I'd ride whenever I could." She walked in and sat down. "I'm printing out material from Control now. A lot of it. It's going to take a while."

Al walked to the door and cracked it, looking out and listening for a moment. "No sirens or flashing lights. Guess the outlaws didn't want to call the police." He started to close the door just as a sheriff's department patrol car came into view. "Wait a second. Maybe I spoke too soon."

The patrol car stopped in front of the three rooms rented by the team.

"We've got company," Al said. "The police." He looked again. "Morales, and he isn't very happy."

"What else is new? I've never seen him when he looked happy," Jenny said.

Al held open the door and Sheriff Morales stepped in, a grim expression on his face. "Let's have the pineapple, Barrone."

"Pineapple, Sheriff? What am I, a fruit vendor?"

"Don't get smart-assed with me! You know what I mean, the grenade."

"What grenade? I don't have a grenade."

"I could search this room and your rental vehicles, you know."

"Go right ahead. You won't find a thing." John was bluffing on that. There were enough weapons in the three rooms to start a minor revolution. He smiled. "And I won't even insist upon a warrant."

Morales sighed and took off his hat, tossing it on

the bed. He looked longingly at John's travel bar. "Is the bar open for me too?"

"Sure. Help yourself."

The sheriff fixed a stiff drink of whiskey and water and sat down. "What did you have in your hand out at the biker bar this evening?"

"A grenade," John said after digging in his top coat pocket. Smiling he said, "This one." He tossed the grenade to Morales.

Morales caught it and said, "Holy shit, man! This is a real grenade."

"Dummy grenades and unloaded weapons can get you killed, Sheriff. You know that."

Morales gingerly laid the grenade on the nightstand and knocked back half his drink. "The bikers found their Hogs. Where is your Ford?"

"Probably on the way to a chop shop." He told Morales what the bikers had done to it.

"Yeah, you'll probably never see it again. That would be incriminating evidence against them."

"I can't believe they reported anything to you."

"Oh, they didn't. Bend Over Betty did."

John blinked a couple of times. "I beg your pardon? Who?"

Morales could not contain his smile. "Mad Dog's old lady," he said with a chuckle. "Bend Over Betty. You want me to explain how she got that nickname?"

"Sure!" Jenny said brightly.

"No!" John said. "I can guess. I think."

"She got smacked around by Mad Dog after she called the office about the motorcycles being taken," Morales explained. "Then she made another call telling us about the grenade bit. I imagine she's going to get the hell beat out of her for that second call." He shook his head. "What a way to live."

"But no one is filing any official charges against us, right?" John asked.

"That is correct. If it hadn't been for Betty, I wouldn't have known anything about it. Were you going to tell me about your vehicle being vandalized?"

"Why, sure, Sheriff," John told him.

"Right," Morales said sarcastically. "I just bet you were." He gave each person in the room a long, careful look. "I don't know who you all are, but you're sure as hell a lot more than private security people. I'd bet my life's savings on that. I ran up against a stone wall trying to check you all past your security business. That tells me you're probably with some super-secret government agency. CIA would be my first guess, NSA my second guess." He paused, waiting for some reply from the trio. None came. "All right," Morales said after taking another knock from his drink. "I know better than to push too hard against a stone wall. I have acquaintances who've tried that and know what it can get you."

"We are what we are, Sheriff," John told him. "But the question that bothers all of us is this: Who are you?"

"I beg your pardon?"

"You heard me."

"I'm the sheriff of this county, and I'm a damn good one too. That's who I am."

"Yes. You're a sheriff who told us there are no out-law bikers and no drugs in your county. That's crap on both counts and you know it."

"This is one of the largest counties in the state, Barrone. And I've got an understaffed and under-equipped department. We do the very best we can."

"I'm not doubting that, Sheriff. But who are you covering for?"

"What the hell do you mean?" Morales flared.

"Are there some county bigwigs mixed up in drugs? Or their kids, perhaps?"

Morales got up and paced the room for a few seconds. He stopped, turned, and stared at John. "I'm going to say this just once, and I will never say it again. Nick Sandoval, Dave Curtis, Morris Grayson."

"And those men are? . . ."

"Find out for yourself, and I wish you good luck."

"What does that mean?"

"They own this county. And their kids, all of them, are shitheads."

"Dope?"

"Everything."

"And their daddies protect them."

"More than that. Their daddies are . . . well . . . I've said too much as it is. You'll see. But if you mention my name, I'll show you that I do have some stroke in this county."

"We'll keep your name out of it, Sheriff. So they've threatened your kids, right?"

That shook Morales. He sat back down and poured another drink. When he again looked at John, his eyes seemed haunted. "That had to have been a real lucky guess, John."

"Sheriff, you did a flip-flop on us once. That got me to thinking. We"—he indicated Al and Jenny— "talked about it. I came to what I felt was the only logical conclusion, other than you being dirty, and I just didn't want to believe that."

"I'm sure as hell not dirty, John!"

"I don't believe you are."

"Thanks for that much."

"Anything else you can tell me that might help?"

Morales paused and sighed. "Well, there is one other thing about the situation that makes it even harder to understand. At least for me. Might as well get it out into the open. You'll hear about it sooner or later. It will just show you what a rotten bunch of bastards those three monied people I mentioned really are."

"What?"

"I mentioned Nick Sandoval."

"Yes. What about him?"

"His wife is my sister."

NINE

"What a great family the sheriff's sister married into," Al remarked.

John nodded his agreement. "Yes, they sound like really solid citizens."

"I think we wandered into a real cesspool here," Jenny said.

"Or worse," John said. "Jenny, bump Control and ask for everything they have on those men Morales named."

"I'll get right on it," she replied. "How about all this stuff I just printed out?"

"Let's see what we've got."

"Well, there are a few pages of useful information," Al said after reading through the printouts send by Control. "The rest is crap. It seems this Nick Sandoval owns the biker bar. Sonny just runs it for him."

"And Dave Curtis's oldest kid, Davy, is a real snake-head," Jenny added. "Eighteen years old and been in and out of trouble since he was in middle school."

John laid his copy of the report aside and shook his head. "Look at the names of some of these outlaw bikers: Pinhead, Big Balls, Hammer and Rammer, X-Man . . ."

"And we can't forget Bend Over Betty," Jenny added with a smile.

"I have a hunch you're not going to let us," John said.

Jenny flashed a grin at him.

"They've all got extensive rap sheets," Al said. "Which should come as no surprise to anyone. Violent bunch of people."

"Worthless," John said. "All of them. There is not one redeeming quality in a single one."

"Let me call in for about fifty pounds of Semtex and I'll take them all out," Jenny said. "And be rid of that damn biker bar as well."

"Control yourself," John told her. He was thoughtful for a few seconds. "However, that is a suggestion to be considered. But only as a last resort."

"That would make a rather large hole in the ground," Al said, looking at John and wondering if he was at all serious.

"Depends on how it was placed," Jenny told him.

"Tell Control we want some C-4," John said.

"Are you serious?" Al asked.

"But not fifty pounds," John added.

They all looked up at the knocking on the door. "Lemmie in, y'all. It's Carrie, from the bar. I'm alone."

Jenny let a very frightened-looking Carrie into the room and to a chair.

"You got off early tonight," Jenny said.

"Naw. I quit and got in my car and hauled ass away from that joint. Look, I'm outta here, like tonight. I've had it with those crazy people out there. I come in here to tell you that all hell is gonna break loose real soon. The bikers is gonna kill you guys."

"When?" John asked.

"Maybe tonight, maybe tomorrow, maybe the next day. Hell, I don't know the exact time or how it's gonna happen. But it's coming. You made them all look foolish. Nobody does that to them."

"You heard them planning to kill us?" Al asked.

"I sure did. And they got the okay from Benny to do it. I was there when he come by. He was pissed to the max, let me tell you he was. And he takes his orders, some of them anyway, from the big guns in the county."

"And who might that be, Carrie?" John asked.

"Damned if I know. I'd tell you if I knew, but I ain't even got a clue."

"Where will you go, Carrie?" Jenny asked.

"I don't know. Hell, I can get a job in any joint. I'm a good waitress and a pretty fair bartender." She stood up. "Look, guys, I gotta shake the dust of this place. You be careful. Real careful."

"You need some money?" John asked.

"Oh . . . naw. I got enough to get me quite a ways. Damn nice of you to offer, though. See you."

She opened the door, and was gone into the night.

"I hope she makes it," Al said after the sounds of Carrie's older-model car faded away.

"I do, too," John said. "If she is to be believed, it took guts to warn us."

"You have reservations?" Jenny asked.

"I have some problems with her overhearing plans to kill us, that's all. Seems to me that would be awfully careless on the part of the bikers." He shrugged. "But I suppose it's possible, considering how angry they must have been . . . and still are."

"What now?" Al asked.

"We get some sleep. I don't believe they'll try anything while we're in our motel rooms. That would be too public. Too many chances of someone else getting hurt or killed." He smiled. "Of course, I could be wrong."

John was the first one up, just as silver dawn was unfolding a new day. He made a pot of coffee and opened the drapes, then sat at the small table, watching the dawn bring the area to life. Jenny wandered in, a cup of coffee in her hand. She sat down at the table and looked bleary-eyed at John.

"You look as though you might be alive," John said.

"I'll let you know in a few minutes. You get any calls?"

"Not a peep."

"What's on the agenda for today?"

"We push the outlaws a little bit more. Let them know we're still around. After you've decided you're still alive, check the computer for our requested info on the big three monied people Morales mentioned."

"I already checked. It came in. Several pages. Nothing really bad on the parents, but the kids are real snake-heads. They're all been arrested about a dozen times, all for minor stuff. Never really punished by the courts for any of it. Except for the one time several of them got busted in a county south of here. They spent the night in the pokey and were sentenced to do some community-service work."

"Did they?"

"No. They never showed up and nothing was ever done about it. The case just sort of went away."

"Money and power talking again. What do you want to bet the young folks are mixed up with the bikers?"

"No bet. They are, according to the sheriff down south of here."

"In what way?"

"The report didn't say. Just said the sheriff strongly suspects they are."

"We getting a new vehicle?"

"It'll be delivered this afternoon. A full-sized Mercury."

Al opened the connecting door and wandered into the room, a cup of coffee in his hand. "I slept like a rock," he said, sitting down on the side of the bed. "Having a hard time waking up. Anything of importance happen during the night?"

"Bunch of reports from Control," Jenny said. "The plot thickens, as some say."

"Anything from the other teams?"

"Nothing so far."

"We'll have to tell them they've been missing all the fun," Al said.

Outside and down the covered walkway, a door slammed and a vehicle cranked up as other lodgers began a new day.

"The Jeeps still in one piece?" Al asked after yawning and taking a sip of coffee.

"Parked right where we left them," John told him, looking out the window and watching a young couple carry pieces of luggage to a vehicle parked by one of the rental Jeeps and open their vehicle's trunk. They stowed the luggage and stood for a moment, chatting. Then the man closed the trunk and leaned up against the Jeep Jenny had been driving.

A wall of flame and smoke erupted as the vehicles parked in that section exploded. All the windows in the motel facing that parking area were blown out, and bloody bits and pieces of the young couple were blasted all over the lot. More cars and trucks were caught up in the hot hell of the blast and exploded, sending lethal bits of metal flying all over the place.

Both John and Jenny were knocked out of their chairs and hurled to the floor by the concussion. Al was blown off the bed and slammed against the wall. The hearing of the three was momentarily impaired by the enormous wall of sound.

Jenny was the first one to crawl to her knees and look around her. There was a loud ringing in her ears and she could just barely hear herself say, "Jesus Christ! Is everybody all right?"

Al pulled himself upright, still sitting on the floor, between the bed and the wall. He was bleeding from a cut on his forehead. He knew Jenny was speaking; he could see her lips moving, but could not hear a word she was saying. He spoke, but could not hear his own voice.

People were walking, running, limping, and staggering out of shattered motel rooms, many of them shaking their heads, trying to clear away the sounds of deep silence. Several fell to the concrete, blood dripping from various wounds. Men and women were crying and moaning. Others appeared numb from the shock of the violent explosion.

John pulled himself up to a sitting position, his hearing gradually returning. "Is everybody all right?" he asked, the words sounding tinny and very far away.

"I'm in one piece," Jenny said. "I think. Al?"

"I'm okay," he replied. "Just have a cut on my head, that's all."

"Our Jeeps were wired to blow," John said, looking out the jagged hole where the window used to be. The entire line of vehicles was a jumble of smoking ruin. "Carrie was telling the truth." Then he remembered the young couple. "Oh, my God! The man and woman."

John got to his feet and stumbled outside. Only

then was he conscious of a thin trickle of blood running down his face from a cut on his upper cheek.

"What man and woman?" Jenny asked, following him outside, pulling on a winter coat over her pajamas.

"The man leaned against the Jeep you'd been driving. That set off the explosion, I guess."

"Very sensitive trigger," she replied. She paused and sniffed the air. "They used dynamite. I can smell it."

"They must have used a lot of it," Al said, coming up behind his friends. "God, what a mess."

"Look there," John said, pointing.

"Oh, gross!" Jenny said as she spotted what John had been pointing at.

It was an arm, blown off at the shoulder. The hand was clenched into a fist.

"It's a woman's arm," Al said.

The parking lot was filling up with fire trucks, cop cars, and ambulances, the smoky early morning air echoing with the sounds of sirens.

"There's a string of intestines hanging over there," Jenny said, pointing.

"Thank you so much for pointing that out," Al said with a grimace.

"You're welcome, and there comes Sheriff Morales."

"I'm wondering if that young couple were the only ones killed," John said.

"I hope that's all," Al said. "Did you see anyone else outside before it blew?"

"No. But my vision was limited by where I was sitting. Here comes Morales, straight toward us."

"Looking like the wrath of God," Jenny said.

"Well, they certainly tried to get you," Sheriff Morales said, walking up. He stared at the trio's various cuts and bruises for a few seconds. "And almost succeeded."

"They killed a young couple," John told him. "That's the woman's arm over there." He pointed. "And I don't know whose guts those are." He pointed to the dangling intestines.

"Good Lord!" Morales said.

A city cop walked up and greeted Morales. "Part of a bumper went through a window and took half the head off a man down at the end of this section, Sheriff. The man's wife suffered a broken arm."

Morales looked at John and frowned. "How many dead so far?"

"Three, Sheriff. But all the rooms haven't been inspected yet." The city officer walked away as another city unit pulled into the parking area.

"I am genuinely sorry about this, Sheriff," John said. "I want you to believe that."

"Yeah, I believe you. Now, I want you out of my county, Barrone. Now, today."

"The practice of running someone out of a community ended a long time ago, Sheriff."

"Legally, yeah, that's right."

"But there are ways, correct, Sheriff?"

"You bet. You really want to push me on this, Barrone?"

"If I have to."

"Then you'd better get ready for some pushing back."

John held up a hand, a signal for truce. "You've got a hell of a problem in this county, Sheriff. Whether you choose to admit it or not. Running us out, or attempting to, won't solve a thing."

"That's a matter of opinions. Your leaving would damn sure make my life easier."

"I'll make a deal with you, Sheriff. We'll shift our base of operations to the county just south of here. How about that?"

"Watson's county."

"Is he the sheriff?"

"Yeah." Morales smiled. Rather strangely, John thought.

"You get along with him?"

"We haven't kissed each other lately." Again that smile.

"Interesting way of putting it. What's his problem with you?"

Morales did not reply.

"All right, let me guess: your tiptoeing around the monied people and their kids in this area, right?"

Morales glared at John for a moment, then turned and walked away, his back stiff with anger.

"How to win friends and influence people," Jenny said. She looked around. "Where'd Al go?"

John glanced around him. "I don't know. I didn't see him leave."

Al rejoined the group, holding a handkerchief over the bleeding cut on his forehead. "Right here. Took me a couple of minutes to find this handkerchief. My luggage is scattered all over the room."

"Worse than my room?" John asked.

"Probably. A car hood came through the window. Took out the bureau before landing in the bathtub."

"I better go see if I can find something to wear," Jenny said. "I can't walk around in my P.J.s all day." She walked back into her room easily enough. The door had been blown open.

"We going to shift the base of operations down one county?" Al asked.

"I think that would be best, Al. We're making Morales nervous staying around here. Not that I blame him one bit. As soon as our car is delivered, we'll pull out."

"I'd better see what I can salvage of my things."

"Yes, me too." He looked back through the broken glass into his room. "God, what a mess."

TEN

The new Mercury was delivered just after noon, and the trio pulled out. They had given statements to the city police, sheriff's deputies, and state police investigators. They had not mentioned anything about the outlaw bikers, and Morales—always hovering close—had not brought up the subject.

"He's worried about his family," John said. "Everything we've gotten on the man suggests he's nothing but squeaky clean."

"How far south are we going?" Al asked.

"Just across the county line. I spoke with a realtor while you two were giving your statements, and told him we wanted to rent a good-sized cabin or house outside of any town, preferably in the foothills and timber. I told him we were on a retreat and needed privacy. He said he was sure he had just the place we were looking for."

"What do you have in mind, John?" Al asked. "I know you've got some kind of plan. You want to let us in on it?"

"We're going to declare war on the outlaws. We're going to bring them to us."

"Just the three of us?" Jenny asked.

"Too many of us would draw a lot of attention and

perhaps spook the bikers off and into cover until we gave up and pulled out."

"It's a good thing we thought to unload the Jeeps and store all our gear in our rooms," Al said. "And it's a damn good thing the state police didn't inspect our rooms too closely."

"On that subject," Jenny said. "I ordered some explosives and caps and timers and so forth. They'll be in Santa Fe tomorrow."

"And so will we," John said. "I want a couple of four-wheel-drive vehicles."

"What did the rental place have to say about the Jeeps, John?" Al asked.

"They were very unhappy."

"I love it!" Jenny said, wandering through the split-level house. "When I retire, this is the type of home that I want."

The house was ten miles from the nearest town and very isolated. The rear of the house butted up against a national forest, lush with thick timber. The house was completely furnished.

"You could roast a bear in that fireplace," Al said.

"Two cords of wood cut, split, stacked, and ready to go," the realtor said. "The electricity is on, the propane tank is full. All the house needs is people."

"We'll take it," John said.

"I'm sorry it doesn't come with bedding," the realtor apologized.

"No problem," John said, walking the agent to the front door. "We've got to go into town to buy food anyway. We'll pick up what else we need."

The trio unloaded the car, and then began the drive into town to pick up supplies and a few articles of clothing, replacing what they had lost during the explosion.

They were just about halfway into town when Al glanced into the rearview mirror. "I think we just might have company. The pickup truck pulled out of that little country store and is staying back."

"Extended cab?" John asked.

"Yes. A very dirty gray color."

"How in the hell could they have found out so quickly about the rented house?" Jenny asked.

"Probably by having half a dozen people in different vehicles watching us," John replied. "Most of these outlaws just look dumb as hell."

"Some of them *are* dumb as hell," Jenny muttered, recalling the fracas at the honky-tonk. Then she said, "Someone had better stay at the house tomorrow. We don't want to leave it unguarded."

"We're leaving it unguarded right now," Al pointed out.

"That's a chance we'll have to take. We've got to pick up supplies. You two go into Santa Fe tomorrow and I'll stay at the house."

"John . . ." Jenny started to protest.

"It's settled. End of discussion."

Al and Jenny pulled out before dawn, promising to return as quickly as possible.

"Take your time," John told them. "I'll be all right."

"He's looking forward to this," Jenny said as they pulled out.

"I think so too."

"He's fifty years old, Al. He should leave things like this to us."

Al smiled as he settled in behind the wheel for the drive to Santa Fe. "You want to be the one to tell him that, Jenny?"

Jenny shook her head. "I think I'll pass on that."

"I thought you would. You saw John work in New York City. You think he can't handle himself?"

"That was in the city. This is going to be much different, and you know it."

"It's his call, and he made it."

"I talked with the others last night. They don't like it either."

"Be that as it may, they don't call the shots. John does. End of story."

"It might be a bad end," Jenny said, then looked out the window and muttered a very vulgar phrase.

Al smiled. "I think he'll be all right. He's looking forward to this. You have to understand just how that picture of what was left of Maria got to him."

"Well, Jesus Christ, Al! It got to all of us."

"Settle down. We've got our assignment for today. We'll do it and get back as soon as we can."

"I should call Control and tell them what John is doing."

"He's already done that. Last evening. They didn't like it either. But he's the boss out in the field."

"Right," she replied. "For better or worse."

John dressed warmly, for the day was cold, the temperature hovering right around freezing, and if the outlaws showed up, he felt that he would eventually end up outside. He carefully cleaned his .45 autoloader and slipped several full magazines in his jacket pocket, zipping the pocket closed. Then he took out his Ruger Mini-14 and field-stripped it. John had always preferred the Mini-14 over the Colt AR-15.

He made another cup of coffee and while it was dripping, fixed some breakfast. He might not get another chance to eat or relax for many hours. John was a veteran of many combat situations and knew only too well the infantryman's credo: Eat when you can, drink when you can, rest when you can. Then he stepped outside and prowled the terrain around the house for half an hour.

Back inside, he finished the pot of coffee and made another pot. He filled a small two-cup thermos and set it on the counter by the back door, just in case he had to exit the house the back way. He would at least have some coffee to ward off the cold. As an afterthought he put some crackers in his pocket.

He fitted a modified battle harness over his coat, then opened a window in the rear of the house and one in the den, cracked them just enough so he could hear any noises close to the house, then sat down with a mug of coffee and waited, his Mini-14 close at hand.

He didn't have to wait long until a slight noise in the timber back of the house brought him to his feet. He picked up his Mini-14, walked to the rear of the house, and looked out. He could see nothing out of the ordinary and didn't expect to, but someone was out there. John knew that wild animals rarely stepped on a branch while traveling through the woods; most made little noise at all.

"Come on, boys," he whispered. "Let's get this show on the road."

Then he heard a noise that seemed to come from the other side of the house.

"The man either shifted locations or there's two of them," John muttered.

He caught a glimpse of a shadow moving through the timber. A two-legged shadow that was moving slowly, carefully. The shadow appeared to be carrying something that looked suspiciously like a rifle.

"Won't be long now," he said, and pulled back the bolt, chambering a .223 round.

Then he wondered about hunters and whether deer or bear season was open. He certainly didn't want to blow a hole in some hunter who was stalking or tracking a deer.

"I should have checked on hunting seasons," he chastised himself. "I sure dropped the ball on that one. But it's too late to worry about it now." The mental picture of Maria's bloody body leaped into his mind and filled him with rage. "Come on, you kidnapping, raping, little-girl-torturing bastards. Make the first move."

John didn't realize it, but he was smiling . . . sort of. More like the grin on a death's head.

"I don't think anybody's at home." The voice came from John's right, just at the edge of the back porch, startling him.

"Two people left," someone called in a stage whisper. "They's supposed to be three in there."

"Well, whoever's in there has probably heard us now," another voice called. "Unless they're asleep or dead. Let's take 'em. Move!"

John tensed and backed up, the Mini-14 at the ready.

But no one appeared. He waited for half a minute, wondering why the holdup.

"I don't like this." The voice from the outside reached him. "Somethin' is mighty queer."

"I ain't goin' in there," another voice said.

The front door was suddenly kicked all the way

open and a man appeared, holding a sawed-off pump-shot. John went belly-down on the floor just as the shotgun boomed, the double-aught buckshot blasting out toward the closed back door.

John shot him, pulling the trigger three times. The .223 rounds hit the intruder in the belly and chest and knocked him backward. He stumbled onto the front porch and lost his balance, falling to the ground.

John rolled to one side and twisted around, still on the floor, just as the back door was slammed open and a bearded man appeared, holding what appeared to be an AK-47.

John gave him several rounds of lead, starting at chest level. The last round struck the man in the face. He dropped the AK and sat down hard in the doorway, his eyes wide open in very startled dying shock.

John quickly rose to his feet. He glanced behind him at the open front door. No one there. He waited, his attention on the back door.

"Son of a bitch!" someone cursed. "This ain't turnin' out worth a shit, boys."

"I'm gone!" another voice yelled.

"Get your ass back here, Jumbo!"

"Fuck you, Toby!" Jumbo said.

John could clearly hear the sounds of running feet, rapidly fading into the cold distance.

"Goddamnit!" Toby shouted. "Acer, you still with me?"

"I'm here, Toby."

"You take Big'un and go around to the front. I'll cover the back."

They brought a damn army with them, John thought. Albeit a very incompetent one.

"He might be on the phone right now, callin' the cops," Acer said.

"Naw. These people aren't cops and they don't want the cops involved. They're somethin' else."

"What?" the man John assumed to be the outlaw called Big'un asked.

"I don't know. But I got the word that they ain't cops. That's all I know."

John stuck the muzzle of his Mini-14 out the side of the open door and gave the outlaws half a mag of lead.

"Holy shit!" a voice hollered. "This guy ain't kiddin' a damn bit."

John slipped in a full thirty-round mag and again blasted the outside air, directing all his fire in the direction of the last voice. This time some of the lead found a target.

"Oh, Christ!" the outlaw yelled. "I'm hit, I'm hit!"

"Where'd he get you, Acer?"

"In the leg. Y'all get me outta here. I'm bleedin' real bad. I think he hit a vein."

"Let's split, man," Big'un called. "This ain't workin' out worth a damn."

"Yeah. We got to get Acer to a doc. Can you get to him, Big'un?"

"Yeah. I'm almost there; couple more seconds. Give me cover fire for insurance."

John bellied down on the floor, behind a wall, just as Toby opened fire.

"We're clear!" Big'un yelled. "Let's get the hell gone from this damn place."

John tried to find a target, using very fast glances out the open door, but the outlaws had backed away too quickly and too deep into the timber.

"I'll see you again, I'm sure," he whispered.

John dragged the body of the outlaw in the front of the house around to the back, then kicked the second body off the back porch and left them both sprawled on the ground. He stood for a moment, trying to decide what to do with them. He shook his head in indecision, and decided to spend the next few minutes picking up all his expended brass.

When that was done, he cleaned up the blood, front and back, and mopped the floor in front of the back door. He knew there was nothing he could do if a good forensics team were to go over the place, but that was unlikely, for he didn't think for a second the outlaws would report the shooting. They would have too much explaining on their own to do.

John looked at the bodies in the backyard for a moment, then said, "Well, to hell with it." He fixed a cup of coffee, sat down in the living room, and drank his coffee and smoked a cigarette.

ELEVEN

John found a tarp in the garage and tossed it over the bodies. Back in the house, he glanced at the clock. It was only midmorning. A lot had happened in a very short time. He checked his phone for messages. Nothing. He walked out onto the porch and looked at the thermometer. The temperature was holding at thirty degrees. He debated for a moment calling Control and advising of the morning's events. He decided he would not.

He built a fire in the den and sat for a time in front of the fireplace, enjoying the soft crackling of the wood as the flames caught and the heat pushed out.

The ringing of his cell phone interrupted his musings. "Anything important happening there, Boss?" Jenny asked.

"Not much," John said. "You made good time."

"The new vehicle was delivered ahead of time as were the other items. We're heading back now. Al's driving the Mercury. We should be back right after lunch."

"Take your time. Enjoy the scenery."

"You sound very upbeat, John."

"No reason not to be. Everything's fine here. See you in a little while."

John went for a walk in the woods behind the lodge,

finding a telltale trail of crimson blood drops. "I hit him pretty hard," John muttered.

He followed the trail for about a mile, until it ended at an old logging road. Fresh tire tracks led back to the main highway. John paused and looked up at the sky: clouding up rapidly. The long-awaited snow was on the way, and it just might be a heavy covering.

John headed back to the lodge, gave the tarp-covered bodies a cursory glance, and picked up an armload of wood and carried it inside. When he went back outside for more wood a few minutes later, the first flakes of snow were falling. He checked the thermometer on the back deck: still thirty degrees.

John sat down in the den and waited for Jenny and Al to drive up.

"What in the hell are we going to do with the bodies?" Al asked after taking a look at the snow-covered mounds behind the lodge.

"Dump them," John replied. "There's a river about ten miles from here. We'll drop them there."

"When?" Jenny asked.

"As soon as we get that SUV unloaded and we can pile them in the cargo compartment. They probably haven't frozen stiff yet. If they have, we'll just bend them until they break."

"Gross, John," Jenny said with a grimace.

John shrugged his indifference. "They're subhuman beings with no regard for the rights of others. Keep that in mind. And keep the picture of Maria in mind when dealing with this scum. It'll make it a lot easier, I assure you." He pointed to the kitchen. "By the way, the coffee is fresh. I just made it."

Sitting in the den with their freshly poured coffee,

Al said, "I didn't pull back the tarp, John. Did you recognize either of those outlaws?"

"No. And I went through their pockets looking for some sort of I.D. They carried nothing. The ones who got away were called Acer, Toby, Jumbo, and Big'un."

"Those names were on the list Control sent us," Jenny said. "Which brings us to this question, Where is Control getting his/her/their information?"

"From sources in various law enforcement agencies, I'm sure. Local, state, and federal."

"This octopus we work for is huge and has quite a number of tentacles," Al said.

"Indeed it does," John agreed.

Jenny stared at John for a few seconds. "You enjoyed the fight, didn't you?"

"I did experience a rather enjoyable sensation from it."

"Fancy way of saying yes," Jenny said.

Al drained his coffee mug and set it on an end table. "Let's get rid of those bodies, gang. They're giving me the creeps."

John field-stripped his Mini-14 and carefully wiped each part clean. The stiffening bodies of the two outlaws were stuffed into the cargo compartment of the new SUV, and moments later were dumped into the river. A few miles down the highway, John pulled off onto an old dirt road and buried his Mini-14 about two feet deep in the ground.

The trio then took a very roundabout route to a truck stop on Interstate 25, many miles south of their rented lodge, and had an early supper. They were back at the lodge just after dark. A sheriff's department car was parked in the driveway.

"Evening, folks," the deputy said, getting out of his unit. "Sorry for the intrusion."

"Perfectly all right, Deputy," John said, shaking the officer's hand. "Is everything all right here?"

"Oh, sure. I'm just checking on a report of gunshots in this area. We got the call about three o'clock this afternoon. Did you folks hear anything?"

" 'Fraid not," John said. "We were driving around down south of here about that time. Had an early supper at a truck stop just off I-25. Snow started picking up and we decided to come on back here. We're new to this area and didn't want to get snowbound miles away."

"I don't blame you for that. The latest prediction is saying this is going to be a major storm. Okay, folks. I just wanted to check here. Got one more place to go, 'bout four miles down the road. You all have a good evening."

"Interesting," John said as soon as the deputy had driven away.

"You think anyone really heard those shots and reported them?" Jenny asked.

"No. One of the outlaws called it in."

"Hoping something would be found around here to bring us to the attention of the authorities?"

"Yes, I'm sure that's it," John replied as they walked on into the house. "And these scummy bastards are really beginning to irritate me."

"I'll make a pot of coffee," Jenny said. "Damn, it's getting colder out there."

John stirred the ashes in the fireplace and laid on some kindling, then put some split wood on, watching it until it caught.

"You drew first blood this day, John," Al said, dumping an armload of wood into the firebox.

"I intend to draw a lot more," John said tersely just

as Jenny walked in, carrying a tray with three steaming mugs of coffee on it.

"You sure slipped into a foul mood in a hurry, John," Jenny said, placing the tray on a table. "Why?"

John turned away from the flames and looked at her, then smiled. "I guess I did, at that. Sorry. Why?" He shook his head. "I don't really know. I . . ."

Headlights turning into the driveway silenced him. He caught a glimpse of emergency lights on the vehicle from the reflection of the lodge lights.

"The police," Jenny said. "I'll let him in."

"Guess again," Al said, looking out the big picture window and smiling.

"What do you mean?"

"You'll see."

Jenny opened the door and stood for a few seconds, staring at the officer. "Ah . . . hello," she finally said.

The officer smiled. "Evening. I'm Sheriff Watson. Mind if I come in for a moment?"

"Not at all," John said, walking to the foyer of the lodge. "Come in out of the weather and get warm."

The sheriff stepped inside, and Jenny closed the door as the sheriff walked over to the fire. "I love a fireplace," the sheriff said. "I find them very relaxing."

"Sheriff Morales didn't tell us everything he knew about you," John said, smiling at the sheriff. "But now I understand why he found my questions and statements about the sheriff of this county amusing."

"Robert Morales is a good man," Sheriff Watson replied. "It's just that Bob and I just don't quite agree on how to treat outlaw bikers. I'm Jimmi Watson, by the way."

John introduced himself and the others and added,

"Not too many women sheriffs, Sheriff Watson. Please forgive our initial shock."

Sheriff Jimmi Watson was, John guessed, in her late thirties. A very attractive woman with short dark hair and unreadable dark eyes. About five feet six. There was no wedding ring on her finger.

"I'm used to it," Jimmi replied. "I'll get to the point. Did one of my deputies stop by here this evening?"

"Yes," John said. "He did. Not more than a half hour ago. After he spoke with us he said he had one more residence to check. About four miles down the road."

Jimmi nodded her head. "That jibes with what Dispatch says. I've been trying to reach him for twenty minutes. I've called the Woodson house. He never showed up there."

"He was all right when he left here," John said.

"Oh, I'm sure he was. I didn't mean to imply that you were under any suspicion. It's just that after he called in from here, we lost contact."

"How about some coffee, Sheriff?" Jenny asked.

"That would be nice. Yes."

"Coming right up."

"Please, won't you sit down?" John said.

"How nice of you, Mr. Barrone, Thank you. But we're all being terribly formal. How about you calling me Jimmi." She smiled and opened her leather jacket, pulling out several sheets of paper. "After receiving this from Bob Morales, I feel I know you all so well."

John returned the smile. "I wondered if Sheriff Morales would alert you to our coming."

"We don't always see eye-to-eye on everything, but we're still good friends."

"Known him long?"

"Since college. He's only a year older than me."

"I've either misjudged your age or his."

"His," she answered quickly and with a smile. "He got married right out of high school. So you're after the bikers, hey, John?"

Jenny brought in a mug of coffee for the sheriff, set it on an end table, and took a chair.

"Thanks. Smells wonderful. The bikers, John?"

"We were investigating the kidnapping of Maria Sanchez. Now we're investigating her murder."

"Who's paying you?"

"A group of people who would like to see justice done."

"In other words, you're not going to tell me."

"I can't tell you what I don't know."

"Bob said you were slippery." She sipped her coffee, her dark eyes never leaving John's face. "But a word of warning. Don't get too slippery with me."

"I wouldn't dream of it."

"Bob is sure you work for the government."

"I can assure you we do not."

"But you have some government ties." It was not put as a question.

"We do not. What we do have is a lot of private money behind us."

"I'll accept that." Jimmi took another sip of coffee and frowned. "John, I don't care if you killed one or twenty outlaw bikers out here today."

John started to speak and Sheriff Watson held up a hand, stilling him.

"Listen to me! This is going to sound very strange coming from a sheriff. But I'm just vocalizing what many, if not most, law enforcement personnel think, but for obvious reasons can't put into words. If there was a shooting out here today, I don't believe for one second you started it. I know how outlaw bikers operate. Since this . . . pack of slime began coming in here, I've been reading up on them, every report I could get my hands on. It's not pleasant reading. In the past year we've had a three-hundred-percent increase in drug use in this area. Amphetamines. Strong stuff. Kids are dying from it; kids are suffering kidney and liver failure. The date-rape pills are flooding this area. Cocaine and heroin trafficking is up by over a hundred percent. The list just goes on and on. Personally, I don't care if you kill every goddamn one of those responsible for the manufacturing and distribution of this poison. Just please do it discreetly."

"We're a private investigation firm, Sheriff Watson. Not a group of hired killers."

"Right," Jammi said. "For your information, I joined the Navy right out of college. Naval intelligence. I didn't put on a uniform for three years. Detached service in and reporting to various . . . ah, civilian intelligence agencies. I'm sure you can check that out . . . and will check it out. Does that tell you anything?"

"Possibly."

"Good. Then we understand each other. I hope." Jimmi knocked back the rest of her coffee and stood up.

"Is your deputy really missing, Sheriff?" John asked.

"Of course not. Well, it's been a very interesting and informative chat. We'll do it again, I'm sure. Nice meeting you all."

"So nice meeting you, Jimmi."

After Sheriff Jimmi Watson had left, John fixed a martini and returned to his chair. "Get busy checking out the sheriff, Jenny. Let's see what Control can come up with."

"Right on it," Jenny said.

"I'm going to shower," Al said. "And go to bed. I think tomorrow just might turn out to be a very busy day."

"You might be right, Al. Good night."

After Al had left the room, John looked at the dancing flames and whispered, "I hope it is a busy one. I hope those outlaw bastards make another try for me."

The wood in the fireplace popped and John smiled.

The next several days turned out to be real yawners. The skies spilled snow all over the place and the skiers came in by droves. Everybody who didn't have to get out in the mess didn't; they stayed home. John, Jenny, and Al stayed snug and warm in the lodge and boned up on the requested info from Control: several reams of it.

"Many more days like this and we're all going to get fat as pigs," Jenny said on the afternoon of the third day.

"Then stop eating," John said with a smile. "That's the biggest container of popcorn I've ever seen."

Jenny stuck her tongue out at him.

"And there must be a pound of melted butter on it," Al said.

Jenny gave him the finger.

"My eyes are getting weary from all this reading," John said, laying aside the printouts. "Give me some of that popcorn. It smells good."

While the popcorn bowl was being passed around and John and Al were digging in, Jenny said, "Jimmi Watson checks out. She was in some hot spots while in the service. She's a sure enough gutsy broad."

"And she's aced one guy and wounded another since she first put on a badge," Al added.

"Her bravery certainly can't be questioned," John said, wiping his hands on a paper towel. "And there is nothing to indicate any dirt anywhere."

"Married briefly," Jenny said. "No serious significant other in her life since the divorce."

" 'Significant other,' " John said with a sigh. "Whatever happened to beau and boyfriend?"

"They went out with the dinosaur," Jenny told him. She grinned and added, "Can you dig it, Pops?"

John gave her a dubious look, much like a long-suffering parent would give an errant child—which Jenny pointedly ignored, while Al laughed—and said, "So she's clean and on the level . . . at least with us. So far," he added.

"She's offering, I think," Al said, "to turn her back while we handle the outlaw bikers discreetly. I believe that was her choice of words."

"We'll deal with the outlaws," John said. "But on our terms, not Sheriff Watson's."

"Which means? . . ." Jenny asked.

"We let them come to us."

"Weather forecast says the snow will be gone by tonight and tomorrow will be bright and sunny," Al said.

"So we do what?" Jenny asked.

"Maintain a high visibility," John told them. "Let the outlaws know we're still around and plan to continue our investigation."

"In other words," Jenny said, just before stuffing her mouth full of popcorn, "be a big fat pain in the ass."

John smiled and replied, "You do turn such a lovely phrase, dear."

TWELVE

The weather prognosticators had hit the forecast right on the button. The next day the sky was a clear blue. The ground was covered with a thick blanket of snow, but the roads, for the most part, were clear. The sun was so bright the reflection bouncing off the snow hurt the eyes.

"Time to go to work," John said. "We'll take the SUV in case we need four-wheel drive."

"Going to stick the needle to the outlaws?" Jenny asked.

"We're sure going to try."

"The same vehicle has passed by the place four times in half an hour," Al said. "That I've noticed, that is."

"Description?"

"Older-model Bronco. Modified. The chassis set up high with those big oversized tires."

"That'll be easy to spot," Jenny said.

"I can't believe they'd be that stupid," John replied.

"You mix stupidity with arrogance and you have a very dangerous mix," Al told his partners.

"For a fact," John agreed. "Let's go stir the mix."

Jenny picked up a large briefcase. "I'm ready. I'll sit in the rear seat."

"What do you have in that thing?" Al asked, pointing at the briefcase.

"Oh . . ." She grinned. "Female stuff, you know? Cosmetics and stuff like that."

"Which way did the Bronco head, Al?" John asked.

"West."

"This may be just a move to get us out of the house so they can booby-trap it," Jenny said.

"Possibly," John agreed. "We'll know when we return, won't we?"

"Homecoming just might be quite a thrill," Jenny muttered, shifting the heavy briefcase from left hand to right.

"John, exactly what are we going to do?" Al asked.

"I'd like to grab one of these outlaws and sweat him."

"I'd like to beat the crap out of one of these ugly miscreants," Jenny said.

"Control your baser instincts," John told her. "Let's go. Al, you drive."

The Bronco swung in behind them before they had driven two miles.

"No doubt about it now," Al said after checking his rearview and alerting the others.

"We'll lead them out away from any homes," John said after quickly checking a map. "There's a road that cuts through this national forest just up ahead. It'll be a right turn."

"We'll need the four-wheel drive, for sure."

"It's on demand. When we slow to make the turn, punch it on." John turned to look at Jenny, seated just behind him. She had taken out a couple of grenades. "Planning to have some fun, Jenny?"

"You bet," she said with a grin. "I checked the fuses on the grenades last evening. They're all five seconds."

"That's nice to know," John said drily.

Al slowed and turned off into the national forest. He punched on the four-wheel drive. The road still had some snow on it, but there was no ice underneath. "Staying with us," he said.

"Good," John replied. "Can you see how many are in the Bronco?"

"Four in that one."

"That one?" John questioned.

"Another Bronco or Blazer just made the turn right behind the first one. Same kind of modified high-tired rig. Three or four in that one."

"Now things get really interesting," Jenny said. "John?"

"Yes?"

"Say we bust up this outlaw bunch here . . . which I sure hope we do. We can't get them all. You know some are going to get away and just start up labs somewhere else."

"Should that happen, we follow. This outlaw bunch is going to be put out of business. Both of you bear this in mind: I want one of these apes alive for questioning."

Al arched an eyebrow at that. "I have to point this out, John, like it or not: These are American citizens. Not international terrorists."

"They are domestic terrorists. Responsible for God only knows how many deaths. They're killing and crippling kids and they don't care. They're hard-core criminals. And the monied people who are behind them are just as guilty and I intend to treat them the same way. You bear that in mind."

"We'd better be able to prove these so-called monied people are behind any of it," Al responded. "Beyond the shadow of a doubt."

"Oh, we will," John said. "Relax your FBI training for a minute."

Al smiled as his eyes cut to the rearview for an instant. The vehicles behind them had made no effort to close the distance. "Training dies hard, John. I really don't object to disposing of hard-core criminals. I just want to be sure, that's all."

"We'll be sure, Al. Jenny, you have anything to add to this short debate?"

"Nope. Let's get on with it."

Al chuckled. "Someday, Jenny, I hope you'll share with us why you hate outlaw bikers with such intensity."

"Maybe I will, Al. Someday."

John knew part of the answer to that, but he didn't want to press Jenny any further about it. That was her business. Whatever the entire reason, John agreed with her. "Our followers getting any closer, Al?" he asked.

"No. Maintaining the same distance."

John looked at the detailed map. "There is some sort of rest area about three or four miles ahead. In this weather it should be deserted. Pull in there. If those bastards behind us want to get this thing started, let's make it easy for them."

"Suits me," Jenny said, opening her briefcase.

John unzipped his small cargo bag on the floorboards at his feet and took out his mini-Uzi.

"Get mine out of my gear bag, will you, Jenny?" Al asked.

"I'm way ahead of you. It's loaded up and ready to stutter."

"If there are vehicles at the rest area?" Al asked.

"Pull in anyway," John said. "We'll wait them out. I want to get this matter started."

"At last report there were about sixty of these out-law bikers involved," Jenny said.

"Good," John replied. "To use an overworked adage: the more the merrier."

"That's certainly one way of looking at it," Al said.

John and Jenny exchanged glances at his comment.

"But on the bright side, they aren't all in this immediate area," Jenny added.

"There's the rest stop," John said, putting a temporary halt to the bantering. "It's deserted."

"And set back a nice distance from the highway," Jenny observed. "That's even better. The trees will help muffle the sounds of battle."

Al smiled as he turned into the rest area. "Are you sure you aren't part Viking, Jenny?"

"Beats me," she replied. "I just don't like drug dealers."

"Or outlaw bikers."

"You got that right."

Al stopped close to the rest-room building and the trio got out, holding their weapons close, partially hidden by their coats. Jenny's grenades were in her coat pockets.

"Keep the vehicle between us and them until we see what they have in mind," John ordered. "And needle them into opening this little dance."

That got John a curious glance from Al.

The vehicles pulled in and stopped just past the entrance to the rest area. The men sat inside, staring at John, Jenny, and Al.

"Eight of the ugly bastards," Jenny said, staring right back. "I recognize a couple from the printouts. The others are new faces."

Just as she finished speaking, the doors opened and

the outlaws began stepping out onto the surface of the parking lot. They were all armed.

"That big fat one with the salt-and-pepper beard is called Popper," Jenny said. "He's a bad one. Did hard time for rape." Her face tightened. "I want him all for myself. The little one with the double barrel sawed-off is Ratface. He's been in the bucket several times for aggravated assault and simple rape. If there is such a thing as simple rape. I want that sorry bastard too."

"You can have them," John said. "Popper and Ratface. What lovely names."

"Time for you folks to pay your debts," one of the outlaws called across the distance.

"Oh?" John raised his voice. "What debt is that?"

"You killed two of ours and shot up Acer pretty damn bad. Now we're gonna even the score."

"Screw you!" Jenny said.

"I believe I just might take you up on that, Blondie. Bend you over and fuck you like a dog."

"In your dreams, Hyena Face," Jenny told him.

"Smart-mouthed bitch," Hyena said. "I'm gonna stomp you after I fuck you."

Jenny laughed at him.

"You're not going to do anything except run your ignorant mouths," John called.

"You're mighty tough-talkin' for an old dude, Pops," another outlaw called.

John smiled at that. "I can back it up, Goofus. Anytime you want to try."

"Goofus? Who you callin' Goofus?"

"You, you goofy-looking escapee from a lunatic asylum."

"Cool it, Hoppy," Hyena said. "I'll handle this."

"Son of a bitch insulted me! He called me a lunatic. I'm gonna stomp him."

"All of you shut up," another outlaw ordered. "Let's get this done."

"I want to fuck that bitch," Hyena said.

"I'd rather kill her," Popper said. "Hell, I think I will." He lifted his weapon.

Jenny raised her mini-Uzi and stitched Popper, the lead slamming into him from his knees to his neck, the impact knocking the outlaw back and into Ratface.

John put lead into Hyena and the outlaw standing next to him. Both went down, their upper torsos riddled and bleeding.

"Son of a bitch!" Ratface hollered, recovering his balance and lifting his shotgun.

John's Uzi stuttered, and Ratface's neck and face dissolved into a mass of blood. He stretched out on the pavement beside his buddy, Popper, both of them equally dead.

Jenny and John blew two full mags into the knot of outlaw bikers. The surprise action took all of five seconds, and in that short span, it left all eight of the outlaws dead or dying. The area in which the bikers had been standing was slick with blood. Al had not fired a shot.

"Make sure they're all dead and take three of the outlaws' weapons," John ordered. "Drop our Uzis beside the bodies and let's get the hell gone from here."

The team had field-stripped their weapons before leaving the lodge, and knew there were no prints on the weapons, the magazines, or any of the brass, which now littered the parking area, twinkling in the bright sunlight. John used Al's Uzi to finish off one who was almost dead anyway. Al grimaced at John's coldness. The glance did not escape John or Jenny.

A minute later, the team had pulled out, heading straight north. Fifteen minutes later, they were out of the national forest. John, now behind the wheel, turned west on a state road. A half an hour later, they were on a major highway, heading south toward Albuquerque. As they rode, Jenny and Al took down the weapons they had taken from the outlaws, and John began stopping along the highway, disposing of the weapon parts. The team stopped at a large mall on the outskirts of the city, and spent several hours walking the mall and shopping, buying things they really didn't need but setting up a credit-card alibi for that morning. Then they drove to a nice restaurant not far from the mall and had lunch.

"Very productive morning," John said.

"I would say so," Jenny said.

"I would imagine that when we get back to the lodge, Sheriff Watson will be waiting for us," Al said, an odd note to his voice.

John nodded his head. "I would be disappointed if she wasn't."

"It's going to be interesting to see her reaction to today's events," Jenny said.

"I want a break from this assignment, John," Al said softly.

"I wondered when that was coming."

"Don't misunderstand me, either of you. I don't want to leave the team. Even if that were possible. It's just . . . well . . ." He hesitated.

"We're a little cold for you, Al?" Jenny prompted.

"Putting it bluntly, yes. New York was . . . different. We were after international terrorists who were planning to kill thousands of people. But these people . . ." He shook his head.

"They were going to kill us this morning," John reminded him.

"So they said. But you and Jenny goaded them pretty hard."

"We told you we were going to do that, Al," John said. "Several times over a period of several days." He held up a hand. "No need to say any more. We can get you a rental car here in the city and you can join one of the other teams and work this matter out in your head. Tell us which team you want to join and I'll advise them you're coming."

"I would appreciate that."

"You know there is only one way you'll ever leave the team, Al."

"I know. I don't want to leave the team. Just out of this assignment."

"All right. We'll get you a car rented as soon as we finish lunch. And I do understand. Eat up, Al. The salad is excellent."

THIRTEEN

Al was gone within the hour, heading out to join Don, Linda, and Paul. John had briefed them as to what had happened and told them to keep an eye on Al.

"You think he's going to try to run?" Jenny asked.

"I don't know. I hope not. I do know that he's got some hang-ups that weren't detected during the interviews or the training."

"If he tries to run, he's a dead man," Jenny said it flatly.

"I know that better than you."

"What do you mean?"

"This organization we work for will put a contract on him and kill him before he can open his mouth. They might already have done that."

"You called Control?"

"Before we left the restaurant."

"And they said? . . ."

"Let's just say they weren't surprised. But I certainly was. In more ways than one."

"Oh?" When John said nothing, she prompted: "You want to explain that?"

"They're paring down the team. Obviously, I didn't know as much about the organization as I thought. I'm still irritated and getting more so."

Jenny was thoughtful for a few miles, alternately looking out the window and at John. He was angry and making no attempt to hide that anger. "I can't blame you for being upset. So what now, John?"

"We go on with the assignment."

"Do we pull in one of the others to take Al's place?"

"I don't think we need to do that. We work well together. So we'll handle it."

"That isn't an order from Control?"

John shook his head. "No. They left that up to me."

"Big of them. We'll give them a gold star."

John smiled for the first time since they had begun the drive back to the lodge. Then he laughed. "You think we can handle it?"

She smiled at him. "Without a doubt. I'm just anxious to hear what Sheriff Watson has to say."

"She might not say anything about it. At least not to us. There is a lot more to Jimmi Watson than meets the eye."

"I . . . I'm not sure I follow you."

"I have a strong suspicion she's one of the standby contact people recruited by Control."

Jenny again fell silent, and was deep in thought for a couple of miles, staring out the window. "So who was our watchdog on the last assignment?"

"I don't know if we had one. I don't believe we did. Jenny, I didn't say Jimmi was a watchdog. I said she was a contact person."

"We weren't sent to New Mexico by chance, were we?"

"Certainly doesn't look that way."

Jenny pointed to the radio, which had been on since leaving the restaurant. "You know damn well those eight bodies in pools of blood at the rest area have been found. Somebody's sitting on the news."

"Three guesses as to who that might be."

"Sheriff Watson."

"Sure. And when it is given to the press, it will be released as the culmination of a deadly quarrel between rival motorcycle gangs fighting over drugs."

"Sheriff Morales will never buy that."

"I'm sure he won't. But Morales won't say a word publicly. He can't afford to. His family has been threatened. And he's taking those threats very seriously."

"Wait a minute, wait a minute." Jenny held up a hand. "I gotta think about this. Something just popped into my head. Is there a possibility that Al might have been planted in the team by Control?"

"Interesting thought, and one I have entertained. That's certainly a possibility."

"Reason I thought that is he sure did a good job on the last assignment. Now all of a sudden he gets hinky. It just doesn't make sense to me."

"Nor to me. Well, we might get the answer someday, but don't count on it."

John and Jenny made it to the lodge, and were having a drink in the den, watching a local TV broadcast, when the news of the dead bikers broke.

When the reporter had finished his story, John and Jenny looked at each other and smiled, Jenny saying, "You called it on both counts, John. A biker war. And I sure see Sheriff Watson's fine hand in this."

"Yes. And I . . ."

The next story on the newscast stopped him cold. He and Jenny listened in shock as the reporter told of Al Durstman's death. ". . . And according to several witnesses, the accident was unavoidable. Durstman's car hit a patch of ice on the bridge and spun out of control. It bounced off the guardrail and went over the side, killing him on impact. He was alone in the car."

"Damn!" John said, using the remote to turn off the TV.

"If there were civilian witnesses, it was just a stupid accident."

"I guess so. But I'm going to do some checking to satisfy my mind."

"I'll notify Control and the other team members," Jenny said.

"Ask Control how they want to handle the funeral arrangements; where to ship the body and so forth."

"Will do." She walked out of the room.

John fixed another drink and sat in the quiet room until Jenny returned.

"Control said Al's death was regrettable," she said. "They asked if you want to consider a replacement. They're waiting for your reply."

"No replacement."

"I'll tell them."

"What about funeral arrangements?"

"They'll handle everything. They said for us to pay our respects at the funeral home—if we want to, that is—and then back off quietly and quickly. They'll get the official police report to us ASAP."

"They have anything else to say?"

"Gamma hydroxybutyrate."

"I beg your pardon?"

"GHB. The date-rape drug."

"What about it?"

"Requests for it have skyrocketed from those assholes around the nation who sell it. It's being manufactured in this area."

"Kill the assholes who sell it," John replied, a very sour note to his voice.

"I agree. But that isn't our job. Control wants us to find out where the lab is and destroy it."

"That will slow it down for maybe twenty-four hours at the most."

"Yes. I know. But that's what we've been ordered to do. Immediately."

"Another lab will just pop up in another area of the country."

"I know."

John sighed. "All right. Tell Control we'll get right on it. First thing in the morning."

"Will do. While I'm doing that, will you fix me another drink?"

"Certainly. Jenny?"

She turned to look at him.

"Sorry I was so cross. My comments weren't directed at you personally."

"I know." She smiled at him. "I liked Al too."

John fixed another drink for Jenny and set it on the end table. He returned to his chair and stared moodily at the flames doing their hot dance in the fireplace. He sat silently and very still until Jenny returned and picked up her drink.

"You ready to use some of those explosives you picked up, Jenny?"

"You bet. When and where?"

"Late tomorrow night. If we get back from viewing Al's body in time, that is. We're going to head back up into Sheriff Morales's county."

Jenny arched an eyebrow at that and waited for John to elaborate.

"Yes. We're going to blow up that damned biker honky-tonk."

"All right!"

"I want to rattle the cages of the monied people

who are in cahoots with the bikers. And there is no better way to do that than by hitting them in the pocketbook."

"And Nick Sandoval owns the biker bar."

"Right."

"And then?"

"Then we start hassling their kids."

Jenny frowned. "Minors, John?"

"I didn't say hurt them. Just hassle them, especially that eighteen-year-old, Davy Curtis."

"That's the one suspected of selling the date-rape crap to kids."

"Right. Him I especially want to talk to."

"How?"

"We'll think of something. After a night's sleep."

"I'm not looking forward to tomorrow."

"Nor am I. But we'll get through it." He lifted his glass. "To Al."

Al Durstman was not badly mangled. At least not his face, and that was all John and Jenny were allowed to see. John did not ask if there were any bullet holes in the body, and the funeral home director did not volunteer any information. Both John and Jenny were relieved to get out of the funeral home's visitation room and back on the road.

"Think we'll ever know the real truth about Al?" Jenny asked as they sat in their vehicle in the parking lot.

"No. And I'm never going to ask." John looked at his watch. "We've got hours to kill before we can head back north. Any suggestions?"

"How about a movie?" Jenny asked with a grin.

"Get serious. I flipped through the movie channels

on the TV last night. I never saw so much idiotic, juvenile nonsense in my life."

"It is kind of dismal, isn't it? And people wonder why the morals in this country have taken such a beating. Well . . . we've checked with the other team members. They had nothing to report. I guess I'm out of ideas. Where is Al's body being shipped? Did you ask?"

"No. Control is taking care of that. We're just friends paying our respects."

"I'd like to get a look at the police report."

"So would I. But I doubt we ever will. As far as we're concerned, the matter is officially closed. That's the word I got from Control when I spoke with them this morning. So forget it." He watched Jenny's eyes as she again glanced at the road that ran in front of the funeral home. "I see it, Jenny. That same pickup truck has passed by three times. And you can bet there is another vehicle or two."

Jenny shook her head. "I know we weren't followed coming down here. I kept an eye out for that. So just how damn big is this group, John?"

"Very large. A lot of local players. And something else: I'm beginning to think the bikers are only very minor players in this game. They're the muscle and the mules and the ones taking the heavy risks."

"Sandoval, Curtis, and Grayson are the head honchos?"

"That's the way I see it."

"All the more reason to blow the biker bar. Get the money people all stirred up, right?"

"I'd like to blow the labs where this deadly crap is being cooked."

Jenny waited, sensing he was not through.

"But they'd be back in business in a week. I can sure see why Control handed us this job."

Jenny started to speak, then paused as the pickup truck once more passed by. "Two of them, John."

"There'll be more waiting somewhere. I'd bet on that."

"So we do what?"

"Head back. Or pretend that's where we're going. Get the map case out, the detailed county maps."

"What are we looking for?"

"A road that wanders off into the mountains and then dead-ends."

"Gonna have us our little private war, are we?"

"I hope so."

They headed out of town, toward the north, Jenny watching the road signs and checking the map. "Take the next exit," she told him. "And put this thing in four-wheel drive. We're going to need it."

"The road that bad?"

"It ain't real great. It's unpaved."

"Then this should prove very interesting." John cut off the main highway and took the road that would lead them, eventually, to the secondary unpaved road. "Jenny, do you have any explosives with you other than plastic?"

"Sure. In my bag behind me."

"What type?"

"Dynamite." She cut her eyes to him and smiled. "Well . . . it's sort of beefed up, you might say."

"Do you mean it's more powerful?"

"Well . . . that's one way of putting it."

"How do you beef up dynamite? Never mind. I'll take your word for it. Can you get it ready while we're moving?"

"It's ready."

John almost lost the vehicle on the road. He recovered and asked, "You mean to say that damn stuff is already capped? And in a bag right behind me?"

She laughed at his expression. "Relax, John. It's not going to blow. It's reasonably safe."

"Reasonably? Dear God!"

"There's our dead-end road." She pointed, then looked behind her. "Several more cars and trucks have joined the chase. This might turn out to be fun."

"If that damn stuff behind me blows, I'm never going to forgive you."

Her eyes twinkling, she said, "There is only a very slight chance of that happening, John."

John cut off onto the rough and somewhat snowy secondary road and fought the wheel for a few seconds. "That's what the jumpmaster said about my chute not opening just before my first jump. It did not fill me with confidence."

"I liked skydiving. It was fun."

"You would."

Jenny again glanced behind her. "I count at least ten people, John. No. Another vehicle has joined the chase. Make that about fourteen people."

"How much further before this road ends?"

"Oh, miles yet."

"It'll probably get worse."

"Sure will," she said brightly. "It narrows down to about one lane just up ahead."

"Wonderful. You ready for a little war?"

"I'm with you, dude. Whatever blows your hat in the creek."

"Then let's do it." John spun the wheel and braked, sliding to a stop.

FOURTEEN

John paused for a couple of heartbeats, then noticed what appeared to be some sort of road faintly outlined about fifty yards behind them. He backed up and turned in, the front of the SUV facing out.

"Get your gear, Jenny. Work around that curve up ahead so the bikers can't see you and circle around. Get as close to them as you can."

"Close enough to chunk some surprises at them, hey?"

"You got it. As soon as they start the dance I'll open fire."

She winked at him. "I'm gone, Pops." She grinned and added, "Take care, John."

John waited and watched, his Mini-14 in hand, a thirty-round magazine in place, a round in the chamber. The outlaws were about a hundred yards away, well within easy range for the 14. But they were staying out of sight, behind their vehicles, which were blocking the road, one behind another, all at a slight angle for maximum cover.

"You fucked up bad this time, Barrone!" a biker shouted, his voice easily carrying the distance. "There ain't nobody livin' around here for maybe eight/ten miles."

"Yeah, old man!" another yelled. "Your ass is in the barrel this time."

"And tell that smart-mouthed, uppity bitch with you she's about to get the fuckin' of her life," yet another outlaw's voice called.

"And when we get done humpin' her I'm gonna beat the shit out of her," another outlaw hollered.

John smiled. He could just imagine what Jenny was thinking, listening to this blather.

"Hey, Barrone! Are you there, or did you fall asleep, you old fart?"

"I'm here, asshole!" John called. "Keep running your stupid mouth about what you're going to do. It's very amusing."

There was a moment of silence from the outlaw bikers, then: "You won't think it's so goddamn funny when we get hold of you, dickhead. I got some real plans for you. Like skinnin' you alive. How does that sound?"

"I'm no scared little girl like Maria, you fathead. I'd think about that."

"You'll scream just like she did, prick. Probably more when we start cuttin' your dick off."

"Took some real brave men to torture a teenage girl. Are you proud of yourselves?"

"She got what was comin' to her, Barrone. She knew better than to talk to you. She knew what would happen to her if she run her mouth."

"What a bunch of yellow-bellied bastards you are," John shouted. "Sorry-assed, no-good slime-bags, that's all you are." *Come on, Jenny,* John thought. *I can't keep them talking for much longer.*

The outlaws opened fire, sending a dozen slugs howling at John.

"How do you like that, Barrone?" one hollered as

the echo of gunfire died away. "Did that wake you up?"

"I'm still here, asshole," John yelled. "Unhit and wide awake. Here have some of this." He clicked his Mini-14 off safety and burned half a mag in their direction. The lead bounced and screamed off vehicles and produced a hail of cussing from the bikers.

"You rotten son of a bitch!" a biker shouted. "Damn you, you'll pay for that. One of your damn slugs done tore up my CD player. Shit!"

"I'm so sorry," John yelled. "But considering the crap you listen to, I feel I did society a favor."

"Crap?" the biker bellowed. "You call my music crap?"

This is becoming ridiculous, John thought. *Where are you, Jenny?*

"I got everything the Dripping Snot Boys ever recorded!" the biker yelled. "And you just ruined their best CD, you bastard."

John sighed. He could just imagine what any group called the Dripping Snot Boys would sound like.

"Hey, you guys!" Jenny's voice cut through the cold air. It was coming from a wooded snow-covered hill just above the bikers' location.

"It's the bitch," a biker said, barely loud enough for John to hear. "Where the hell is she?"

"I can't see her. But I think she's somewhere up yonder in them woods."

"She's close," another said. "How the hell did she get up there?"

"She circled around, you idiot," another said. "And she's got a clear field of fire to us. Y'all give her some lead. Maybe we'll get lucky."

"Aw, come on. I don't want her dead, Jack. I want to fuck her."

"Fuck your fist, Woody," Jack replied. "I want these people dead and out of our business."

A small object was thrown out of the woods. It arced high and slowly began falling, landing just in front of a pickup truck.

"What the hell is that?" a biker said. "Is she throwin' rocks at us?"

The "rock" exploded, sending a shower of snow, dirt, and other debris all over the bikers and the vehicle. The windshield was shattered and one biker went down, his face a mask of blood and shredded flesh from the shrapnel. He lay on the ground, screaming in pain.

"Jesus Christ!" an outlaw shouted. "Dynamite!"

Another object came hurtling out of the nearby woods. It landed in the bed of the pickup truck with a thonk and blew. Pieces of metal were sent flying in all directions as the bed was ripped apart. The jagged metal tore into the flesh of a couple of outlaws and drove them to the ground. The rear tires of the pickup were blown off and then the gas tank exploded. Two more bikers were knocked to the ground, one with part of his head missing and his brains hanging out, his head torn open by a large piece of metal.

"Son of a bitch!" Woody yelled, staggering to his feet, lurching from behind cover.

John shot him in the knee, the .223 round shattering the knee cap and knocking the outlaw back to the churned-up snow, hollering in pain.

Jenny tossed another highly volatile homemade grenade. This one landed in the center of the confused bikers and sputtered for a couple of seconds before exploding.

"That's all for me," Jack said, most of his hearing

momentarily gone from the explosion. "Let's get the hell gone from here."

"What about Woody and the others?"

"Leave 'em. Come on. Every man for themselves!" he shouted. "Run."

Jack ran for a vehicle and made it. The two who ran with him didn't. Jenny shot one in the head and John aced the other, blowing his spine apart, the fragments of lead piercing his heart. Both men suddenly slumped to the ground, dead on impact with the snow.

Another group of outlaws ran for the last vehicle, an SUV, and made it, cranking up and spinning away.

The last knot of bikers ran for another vehicle, parked on a curve just off the road. Jenny gave the engine a half a magazine of lead and smoke and steam began rising from the perforated hood and the punctured radiator. The outlaw bikers kept right on running, heading back up the road as fast as they could.

John drove down to the battle site and looked at the carnage. Woody was still alive, moaning and groaning in the bloody snow, his left kneecap busted, the leg useless.

"Want to go for a ride?" John asked him.

"Fuck you!" Woody said.

"No, I don't think so. Your leg hurt you some?"

"Hell yes, it hurts, you son of a bitch!"

"Oh, that's too bad."

"Go to hell, you government asshole."

"I don't work for the government."

"Huh? Sure you do!"

"I'm sure I don't."

"Morris said you did."

"Who is Morris?" John knew perfectly well who Morris was: Morris Curtis. One of the money men behind the bikers.

"Fuck you! I ain't sayin' no more."

"Very well. I'll just leave you here and maybe your buddies will come back for you."

"Sure they will."

"It's cold out here, buddy. You willing to bet your life your buddies will be back?"

Woody hesitated for a few seconds, indecision on his face. "Yeah, I am."

"Suit yourself. Don't catch pneumonia lying there in the snow. Or bleed to death." John picked up Woody's rifle, which was lying several feet away, out of arm's reach, and turned away as if to leave.

"Wait a minute!" Woody said. "Man, you can't leave me here. Hell, I can't walk."

"I offered you a ride, remember?"

"Straight to jail? No, thanks."

"Who said anything about jail? I didn't."

"What do you mean?"

"I mean, I can take you to a doctor that will fix you up and ask no questions. And it won't be reported to the police."

"Why would you do that?" Woody had struggled out of his jacket and wrapped it around his wounded knee.

"In exchange for information."

"Forget it."

"All right. See you." John turned away and started to walk off. He had taken only a few steps before Woody called after him.

"Wait a minute, man! I mean, shit, I'll die out here."

John stopped and turned around. "Make up your mind."

Woody hesitated just as Jenny strolled up and stood a few yards away, watching and listening. "I have a suggestion," she said. "Why not just shoot the bastard in the other knee and leave him here to die? His buddies won't be back; they're still running away."

"Oh, shit, lady!" Woody hollered after taking a quick look at Jenny's grim, unsmiling expression. "I mean, hell, you can't be serious!"

"The hell I'm not," Jenny replied. "I'll be only too glad to do it. I hate you bastards."

"I never done nothin' to you personal!" Woody hollered.

"You're alive," Jenny told him. "That's enough for me."

"You 'bout a cold bitch."

"That's me," Jenny agreed.

"What about it, outlaw?" John asked. "Medical treatment for information, take it or leave it."

"All right, all right. I'll take it. Hell, I ain't got no choice, do I?"

"No, you haven't. None at all."

"What do you want to know?"

"Everything. And when we get you in our vehicle, you'd better start talking and you'd better not stop. If I sense you're lying, I'll throw you out on the highway and you can rot."

"Jesus!" Woody said. "And people call us hard. You folks take the cake."

"Let's get him in the car," John said. "Then you drive, Jenny. I'll sit in the back with our friend."

"I don't trust the son of a bitch," Jenny said.

"I don't either. But we'll see what he has to say, then decide what to do with him."

"I'm gonna level with you!" Woody hollered. "I swear I am."

"You'd better."

John and Jenny got the biker to his feet and into

the rear seat of the SUV. Woody was almost crying from the pain in his shattered knee.

Jenny looked back at him, her eyes cold as ice. "If you lie to us, outlaw, I personally will shoot you in your other knee and shove you over the side into a deep ditch. And don't you ever doubt that for one second."

"Can you gimme something for the pain?" Woody begged.

"No," John told him. "Grit your teeth and bear it. It's a long ride to the doctor. Start talking, outlaw, and don't stop. If you do, you know what's going to happen to you."

"I understand."

John clicked on a small, battery-operated tape recorder. "We're waiting."

Woody sighed and started talking.

FIFTEEN

Woody talked, Jenny drove, and John listened and recorded. Woody talked a lot, and when he finished, John had no doubts about him telling the truth. Woody had filled in all the pieces of the puzzle, implicating Nick Sandoval, Morris Grayson, and Dave Curtis and several of their teenage kids. Woody then leaned back in the seat and closed his eyes, seeking some relief from the pain in sleep.

"What a miserable bunch," John said.

Jenny nodded her head. "I heard. And these punk kids are not only into all sorts of dope, but also into making porno films at private parties which their parents don't supervise. According to Woody, they don't even stick their heads into the kids' suites of rooms to check on them."

"The kids have their own private quarters, not attached to the main house. Incredible."

"Very rich and very stupid parents," Jenny said.

"Inherited money, Jenny. Money their parents and grandparents and further back than that made, some of it going back to the last big gold strike in Alaska around the turn of the century."

"Your parents were rich, John. With old money. But I'll bet they didn't give you free rein."

John chuckled. "You can say that again. My dad believed in hard work. We earned what money we got. I . . ." He paused as Woody's breathing became louder and more labored. "I think we've got a problem back here." He tried to wake Woody, but there was no response. "I *know* we've got a problem."

"People don't die from getting shot in the knee," Jenny said. "And you've stopped most of the bleeding."

John quickly ripped open Woody's shirt and placed his hand over the biker's heart. It was beating very fast and seemed very irregular.

"Jenny, I think he's having a heart attack or a stroke."

"What can I do?"

"Nothing. Just keep on driving. We're still an hour away from the doctor."

"You think he'll make it?"

"Damned if I know. He looks terrible."

"That's the way he always looked. What else is new?"

"Be charitable, Jenny. I think the man is dying."

"Of what, hard living?"

"That certainly might be the case."

A few minutes later the outlaw biker convulsed, stiffened, and died.

"Great," Jenny said after Woody's last gasp. "Now what?"

"We dump him."

"I'll look for a spot that would be appropriate for a rapist, murderer, doper, and all-around asshole."

"You're such a caring, considerate person, Jenny."

"That's me, to a T."

Jenny turned off on a county road and drove for several miles before coming upon an unpaved road.

A mile down that road, Woody was dumped into a ditch and John and Jenny headed back for the lodge.

Sheriff Watson's unit was parked in the driveway when they got back.

"Sheriff Watson," John greeted her. "How nice to see you."

"I'm sure you're both overjoyed," Jimmi replied. "Let's talk in the house. It's getting colder out here."

John started a fire while Jenny volunteered to make a pot of coffee. "What's on your mind, Sheriff?" John asked, turning away from the fireplace.

"Your friend's death was a pure accident, Mr. Barrone. I've gone over the MVA reports and run checks on the witnesses."

"Everything checks out?"

"All the witnesses are solid-citizen types. Not from this area. A young mother traveling with her two preschool-age kids, an engineer from the southern part of the state, and a retired couple from back East."

John said nothing.

"Did you have an interesting day, Mr. Barrone?"

"Not really. After paying our respects to Al we drove around a bit before heading back."

"Didn't run into any trouble?"

"Not a bit."

"Horseshit!"

"I beg your pardon?"

"I received word about an hour ago that state police and sheriff's deputies report quite a battle took place south and west of here. Lots of blood and bodies. All the bodies outlaw bikers. Explosives were used."

John shook his head. "We certainly live in a very violent time. I wonder if television and the movies have anything to do with it."

Jenny walked in just then with the coffee and placed

the tray on a table. "It's lack of discipline at home and in the schools," she opined. "Personally, I blame it all on the liberals."

"Really?" Sheriff Watson said, sugaring and creaming her coffee.

"You bet." Jenny sat down on the couch and picked up her coffee mug.

"Well, anyway, at least what happened today happened outside my jurisdiction. It isn't my problem."

Neither Jenny nor John had anything to add to that.

Jimmi Watson smiled. "But I have to say, this is really bad coffee."

John jerked a thumb toward Jenny. "She made it."

Jenny shrugged that off. "Cooking is not my forte."

"But you're pretty good with explosives, right?" the sheriff asked.

Jenny smiled and did not reply.

Jimmi held up a hand. "Okay, okay. I won't press anymore. I'll just say congratulations on a job well done."

"And what job would that be?" John asked.

Before Jimmi could reply, the front window blew in, shards of glass flying all over the den, the panes shattered by gunfire.

The three of them hit the floor, Jimmi clawing for her holstered weapon. Jenny and John belly-crawled over to a closet, grabbed weapons and pouches of magazines, then took positions around the den.

"You wouldn't happen to have another one of those Uzis, would you?" Jimmi asked.

"Coming right up," John told her. "And by the way, we are licensed to have them."

Another long volley of gunfire stopped conversation for several seconds.

"Rotten bastards!" Jimmi said as John slid an Uzi over to her.

"You have a radio and we have phones," John said as the gunfire momentarily abated. "Why don't you call in for assistance?"

"I might do just that," Jimmi replied. "After I assess the situation."

"Of course," John said as he and Jenny exchanged glances. "You feel confident that we can handle this."

"Don't you?" Jimmi retorted.

"But of course. Any suggestions as to how we should mount our defense, Sheriff?"

"We kill the bastards."

Jenny laughed. "That's simple enough."

"This was just a sample of what's in store for you people!" The shout came from the cold outside. "We'll be back. You can bet on that."

Those inside the lodge remained behind cover, waiting in silence. No more shouts came, no more gunfire.

"Jimmi, you recognize that voice?" Jenny asked.

"No."

John studied the bullet-shattered windows for a few seconds. The bottom half of the windows were intact.

"I see it," Jenny said, following John's eyes. "You think they deliberately kept their fire high to avoid hitting anyone?"

"Could be. If so, why?"

"A warning, maybe."

"To whom?" Jimmi asked. "You people or me?"

The three of them listened as the sounds of fast-moving vehicles gradually faded away into the night.

"Now I'll call it in," Jimmi said, walking over to the phone and punching the numbers.

John took a flashlight from a drawer and went out the back door, circling around the house. After a moment of searching he found the brass twinkling under the beam of light. Using the small end of his ballpoint pen, he picked up a casing and looked at it. It was a .308. Another was a .270. Yet another casing was from a 7mm. The last one he picked up and studied was from a .30-30. "Now that is interesting," he said.

"What is?" Jimmi said, walking up. "What did you find?"

"Lots of brass. Take a look at these casings. Check out the calibers."

Jimmi looked at them and frowned. "These are from hunting rifles."

"Yes. The outlaw bikers big hunters?"

"Are you serious? Hell, no. If they did hunt, which they don't, they'd poach. What are you getting at?"

"New players in the game."

"Who?"

"I don't have a clue. Yet. That voice was young-sounding to me. Did you pick up on that?"

"Now that you mention it, yes, I did."

"Awfully small footprint here," Jenny said, working the beam from her flashlight over the trampled snow. "A very young boy or a girl."

"I'll opt for the girl," John said. "Yes. Maybe one of the teenagers from the big three."

"Sandoval, Curtis, and Grayson?" Jimmi asked.

"Yes."

"You reached that conclusion just from looking at a footprint?" Jimmi asked. "A judge would fall out of his chair laughing."

"I'm sure he would. But did I say anything about the legal system?"

"No. Let's back off and keep this area as sterile as possible. Let my people work it. They'll be here in a few minutes."

"Suits me. Let's go back inside and wait where it's warm."

Sheriff Watson and her deputies collected what evidence there was, took pictures, and the deputies left.

Just before Jimmi left, she said, "I'll notify the real-estate agent tonight and tell him I was the target. That'll get you people clear. I'll send someone out in the morning to repair the damage. Okay?"

"I have a question," Jenny said. "Do the kids of the big three money men get down in your county often?"

"Yes. Usually on the weekend. But they almost always behave themselves . . . as much as kids ever do, that is. Just minor crap. Playing their radios too loud, driving too fast. Stuff like that. They know I don't kowtow to their parents."

"Never?" John asked.

"Never. And you can bet my God I never will. I picked up Sonny Grayson last year and held him in juvenile detention for several hours until his father, Morris, came down and got him. Morris tried to verbally intimidate me, and I finally told him if he didn't shut his goddamn mouth I'd put *him* in jail. None of them have had much use for me after that."

"Sounds like a wonderful family," John said.

"They're rich white trash," Jimmi said bluntly. "Shit-sorry right down to the bone. Every damn one of them."

"Even Sheriff Morales's sister?" Jenny asked.

"She's just as bad as any of them. She was a gold-digger in high school. She and Sandoval deserve each other."

"Sheriff Morales might not agree with you on that," John said.

"Oh, he knows it. Believe me he does. Look, I gotta go. I'll check back with you in the morning. See you."

"What now?" Jenny asked after Jimmi had left.

"We get a few hours sleep and then we drive up to the biker honky-tonk."

"Oh? We going after a late-night beer?"

"No. You're going to blow it up."

SIXTEEN

The biker honky-tonk was dark and no vehicles were parked around it.

"We're doing Sheriff Morales a favor. He ought to thank us," Jenny said, as they drove past the joint for the second time.

"Something tells me he won't."

"I'll set the timers for thirty minutes. That will give us plenty of time to be out of the vicinity."

"I want to be miles away when that stuff explodes," John said, as he turned down a road that ran beside the beer joint. He pulled off the road and parked. "I have never been a fan of pyrotechnics."

Jenny smiled. "I love it!"

"Come on, Boom-Boom," John said. "Let's do it."

John watched as Jenny placed what looked to him like a small satchel charge and set the timer. "That's it," she said. "Let's get gone from here."

The two of them walked swiftly away as John asked, "Are you sure that little bag of explosives is going to bring down the entire building?"

"There won't be enough left of that place to use as kindling wood. Trust me."

"I guess we'll hear all about it on the local TV news in a few hours."

Just as they reached their vehicle, they paused as a

car approached the honky-tonk, slowed, and turned in, pulling around to the rear of the building. Through the thin timber they could see two men get out, one of them holding what appeared to be a briefcase. A few moments later, another car drove up and pulled in. Two men got out and opened the trunk, taking out several large suitcases.

"Well now, the plot's thickening up like pudding," Jenny whispered.

"Another car coming," John said. "Well, well," he added as the third vehicle pulled around to the rear of the building. "Look at that, would you."

"That's a sheriff's department unit," Jenny whispered as the driver got out. "But it isn't Sheriff Morales. I can tell that even from here."

"How much time do we have before that stuff blows?"

Jenny looked at the luminous hands of her watch. "Twenty-one minutes."

The moon was very bright, but the distance was so great neither John nor Jenny could make out the features of the men. However, they could tell they were all men. And of course, they could not hear a word being said.

The briefcase was passed to the two men who had unloaded the heavy cases, then the cases were put into the trunk of the first car. Then the deputy was handed an envelope.

"Payoff," John whispered. "And I'll bet you that's dope of some kind in those cases."

"I wouldn't bet against you." Jenny looked at her watch. "Seventeen minutes."

"What's going to be left of those men in front of the building?"

"If the concussion doesn't kill them, they might be

thrown a considerable distance. And if the falling debris doesn't crack a skull or break a back or neck, they might come out of it alive. But I wouldn't take any bets on that."

"Slim to none," John said.

"With slim coming in a real poor second."

"Well, hell! Now they're all going to have a cigarette and chat for a while."

"All we can do is watch and wait. We're too far away to be in much danger."

"*Much* danger?"

She smiled in the moonlight; really a very pretty lady. "We'll feel it when it blows, that's all." She turned her head and muttered, "I hope."

"I heard that!"

"Don't worry about it, John."

"Look! They're getting in their cars. Damn! All of them getting into one car . . . that's a Lincoln Town Car, isn't it?"

"Looks like it. I can't tell from here."

"They must have gotten cold."

"They're not alone. It must be about twenty-five degrees out here."

"But the wind isn't blowing."

"Whoopee."

John contained his laughter at Jenny's sarcastic reply. "I thought you said you liked the cold."

"I do. In small doses, when I want it, and when I'm moving around to keep the blood flowing. I'm freezing my butt off out here!"

"You need it after all that buttered popcorn you ate the other night."

"Are you implying my ass is getting big?"

"I didn't say that. You have a very shapely derriere."

"Thanks. Yours ain't bad either . . ." She paused. "For an old dude," she said with a soft giggle.

"Thanks . . . I think. How many minutes to go?"

"Twelve."

The minutes ticked by, very slowly it seemed, and the men in the car showed no signs of leaving. John and Jenny watched and waited in silence in the cold night air.

"Four minutes to go," Jenny said, breaking the silence. "Let's move closer to our car and get ready to get the hell gone from this area."

"Depending on the location of any sheriff's department units, we should have a few minutes to get clear once the honky-tonk goes up," John said. "Providing this road doesn't become blocked by debris from the blast."

"And we don't get a commode through the windshield," Jenny said, leaning up against their SUV.

"What the hell type of explosives did you use?" John asked.

"A very powerful type. According to the military, still in the experimental stage."

"Oh, hell!"

"It works quite well. It's just very volatile, that's all. Control was hesitant to send it to me."

"And you've had it in the lodge?"

"Oh, sure. It's quite safe. Sort of like C-4."

"But a lot more powerful."

"Right."

"How long before this spectacle erupts?"

"About ninety seconds. I think we'd better get into the car."

"I was about to suggest that. We'll take the chance they won't see the interior light come on."

"Won't make any difference if they do," Jenny said. "It's too late now."

In the last few seconds before the charge went up, John cranked the engine and turned up the heater fan. There was little chance the men sitting in the car talking could hear the SUV's engine being started. And even if they had a window cracked to let in fresh air, it was too late now. The biker honky-tonk was about to blow.

And blow it did!

The building went up with an earth-rocking blast that bent nearby tree limbs. The rear of the concrete-block building seemed to swallow the front, and then the entire structure disappeared. Concrete blocks— among other things of now-unidentifiable origin— were sent flying high into the air, in all directions. A beer cooler landed directly on top of the car in which the five men were sitting and mashed the roof flat. The cooler's lid flew off and spewed exploding beer bottles, drenching the car and the immediate area around it. Urinals and commodes and part of the long bar dropped from the sky, along with pieces of tables and chairs. The patrol car and the other civilian vehicle were turned over on their sides and their windows blown out.

"Well, that's that," Jenny said.

"I agree wholeheartedly," John said, dropping the transmission into gear. "We're gone."

John and Jenny slept until late morning, had a leisurely breakfast, then took their coffee into the den, waiting for the local news to come on the TV.

"I was sure Sheriff Watson would have paid us a visit by now," John said.

"Or Morales."

"Or both."

When the news came on at noon, the explosion of the biker honky-tonk was the lead story. Five men had been killed. One of them was Nick Sandoval's younger brother, another was a county official, and another was one of Morales's deputies. John and Jenny were not familiar with the names of the other two, and the newscaster did not elaborate. A large amount of cash and drugs was found in the car with the dead men, four of whom had been crushed to death by a large beer cooler. The deputy had been thrown from the car and his skull had been crushed by a falling urinal.

Jenny almost cracked up at that.

"It isn't funny, Jenny," John said, trying his best to maintain a straight face.

"The hell it isn't! One dirty deputy on the take killed by a falling pisser. What an epitaph that would make."

"I don't even want to think about it."

Jenny was still laughing as she held up her coffee mug. "More coffee, John? I'm going to make a fresh pot."

"Yes, please. I'm going to step outside for some air. Try not to blow up the coffeepot."

"Funny, John. Very amusing."

Still chuckling, Jenny headed for the kitchen, and John stepped out onto the front porch. The noon air was crisp, the temperature in the upper thirties. There was no traffic on the road in front of the lodge.

Morales had told John that he was sure some of his deputies were dirty, on the payroll of the Big Three: Sandoval, Curtis, and Grayson, the money men. *Well,* John thought, *you now have one less on the take, Sheriff.* And there was no doubt in his mind that both Watson and Morales knew perfectly well who had blown up the honky-tonk . . . or at least strongly suspected.

And John was wondering when the Feds would make their appearance in the area. The number of bodies was rapidly mounting. It was only a matter of time.

John took another couple of deep breaths of the cold, clean air and went back into the lodge. He could smell the aroma of fresh-brewing coffee.

"Smells good, Jenny," he called.

No reply.

John frowned. A fire was burning in the fireplace, but there was a draft of cold air chilling his legs. He walked into the kitchen. The back door was open.

"Were you raised in a barn, Jenny?" he called, figuring that would get a sarcastic response from her.

Silence greeting him.

John stepped out onto the back porch and looked around. The porch had been swept clean of snow, but there were new footprints in the snow behind the lodge. Large footprints, leading off into the timber. They were not Jenny's.

Jenny was gone.

SEVENTEEN

John followed the tracks as fast as he could. The tracks made a half circle and ended back at the highway, about a hundred yards from the lodge.

John returned to the lodge and began gearing up as quickly as he could. He was going to get Jenny back if he had to kill every outlaw biker in the north half of the state.

Just as he was loading up the last bit of gear, a van and a car pulled in the drive and the real-estate agent got out.

"The lodge is all yours," John said before the agent could speak. "I might be back today or tonight. I might be gone two or three days . . . or longer. Just lock it up before you leave. Okay? Fine," he said before the startled agent could reply. "See you." John got into the SUV, backed around the van and the car, and was gone.

He headed west, the direction the tire tracks he'd found had taken. A set of tracks was all John had . . . for now. But he knew where to get more information. And more importantly, how to get it.

While he drove, he called Control and told them what had happened.

"Do you need assistance, John?"

"No. Just bringing you up to date. I'll be in contact." He broke the connection.

John drove until he came to a crossroads, then pulled over and studied the printouts they had received from Control earlier: printouts that listed known addresses of many of the outlaw bikers. Most were in Morales's county, but a few resided in Watson's jurisdiction. John studied the map for a moment, then headed into the country.

He drove for several miles before turning into the driveway of a ramshackle house: a mobile home with a very amateurishly built wood-frame addition. There were several cars and trucks parked around the hovel, and he could see the tarp-covered shapes of several motorcycles parked under a shed. John parked and got out, carrying a sawed-off pump 12-gauge riot gun loaded with double-aught buckshot in his left hand. In his right hand he carried a grenade, the pin pulled, his fingers holding down the spoon.

A window was jerked open and a man shouted, "Get off this property, Barrone!"

John stepped behind an older-model pickup truck and shouted, "Get your scummy asses out here and talk to me."

"We got nothin' to say to you, prick."

We. John digested that. More than one in there. "Get the hell out here."

"Fuck you, old man."

John popped the spoon and tossed the grenade.

"Oh, shit!" he heard a man holler. "Get down! That's a grenade!"

The grenade blew, demolishing the rickety wood front porch and tearing a hole in the side of the old mobile home.

"Jesus Christ!" someone yelled from inside the mobile home. "Somebody kill that bastard."

A man appeared by the side of the mobile home, between the pigsty and the shed, holding a rifle. He pointed it at John. John shot him, the double-aught buckshot slamming the man backward and dumping him in the thin covering of snow. The rifle was flung several yards away.

"I'm done!" the voice shouted from the mobile home. "I'm comin' out. Good God, man, you're nuts!"

"Step out with your hands where I can see them. And they'd better be empty."

The belly-shot biker thrashed in the snow and mud and screamed in pain. "Jimmy! Kill that crazy bastard and get me to a doctor. Goddamn it, do it!"

The biker called Jimmy jumped out through the freshly blasted hole in the side of the mobile home, where the front door used to be, a pistol in each hand. John blew his legs out from under him. He hit the ground, losing one pistol. He raised the other pistol and cursed at John. John blew his hand off.

The outlaw biker screamed and rolled on the ground, blood spewing from his shattered legs and the stump of his right arm. A woman appeared in the jagged hole that was once the front door, her hands in the air.

"Don't shoot, mister!" she shrieked, "For God's sake, don't shoot!"

"Get your ass out here!" John called as he punched fresh loads into the shotgun.

"I got to hep Jimmy and Luddy!" she said, jumping down to the ground.

"You talk to me. Then you can help them."

"My fuckin' hand is gone!" Jimmy yelled. "Where's my hand? Don't let the dogs git it."

John walked over to the woman. "Get on your knees," he commanded.

The woman dropped to her knees and began mumbling prayers she probably had not recited since childhood.

"The people who took my partner, Jenny . . . where did they take her?"

"Don't tell the son of a bitch!" Jimmy yelled.

John coldly shifted the muzzle of the shotgun toward the wounded outlaw. "Shut up!"

"Fuck you, Barrone! When my boys get through with that uppity bitch, you won't be able to recognize her! I just wish I could be there to see 'em carve on her."

John shot Jimmy in the head. The outlaw biker's head exploded in a mass of blood, bits of bone, and tissue.

The woman began screaming and waving her arms and puking down the front of her shirt.

John placed the muzzle of the shotgun against the woman's head. "Talk to me, you worthless bitch! Right now. Talk to me or die."

"I'll tell you anything you want to know. Dear God, don't kill me!"

"Where did your scummy-assed friends take my partner?"

"I don't know for sure."

John pushed the muzzle of the shotgun harder against the woman's head.

"I swear to God that's the truth, mister! I don't know for sure."

"Then tell me what you do know."

"They took her up Lost Canyon Road. That's all I know."

John felt sure she was lying. "Get up, goddamn you, get up on your feet."

John shoved the woman toward his SUV. He took out the county map and spread it on the hood. "Show me, and you'd better be right."

The woman's hand was shaking badly as she pointed toward a spot on the map. "That's the road. It dead-ends after a few miles. That's where they took her."

"How many of them?"

"Jesus, man, I don't know for sure."

"Guess."

" 'Bout a dozen, I reckon. A whole bunch of them, for sure. I got to pee, Mr. Barrone. Real bad."

"Cross your legs and hold it. Who is the leader of this bunch?"

"There ain't but one leader. Benny Ballinger."

"Is he with this bunch?"

"Yeah. Him and Griz and Chink and a lot of others. They might be two or three dozen for all I know. I got to pee, man!" She cut her eyes. "Is Luddy dead? He ain't moving none."

"Probably. If he isn't, he will be soon."

"You 'bout the coldest man I ever did see. What am I gonna do now?"

"You're going to go into that shed over there and pee."

"Can't I go in the house and use the sit-down?"

"No. Go squat."

"Are you goin' to watch?"

"Hell, no. Move. Hurry up. We're pulling out. You're going with me."

"Why?"

"Because if you're lying to me about this Lost Canyon Road, I'm going to kill you."

"I swear I'm not lyin'."

"We'll see. What's your name?"

"Peggy."

"All right, Peggy. Go pee."

The woman hurried off to the shed, returning in a few moments. "I feel a lot better now."

"Wonderful. Get in the vehicle."

She paused and looked down at Jimmy. "He wasn't much to look at alive. But he's sure as hell no beauty now, is he?"

"Get in," John said wearily. "You show me the way."

As they headed out toward Lost Canyon Road, Peggy asked, "Is there going to be shootin'?"

"Probably quite a lot."

"Once we get there, can I haul ass?"

"Yes. I'm sure they'll be lots of cars and trucks for you to choose from. Maybe a motorcycle or two."

"Good. I wanna carry my ass back to Mobile. That's where I'm from."

"I'm sure Mobile will be overjoyed at your return."

"You talk funny, you know that?"

"Blame it on my parents. It's all their fault."

"Yeah? Me too. How about that? We have something in common."

John sighed. "Will wonders never cease."

"Slow down and turn right up here. About three or four miles up this road, hang another right. It's about seven miles up that road. Set way back off the road. Does this thing have four-wheel drive?"

"Yes."

"Good. You're going to need it."

"*We're* going to need it."

"What? Oh. Yeah. Right."

"How well armed is this bunch?"

"They got lots of guns. All kinds of guns. Pistols, rifles, shotguns. And some of those Russian guns?"

"AKs?"

"Yeah! That's it. I 'member 'em talkin' 'bout 'em."

"Is there a lookout on guard?"

Peggy smiled. "I wondered if you was gonna ask about that."

"There is and you weren't going to tell me, were you."

"I guess not."

"Now I know just how far I can trust you, don't I."

"I reckon so."

"Give me one good reason why I shouldn't kill you right now?"

"Oh, man! Look, I'll be square with you from now on. I promise I will. You have my word."

"Your word? Is that supposed to mean something?"

She was silent for a couple of minutes. "It used to mean something."

"Before you got involved with outlaw bikers."

"Naw. Long time 'fore that. Look, stop after you've gone 'bout five miles on the canyon road. You'll have to walk it from there. It'll be safer. I'm not kiddin' you. I'm bein' straight with you 'bout this."

"All right. It's your life, Peggy."

"Yeah. I know that. I ain't goin' up to the shack with you. You can kill me if you want to. But I ain't goin'. It's suicide for you and I don't want to be a part of it. That blond bitch is probably dead by now anyways. At least she's been gang-shagged, you can bet on that."

"We'll see."

***

"Come on, Griz," Tubby said. "What are we waitin' for? I want some of that snatch. Let's do the bitch."

"Yeah," a biker called Big Hurt said. "That's prime pussy, man."

Griz shook his head. "After we deal with Barrone. Then we'll all have some fun."

"How do you know Barrone will be here?" Nutcutter asked. "He don't know where this place is."

"I don't think it will take him very long to find out. Wouldn't surprise me none to see him pop up here any minute."

"He ain't no magician," Big Balls groused. "He's just a human person. And an old one, at that."

"He's not as old as he looks," Griz said. "It's that gray hair that makes him look older. Our guy in Morales's department said he was around fifty."

A biker called X-Man stood up, rubbing his crotch. "I wanna get her to suck me off. How about it, Griz?"

"You try to stick that thing in my mouth and I'll bite it off!" Jenny yelled. She was tied to a straight-backed chair in a corner of the old house.

"Leave her alone," Griz said. "We'll all get our turn at her soon enough."

"I wanna see her tits," Mean Jeans said, walking over to Jenny. "She's sure got a nice-lookin' set."

"Then look at her tits," Griz said, getting tired of the topic. "I don't care. I just don't want everyone gettin' all excited and linin' up for a hump. Not yet."

"I agree with Griz," Hammer said. "Let's deal with her partner first."

Mean Jeans walked over to Jenny and ripped open her shirt. "Shore fills that slingshot up nice, don't she?" He hooked his fingers into the front of her bra and tore it open. "Look at them nipples."

Jenny kicked him in the balls. Mean Jeans hollered

in sudden pain and doubled over, holding his crotch and cussing.

Griz and the others laughed. Hammer said, "I think I'll look at her tits from over here, Mean Jeans. It's safer that way."

"Yeah," Hammer's buddy, Rammer, said. "Mean Jeans ain't gonna do no humpin' for a while yet."

Mean Jeans straightened up and slapped Jenny. The blow knocked her to one side, dumping Jenny and the chair to the floor.

"Leave her alone!" Griz ordered. "Let her lay there on the floor. She can't go nowhere." He walked to one of the front windows and looked out. "Come on, Barrone. Let's get this over with."

EIGHTEEN

"Tooter will let us know if Barrone comes up the road," Big 'un said.

"Barrone is no Girl Scout," Griz said. "Tooter might not be alive as we speak."

"How come you so damn sure Barrone is comin'?" Pisspot asked. "He don't even have no idea where this place is."

"All he had to do is call Morales or Watson to find out where every biker in this area lives. Then he pays them a visit."

"They wouldn't talk!"

"Don't bet on that. Barrone is tough, boys. And he'll kill without blinkin' an eye. Him and that bitch over yonder is ex-government people. CIA types, I figure. From out of the operations section of that agency. You watch a couple of your buddies get killed right in front of you, and you'd talk. You'd sing like a bird, and don't tell me you wouldn't."

"They's twenty of us here, Griz. You think that bastard's gonna attack us?"

"Yeah, I do. Stoneballs, bump Tooter on the two-way. See if he's seen anything."

"I tried a couple of minutes ago. No reply."

"Try again."

Stoneballs tried to raise Tooter. Nothing.

"He don't answer, Griz."

"Maybe he's takin' a leak or a shit," a biker called Snag said.

"Maybe he's dead," Griz said flatly. "Or got knocked in the head and is trussed up like a hog."

Tooter was lying facedown in the rocks above the road. His skull had been fractured by the butt of John's Mini-14 and he was quite dead. John was slowly working his way along the ridge above the old cabin, pushing a very reluctant Peggy ahead of him.

"That was awful what you done back there with Tooter," she admonished him. "He was a nice guy."

"I'm sure he was. How many innocent people did he have a hand in beating up? How many girls has he raped? How many hours has he spent making illegal drugs that are being sold to kids?"

Peggy had no response to any of John's questions.

"If you're thinking of shouting out a warning when we get to the cabin, don't," John warned her. "I think you know by now I will kill you."

"I believe you," Peggy said. "But them's my friends you're about to shoot."

"You need to choose a better class of friends."

"You say. They always been good to me."

"They only beat you when you need it, right?"

"That's right."

"Pitiful. Keep walking."

"My feet hurt and I'm cold," Peggy complained.

"Just one of life's little tragedies. Move."

"What do you have in that pack on your back?"

"A sack of surprises."

"You're a mean man."

"You don't know how mean, Peggy."

"I got a pretty good idea."

"Keep that in mind. There's the cabin. Damn big place."

"Used to be a hippie place back in the late sixties, I was told. Peace-and-love people. It was deserted for years and finally bought for back taxes."

"By Sandoval, Curtis, and Grayson?"

"Yeah. You know a lot, don't you?"

"I try. Stop here and sit down, right over there."

She slumped to the cold ground and glared at John. "You work for the government, don't you."

"No. I don't."

"Then who the hell are you?"

"A concerned citizen."

"You 'bout a smart-assed bastard, that's who you are. I don't like you at all."

"How sad. I'm heartbroken." John stared at the barnlike structure below.

"I hope Griz and them others kill you," Peggy said.

"I'm sure they'll try."

"*Help!*" Peggy screamed, jumping to her feet. "Griz! Barrone's here. Help!"

"Who the hell was that?" Hook said. "Somebody's yellin."

"Sounded like Peggy," Pisspot said. He jerked a thumb. "Up yonder, above and behind us."

Peggy hesitated, not understanding the smile on John's face. Then she took off running down the slope.

John stood and watched her go. "Good riddance," he muttered.

* * *

"Help!" Peggy shouted, almost losing her footing on the muddy slope. "Open the damn door, I'm comin' in."

The side door of the large old house was open and Peggy ran in, almost falling to the floor. "Barrone killed Jimmy and Luddy. He's up yonder behind the house, up in the rocks."

"Alone?" Griz asked.

"Yeah." She cut her eyes toward the trussed-up Jenny. "He come after that bitch. Y'all been playin' with her tits?"

"Hell with her tits!" Griz said. "How'd you get away from Barrone?"

"I run off."

"Just like that?"

"Yeah."

"Too easy. He's got something up his sleeve."

"Hell, Griz," Snake said. "We can use the cunt for bargainin'. We stick a gun to her head and Barrone ain't gonna do nothin' 'ceptin' back off."

"And if he don't and we was to kill her? Then what? Think about it. We got our orders from Sandoval: We need the information that's in that broad's head. That's what's important."

"Yeah," Snake reluctantly agreed. "I guess you're right about that."

A tremendous thump echoed from the roof of the old house.

"What the hell was that?" Big Train asked, looking around him.

"Something hit the roof?"

"Grenade?" Tubby wondered.

"Naw. It would have gone off by now."

Up on the ridge, among the rocks, John smiled and picked up another baseball-sized rock, took aim, and let it fly. This rock went right through a window.

"Shit!" Bend Over Betty hollered. "He's chunkin' rocks at us. Do somethin,' Mad Dog."

Mad Dog looked at her. "What the hell do you want me to do, you dumb bitch? Throw 'em back at him?"

"Shoot the son of a bitch, you ugly bastard."

"Knock it off, both of you," Griz ordered. "Let's get organized here. Grab your weapons and get into position like we talked about. Move."

Up on the ridge, John was sitting behind a cluster of boulders, munching on some crackers he had grabbed before leaving the lodge. Finished, he carefully stowed the remainder of the crackers in his pack and took a sip of water. He got to his feet, holding another rock. He let it fly and it sailed through another window. A faint cry reached him and he grinned.

"The son of a bitch hit me in the head!" Greaseball hollered. "I'm bleedin'! And there's a big knot comin' up on my head. I'll kill that bastard!"

"Before you do that, you have to spot him," Griz said sarcastically. "Have you got him located?"

Greaseball ignored Griz, muttered something under his breath, and pressed a bandanna to his bleeding head.

"All I know is he's up yonder," Chink said, pointing. "About forty or fifty feet above us. This ain't worth a shit, people. It ain't workin' out the way we thought it would."

"You got a better plan?" Griz asked.

"Give him the woman and let's get the hell out of this area. We can set up somewheres else. Them three money men and their goddamn snooty kids ain't worth dyin' for."

"Aw, come on, people!" Snake said. "He's one man. That's all. Just one man. They's twenty of us here—not countin' the girls. We ain't got no choice in the matter 'ceptin' to fight. So, by God, let's get to it and kill the old bastard."

"He ain't that old," Peggy said. "He's in damn good shape too. And he's mean as a snake. He killed Jimmy and Luddy and never even batted an eye."

"I'm against rushin' him," Stoneballs said. "He's got the high ground and rushin' him would get a lot of us killed."

"Let's just wait and see what he does," Griz said. "We got time. And he ain't gonna call for no help. He's workin' alone." He looked at Big Tit. "Go make some coffee. A lot of it. And fix somethin' to eat too. I'm hungry. All you women go make yourselves useful."

"What about her?" Snake said, jerking a thumb at Jenny.

"Put a coat on her and toss her in the basement. Get her the hell out of the way till we get this matter settled."

"Can I fuck her?" Tubby asked.

"No, damn it!" Griz said. "Good God, Tubby. We're in a fight for our lives here and all you can think about is pussy. Take the damn woman to the basement and leave her."

"I carry the chair too?" Tubby asked.

"No, Tubby," Griz said with a lot more patience

than he felt. "Untie her and walk her down to the basement. Tie her to a damn post."

"Okay, Griz, okay. Don't get all pissed off."

Griz moved to a window and cautiously looked out, being careful not to fully expose himself. He couldn't see anything but rocks and mud and dirty-looking snow. "What the hell are you waitin' on, Barrone?" he muttered. "Stop throwin' rocks and get to shootin'. Let's get this show on the road."

Up on the ridge, John waited. He didn't want to start shooting for fear he'd hit Jenny. If she was still alive, that is, and he felt sure she was. Jenny was taken, he believed, for two reasons: to get any information they could out of her, and to draw him out.

John doubted that Jenny had told the outlaw bikers anything—yet. But under torture, anyone could break.

He decided to shift positions and get closer to the house. He cautiously worked his way through the rocks until he was directly behind the huge old house. There were no curtains covering the windows, so he could see into the kitchen. Several women were busy in there. One man was squatting or kneeling behind the center window. He was holding what looked like a Russian AK-47.

Then John spotted the outside doors to the basement. "Well, now," he muttered. "Let me check on this." He took a small pair of binoculars from his rucksack and adjusted the focus. The doors seemed to jump at him. The old double doors were secured with only a wooden peg stuck through the hasp. "Interesting," John muttered, stowing the binoculars.

He saw a way he might reach those doors without being spotted. But if he got trapped in the basement, it might prove to be rather unpleasant, he reminded himself.

"Oh, what the hell." he said. "Let's do it."

John began working his way down the ridge.

The women working in the kitchen were talking to the outlaw on guard, distracting him. John slipped down to the rear of the house without being seen. He pressed up against the cold wood and thanked the Gods of War for smiling on him.

Slipping over to the slanted double doors, John listened. He could hear no sounds coming from the basement. Working as quietly as possible, he pulled the wooden peg from the hasp and opened one side of the heavy doors. The basement was dimly lighted by a single bare bulb hanging from the ceiling. John idly wondered how much it cost somebody to have electricity run this far from the highway.

He began the slow descent down the stairs. He heard a faint thumping sound coming for a dark corner of the basement. He stepped down into the basement and spotted Jenny. Working quickly, he cut the ropes that bound her and removed the duct tape that covered her mouth.

"You all right?" John whispered.

"Just pissed off to the max," Jenny said, rubbing her wrists to restore normal circulation. Then she tucked her shirttail into her jeans. "You wouldn't happen to have a safety pin on you, would you?"

"Sorry, no. But I do have a spare pistol in my pack."

"I'll take it. What now?"

John handed her the 9mm and spare magazines. "We get the hell out of this basement and up into the rocks."

"And then? . . ."

"We start a dialogue with the bikers."

"You've got to be kidding."

"Well, sort of a dialogue."

"That's better."

John replaced the wooden peg in the hasp of the basement door, and a couple of minutes later he and Jenny were back among the rocks above the huge old house.

Jenny looked into John's pack and smiled when she spotted the grenades. "Did you bring any C-4?"

"No."

"Too bad. I could have brought the damn house down with that."

"I would like to have some of these people alive for questioning."

"How much confirmation do you need about who is involved in this mess?"

"How much did you hear while you were with them?"

"Enough to know that Sandoval, Curtis, Grayson, and their older kids are involved up to their asses. Also the names of several very prominent community leaders and their wives and kids and friends."

"Did they mention where their labs are located?"

"No."

"Pity. Jimmi and Morales would like to have that information."

"John?"

"Yes?"

"I'm freezing my ass off. It's cold up here in these damn rocks. Can we get this show on the road?"

"How would you like to start it?"

"By shooting a couple of those outlaws and castrating a couple more."

"Bloodthirsty, aren't you?"

"You better believe it."

John picked up a baseball-sized rock and handed it to Jenny. "You think you can hit the house from here?"

"Of course. I could do that with my eyes closed."

"Think you could put that rock through the kitchen window?"

"Piece of cake."

"Okay. Do it."

"You're enjoying this, aren't you?"

"So far. Traveling with Peggy was a real treat. Very intellectually stimulating."

"I'm sure."

Jenny hefted the rock and eyeballed the distance. Then she let it fly. It crashed through the kitchen window, hitting Bend Over Betty on the ass and startling the biker who was supposed to be on guard.

"Shit!" Betty hollered. "I been shot!"

"No, you hasn't," Gatepost, the guard in the kitchen, said. "You got hit in the butt with a rock, you dumb bitch."

"Hey!" Hook hollered after looking down into the basement. "That bitch is gone. She got loose."

"What?" Griz said. "How'd she get out?"

"How the hell do I know? But she's gone."

"Check the basement careful."

"Hey, you bastards!" Jenny yelled from the rocks. "Come on out and get me if you've got the balls to do it."

"That damn mouthy cunt!" Pinhead said.

"Forget the basement," Griz said. "Some of you go get that bitch."

"You can bet she hooked up with Barrone and she's got a gun now," Mad Dog cautioned. "Waitin' for us to show ourselves."

That stopped them all cold, all looking at Griz. After a few seconds of cursing, Griz picked up a rifle and said, "Let's end this right now. They got the back covered good. So we start slippin' out the front. One by one and circlin' around. We can put them in a box."

"Who goes first?" Tubby asked.

"Any volunteers?" Griz asked.

"Hell, I'll do it," Hammer said, picking up a shotgun. "Y'all give me some coverin' fire from the back."

The outlaws crowded into the kitchen and an adjoining bedroom.

Jenny was peeping out through an opening in the jumble of rocks. "That got their attention. They're getting ready to attack."

Her words were still dangling in the air when the outlaws opened fire from the rear of the house.

John and Jenny hugged the ground, bullets whining all around them.

NINETEEN

While John and Jenny were belly-down on the ground, behind the rocks, Hammer and his buddy Rammer charged out the front of the huge old building, Hammer going to the left, Rammer to the right. A few seconds later, X-Man followed them, heading straight for the ridge and the rocks directly behind the building.

"X-Man disobeyed orders," Griz said. "He's gonna get killed. The dumb bastard."

X-Man made the beginning of the upward-sloping ridge and began firing his AK.

"They ain't returnin' the fire," Tubby said. "What's the matter with them?"

Griz smiled grimly. He knew what was happening, and he admired the courage of Barrone and the woman. "In a few seconds, the bitch is gonna have X-Man's weapon and a bag full of ammo. Damn!"

The clattering of the outlaw's AK suddenly stopped as he disappeared into the rocks. A few seconds later, his body was pushed out, minus his weapon and his rucksack filled with spare magazines. The body rolled slowly down the ridge.

"Well, shit!" Tubby said. "What happened?"

"They killed him, you idiot," Griz said. "They saw

him comin' and laid in wait for him to crest the ridge."

Meanwhile, John and Jenny had split up, John taking the right side, Jenny, now armed with an AK-47, the left, and waited for Hammer and Rammer to make an appearance.

Jenny spotted Hammer, panting and struggling his way up the ridge, and dusted him with AK rounds.

"Whoa, shit!" Hammer yelled, throwing himself belly-down on the cold and rocky ground as the lead howled around him.

"You hit?" Rammer hollered, giving away his location to John.

John pulled the pin, popped the spoon on a grenade, and tossed it.

The explosion peppered Rammer's legs with shrapnel and sent him screaming and rolling down the ridge.

"Damn!" Griz muttered as Rammer's bloody body came to rest on level ground behind the building.

"Help me!" Rammer yelled. "My legs is all tore up. Somebody help me."

"Nobody goes out there," Griz yelled.

"We got to help him!" Bend Over Betty said.

"You try and you're dead," Griz told her. "They'll shoot you. That's an old trick. Rammer's on his own."

"Give me some goddamn coverin' fire!" Hammer yelled. "I got to get out of here."

"Here, you assholes!" Jenny yelled. "Have a present from me." She hurled a grenade toward the rear of the house.

"Oh, shit!" one of the outlaws in the kitchen yelled, spotting the grenade just before it rolled under the rear of the building. "Get out of here."

The grenade blew and took out half of the kitchen.

Part of the structure collapsed and dumped debris on those in the kitchen. Big Balls got conked on the noggin by part of a beam that knocked him goofier than he normally was. "I didn't do it, Mr. Ballard," Big Balls said, hurled for a moment back in time to his high school days in Los Angeles. "It was somebody else raped that chick in the gym. Not me."

"What the hell are you talkin' 'bout?" a biker woman called Fireball asked as she pushed part of a table off her legs and crawled over to the delirious biker.

"She wasn't no good no way," Big Balls said. "She just laid there like a stump an' bawled and hollered. I know it must have got good to her."

"Anybody killed back yonder?" Griz yelled from the next room.

"No, but Big Balls is out of his head," Fireball yelled. "Talkin' crazy."

"Hell, that's normal for him."

Back on the ridge, John looked over at Jenny. "Any people in that house you feel society would miss?" he asked.

"Hell, no. Just a bunch of sorry white trash, that's all."

John chuckled. "That's a good old Southern expression."

"It fits that bunch down there. You want to spray some lead around?"

"Yes."

"Let's do it."

John and Jenny let the bullets fly, changing mags as quickly as they could. While they were filling the old house with lead, Hammer managed to crawl to safety. He rolled down the slope and made a run around some old falling-down sheds just to the rear and to one side of the main structure. There he stopped and caught his breath and pondered his situation, reaching the conclusion that this wasn't worth a shit for nothin'. But he knew if he tried to reach the house, he'd get his ass shot off. He decided he'd just sit right where he was and wait things out.

Big Tit got grazed by a bullet in her ample butt and started hollered and bawling. Bend Over Betty got conked on the head by a flying piece of wood off a beam and was knocked to her knees, bleeding from the forehead. Peggy made a dive for what she thought was a closet, and knocked herself stone-cold goofy . . . it was another set of stairs leading to the basement, and her head made contact with every step.

Just when the outlaws thought it might be over for a few minutes, Jenny chunked another grenade. The minibomb bounced through the debris on what was left of the kitchen floor, and ended up in the hallway leading to the main living room.

"Holy shit!" Griz hollered, just about a half second before the grenade exploded. He dived for the floor, behind a couch.

When it blew, it took down much of the center of the house, collapsing part of the roof. A huge dust cloud slowly enveloped the house.

"Shift to the left," John said to Jenny. "About a hundred yards. Move, while we have some cover."

"Cover the road?"

"Yes. Let's go."

While the outlaws were coughing and hacking up dust and cobwebs and spitting out bird droppings and rat shit, Jenny and John slipped away and took up positions in the rocks above the road and about a hundred yards west of the house.

"They're in a box canyon," John said. "They can't

get out without making a run past us." He dug in his pocket and tossed Jenny the keys to the SUV. "The vehicle is about a mile and a half down this road. There's a winter coat in there for you. Fill up a rucksack with ammo and grenades, and the box you left in there the other day is still there, in the backseat."

Jenny grinned.

"I thought you'd be pleased to hear that. There are emergency rations in the storage area as well. Bring back all you can carry. All you think we'll need. I'll hold our bikers at bay."

"I'll be back as quickly as possible."

"Take your time. The outlaws aren't going anywhere."

Big Balls was staggering around the house, holding his aching and bleeding head and cussing. Griz was sitting on the floor in the living room, trying to come up with a way to get out of this mess. So far he had not been able to think of anything.

From his vantage point in the rocks, about a hundred yards up the road, John picked up the AK Jenny had left behind and began putting lead into the many vehicles parked in front of the old hippie home. Steam began rising from punctured radiators, and vehicles began to sag as John blew holes in tires. One vehicle briefly caught on fire as one of John's bullets punctured a gas line.

"That rotten bastard and bitch," Griz said, chancing a quick look out a window.

"I think Rammer is dead," Big Un called after looking out the ruined rear of the house. "Leastways, he ain't movin'."

"Where's Hammer?" Griz asked.

"I don't know," Gatepost replied. "But I don't think he's still up in the rocks. I think he made a run for it."

"Run . . . where?" Griz called.

"Damned if I know."

"What the hell are we goin' to do, Griz?" Pinhead called from the other side of the house. "It's gettin' damn cold in here."

"To be honest," Griz replied, "I don't have no fuckin' idea."

"Thanks a lot."

"You're welcome."

John had tired of shooting at the vehicles, and put a dozen or so rounds into the house, sending everyone who had gotten to their feet diving for the floor. A couple of the women started crying and begging for Griz to do something.

"What the hell do you want me to do?" Griz yelled. "Good God! I'm in the same spot as the rest of you."

"We got to get out of this trap, Griz," Greaseball said.

"I know that," Griz replied. "*How* to do that is what I don't know."

"You want us to start thinkin' about a way?" Snag asked.

"I think that would be very nice of you," Griz told him, doing his best to keep control of his rising temper. "Why don't you do that?"

"I been doin' it," Snag said. "I can't come up with nothin'."

"Wonderful," Griz muttered, just as John opened fire again, sending everyone in the house scurrying for cover.

Jenny came panting back and flopped down beside John. John cringed as the heavy rucksack she was carrying hit the ground hard. She laughed at the expression on his face.

"Relax, John. This stuff won't go off by impact." She grinned. "Usually, that is."

"What are you going to do with it?" John asked. "We're a little far away for throwing."

"I'm working on something. I thought it might be nice to seal their fate for a while . . . in a manner of speaking."

John looked at her for a moment, then smiled. "Ah, yes. As in blocking the road, perhaps?"

"You got it."

"Very good, Jenny. I like it."

"Me, too. Now let me have my rifle back. I want to burn a couple of mags into that damn house and hope I hit something subhuman."

Jenny uncorked a full mag into the house, working from front to back, the rounds knocking holes in the old structure.

"You feel better now?" John asked.

"A little bit."

"You want to tell me what happened in there while they had you?"

"Let's just say they were making plans to gang-bang me, and one of those cretins wanted me to suck his dick."

John sighed and grimaced.

"But this is that bastard's AK," Jenny said. "I hope he's sucking the devil's dick right about now."

John looked pained for a moment, then shook his head. "The women in the house?"

"Just as bad as the men."

"I gathered that from the one I convinced to lead me out here."

Jenny burned another round into the house, then

smiled and laid the AK aside. "I think I'll go to work putting some charges together."

John looked at the rocks on the other side of the narrow road. "Then you can effectively seal them in?"

"It'll take them a while to dig out."

"And then what do you propose we do about the drug situation?"

That got John an odd look from Jenny. "I don't follow you."

"I believe we were sent here to stop the manufacturing and sale of illegal and dangerous drugs, were we not?"

"That's true."

"How is sealing this bunch in for a few hours going to stop that? As soon as they dig out they'll be right back in business."

"Are you playing devil's advocate, John?"

"In a way, yes."

"Are you proposing we execute them all? If so, how do we accomplish that?"

"I'm not suggesting that. I'm just asking a question."

"You want to try to have some sort of intelligent conversation with that pack of subhuman beings?"

"It might be worth a try."

"You'd be wasting your time."

"That's probably very true, Jenny."

"Your Boston upbringing is surfacing."

"Perhaps. Want to give it a try?"

"All they're going to do is lie to you. Anybody would to save their life. You know that." She shrugged. "But it's your show, John."

"Let's give it a try."

"Go right ahead. I'll just sit here and think of all the ways I can say, 'I told you so.'"

John smiled and moved a couple of dozen yards closer to the house, being careful to stay in the rocks and not offering any clear target. "Hello, the house!" he shouted, his voice carrying clearly in the cold air.

"What do you want, Barrone?"

"To talk. How about it?"

"Talk about what?"

"Your staying alive."

"We're alive."

"Don't be a fool. You can't get out. You're trapped. We can bring that house down around you anytime we like."

"You say! We got people comin' to help us. You're the ones is gonna die."

"You're doing great, John," Jenny said, working with something that looked a lot like Silly Putty. "Keep it up."

John ignored her sarcasm. "I'll make a deal with you!" John shouted. "You give up your labs and dope dealing and you all can walk out of here."

"Ride out," Jenny corrected. "On their stupid-looking motorcycles."

"You go to hell, Barrone!"

"Told you," Jenny said.

John ignored her. "This is the last offer you're getting," he called. "Take it or die. The choice is yours."

A wild chorus of shouts and profanity was the bikers' answer.

John sat down and looked at Jenny.

She smiled at him. "Now we go to work, Boss."

TWENTY

"You keep them talking or shoot them or whatever," Jenny said, slipping into the backpack she'd retrieved from the SUV. "I'm going to go have some fun."

"Where will you be?"

Jenny pointed to a high point above the rear of the house. "Up there."

"Lots of boulders up there," John said.

"Sure are. But they won't be there for long."

"Have fun."

"I will. It'll take me a few minutes to circle around and get in place. Then a few minutes to plant the charges and get clear. When I yell, you look out. There'll be rocks flying in all directions."

"I would tell you to be careful, but knowing you, that would be a waste of breath."

She grinned at him and was gone.

"All of a sudden it got quiet," Big Balls said inside the house, rubbing his sore head. "What are them people doin' now?"

"How do you feel?" Griz asked. "Are you thinkin' clear now?" *As clear as you're capable of,* he silently added.

"Yeah. I'm thinkin' about cuttin' Barrone's nuts off, real slow, and skinnin' that bitch from neck to ankles just to hear her holler. I get a hard-on just thinkin' about what I'm gonna do to that cunt."

"Wonderful," Griz said. "That would be a sight to see. Hell, I'll even help you." He looked around him at his battered followers. "You've had time to think about Barrone's offer. Anybody want to take him up on it?"

The answer was unanimous and loudly proclaimed: "No!"

"All right. That's settled then. Let's get our wits about us and get ready to fight. Get geared up, people."

Jenny reached the spot she had pointed out to John and settled in, planting the first charge under a huge boulder. She moved a few yards to her right and planted another charge, smiling as she worked. "This one's for you, Maria, and for you, Al." She moved to another spot and went to work. "And this one's for me." She carefully set the timers on each charge and got the hell out of there.

"Now, John!" she shouted. "Right now!"

"Now, what?" Gatepost asked, looking around him. "What's that dippy broad shoutin' 'bout?"

"I guess we'll know in a few minutes," Griz said as he walked to the only part of the rear of the house that was still intact and peeked out what used to be a window.

Actually, it was considerably less time than that.

Griz was peeking out the broken window when the charges, about a hundred feet above him, blew with an enormous roaring sound.

"Oh, shit!" Griz said. "Run!" he shouted. "Everybody, get to the front of the house. Run! The whole damn mountain's comin' down on us."

Not quite the entire mountain, but enough of it.

Boulders came bouncing and sailing down, landing on the huge old structure, destroying the entire rear of the old hippie house in the canyon. Chink just missed getting crushed like a bug when a boulder about the size of a small car came crashing through the roof and landed about a foot from him, crashing through the floor and coming to rest in the basement. It scared him so bad he almost pissed his pants.

"Holy shit!" he shouted. He jumped to his feet and ran out of the room, colliding full force with Nutcutter. Both of them smacked heads and knocked each other silly. They stretched out on the buckled floor, momentarily out of it.

"Help!" Peggy yelled from the basement. She had been staggering around, trying to recover from tumbling down the long flight of stairs. "Somebody help me get out of this damn place."

"Use the damn stairs," someone yelled.

"There ain't no goddamn stairs," Peggy screamed. "They're all gone."

"Use the back way," Griz yelled.

"I tried. The doors are blocked by something. You can't even see no daylight 'tween the cracks."

They were covered by about a ton of dirt.

"Uh, Griz," Fireball said. "I got an idea."

"What is it?"

"Use one of the cell phones to call for help."

"We only brought one in. I tried to use it when this crap first started. The damn thing is busted or something. It won't work."

"Where are the others? Hell, everybody's got one."

"Outside, in the cars."

High above, Jenny started chunking grenades. The outlaws all heard the grenade hit what was left of the roof.

"Oh, crap!" Bend Over Betty said. "I know what that is."

The grenade caught on a pile of debris in the attic and exploded, sending more dirt and bird droppings and rat shit and broken boards showering down.

"Get me out of this damn spooky place!" Peggy screamed. "I'm goin' crazy down here. Somebody help me."

Another grenade landed on the roof and started its slow roll. But this one rolled through a hole and landed in what was left of the living room before it blew. Ax and Ox had turned to run just as the mini-bomb exploded. They both got peppered in the ass with bits of hot metal.

"Whoa, shit!" Ax hollered, grabbing at his punctured butt.

"My ass is on far!" Ox yelled, doing a very original little hoochy-coochy step in the middle of the floor.

"Help!" Peggy hollered. "I think they's rats down here. It's dark and I can't see. Help!"

"Somebody look at my ass!" Ax yelled.

"Mine, too!" Ox said.

"I've seen both your asses," a biker broad named Bouncy said. "I don't care to see them again."

"Well, fuck you!" Ax said.

"No, thanks," Bouncy replied. "I've done that too. Once was enough."

"Somebody's got to do something," Snake called.

"Feel free to act on your suggestion," Griz said, trying to brush all the rat crap out of his hair. "Just anytime you feel up to it."

Jenny waved at John, signaling she was through and coming back. John waited until she was clear, and began once more potshotting at the house.

"You're dead, Barrone!" Pinhead yelled from the house. "I'm gonna kill you slow, you bastard."

"And I'm gonna skin that bitch alive!" Big Balls screamed.

"After I get through with her!" the biker bitch called Hot Pants shrieked. "I'll cut her tits off!"

"What lovely people," John muttered, pausing long enough to lay the AK aside and take a sip of water.

Peggy had stumbled around in the dark and found a ladder by tripping over it and falling on her ass. After doing some high-powered cussing, she managed to get the ladder in place and slowly climb out of the basement. She got almost to the top and held out a hand for someone to help her.

"Here," Pisspot said, extending a hand. "Grab hold."

Peggy grabbed his hand just as the rung she was standing on broke. Pisspot and Peggy tumbled back into the darkness of the basement, both of them cussing and bellowing.

"This is worse than the Keystone Cops or the Three Stooges," Griz muttered. "We're all falling apart."

"I think we ought to make a deal with Barrone," Gatepost said. "Take him up on his offer. We'll kill him just as soon as we're free from this damn place."

"And then I can fuck that Jenny bitch," Chink added. "Fuck her hard and long. Make her holler."

Griz looked at Chink and slowly shook his head in disgust. He turned his attention to Big Balls. "You trust Barrone to keep his word, Big Balls?"

"Do we have a choice? If we stay here we're all gonna get killed."

"Get us the hell outta here!" Pisspot hollered from the basement.

"Somebody get them out of the basement," Griz

said. "Then we'll talk about makin' a deal with Barrone."

"Decided not to block the road?" John asked as Jenny plopped down beside him.

"I'll do that from the other side of the road. I wanted to have some fun with the outlaws first."

"I believe you succeeded admirably. The house is virtually destroyed."

Jenny was studying the rocks on the other side of the road. "I think I can seal them off for a long time. At least they'll never get their vehicles out . . . not without the help of a lot of earthmoving equipment."

"Have at it."

"I believe I will. See you in a little while."

"I'll be right here."

Jenny stuffed her rucksack full of explosives from the backpack and slipped away. John picked up the AK and started putting rounds into the house.

"This is ridiculous," Griz said between shots. "Two damn people pinning down two dozen people. This happens in the movies, not in real life."

"We gotta get clear of here, Griz," Hook said. "What's left of this old house is gonna fall in on us and kill us all."

"I ain't surrenderin' to that old dude," Greaseball said. "Hell, he ain't the law. He don't have no authority at all."

"Here comes Hammer!" a biker bitch shouted. "He's gonna make it."

Hammer hit the front porch—what was left of it—and fell into the ruined living room. "Son of a bitch!" he said. "I'm freezin' and I'm hungry. Is there any coffee?"

"No. The fire is out and the kitchen is destroyed," Fireball replied. "That answer your question?"

"I'm sorry I axed."

"Is there any vehicle that hasn't been shot all to hell?" Griz asked.

"I don't think so. We parked them all in a line and Barrone took them out in order. Like shootin' targets in a shootin' gallery. Where's Rammer?"

"I think he's dead. Out back. He hasn't moved or hollered in a long time. I think he may have bled to death."

"Big puddle of blood all around him," Greaseball said. "That grenade must have hit a big vein or something. He's gone, Hammer."

"X-Man?"

"Dead."

"I been hearin' all that talk 'bout a deal. I don't trust Barrone and that bitch. I think they're here to kill us. Any damn way they can."

"But if they're not government, and I don't believe they are, like I used to," Chink said, "who the hell are they?"

The question was met with silence.

John started blasting away at the house again, and everyone hit the floor.

"Shit!" Griz hollered. "I can't take much more of this."

"Somebody get us out of this damn basement!" Pisspot hollered.

"I can't take much more of that either," Griz muttered.

TWENTY-ONE

Tubby crawled over to Griz. "Maybe it's time for us to haul our asses out of this area, Griz. Have you give that any thought?"

"Sure. But where would we go? And could we ever get as well connected as we are here?"

"We'd be alive."

"We're alive now, Tub. And when we get out of this box, and we will, Barrone and that bitch of his is dead."

"You promise this time we'll kill them?"

"Bet your ass on it."

"All right. That's good enough for me." He studied Griz's face for a few seconds. "How do we get out of here?"

"I ain't got no idea, Tub."

"Me neither."

In the rocks on the ridge, John was getting cold and rapidly tiring of the siege. The outlaw bikers were cruel, vicious, and lacking in any socially redeeming qualities. John would be the first to admit that. But they were also, for the most part, stupid. Most of them behaved as if they possessed the I.Q. of an oyster. John didn't feel sorry for them any more than he would for a vicious and uncontrollable dog. He just felt . . . hell, he didn't know what he felt or how he felt. He was just tired of it.

He checked his watch and looked over at the ridge where Jenny was working. She'd been gone about thirty minutes. Then he looked up at the crest of the ridge and saw her, waving her arms at him.

"Okay," he shouted.

Jenny disappeared from sight.

"Okay what?" Greaseball asked after hearing the shouted acknowledgment. "What the hell is them two doin'?"

"Whatever it is," Griz said, "you can bet we ain't gonna like it." He paused and frowned. "I hate them two."

The moments passed in silence and John waited, wondering when Jenny was going to set off the charges. He was startled when she suddenly appeared beside him. The woman could move like a ghost.

"Let's get out of here," Jenny suggested. "That whole damn ridge is going to come down in five minutes."

The couple slipped out of the rocks and off the ridge, and were walking back up the snowy, muddy road toward their SUV when the charges blew. They turned and watched as a miniavalanche was created, tons of rock and dirt blowing and sliding down, covering the narrow road.

"About twenty feet deep," John guessed.

Jenny smiled. "That road just might be closed permanently."

"We've bought some time," John said. "For all the good it's going to do us."

They turned and walked on in silence for a few moments. "We didn't accomplish very much, did we?"

"Not a great deal. We still don't know where the labs are."

"But we did put a honky-tonk out of business."

John nodded his head. "That we did. But damn little else."

"So what happens now?"

"We call the other teams and see if they've managed to do any better."

"Why are you so down, John?"

"I'm not down so much as I am angry."

"At me?"

"Oh, no. At . . . well, what the hell makes, creates people like these outlaws? You've read the reports from Control on them. Many of them came from good, decent families. What the hell happened to them along the way?"

"You really worried about it, John?"

"Not really. I think they're trash and that's all they ever will be. Maybe it's what they want to be. No, what is puzzling me is something that popped into my mind while I was lying back there on that ridge."

"And that is?"

"We're missing something, Jenny. Start adding things up and the arithmetic is all wrong."

"There's the SUV, John," she said, as they rounded a bend in the road. "Save it until we get going and warm up."

"I'd like some dry clothes and about a quart of hot coffee."

Jenny laughed. "I would love to see the bikers about now."

Griz took a long look at the blocked road and verbally exploded. "Those goddamn rotten no good . . ." Griz filled the cold air with wild profanity. He cussed and kicked at rocks and waved his arms and jumped up and down until he was near exhaustion.

As big as Chink was, he backed away from Griz when the biker became this angry. Griz had a very volatile temper when angered.

When Griz stopped to catch his breath, Chink said, "If you're all through jumpin' up and down like a monkey, Griz, maybe you can tell us how we're gonna get out of here."

"We're gonna walk out, you dumb son of a bitch! Unless you can figure out a way for us to grow wings and fly out."

"And the cars and trucks?" Greaseball asked.

"Well, Grease, I guess we'll just have to leave them." Griz's sudden and highly explosive anger was gone, leaving as quickly as it came.

"We got some dead bodies," Pisspot said.

"I know that, Pisspot. We'll bury them. Won't say anything about it. There ain't nobody gonna miss them."

"That don't hardly seem right," Peggy said.

"Who the fuck axed you?" Hammer said.

"I'll say a prayer over them," Bend Over Betty volunteered.

"You? Say a prayer?" Mad Dog asked. "This is something I gotta hear."

"I know some prayers. I was a little girl once. I used to go to Sunday School too. When I got some older, I used to fuck the preacher. How does that grab you, asshole?"

"You fucked the preacher?" Fireball said. "That's disgustin'!"

"They got a dick just like ever'body else," Betty said. She turned to Mad Dog. "You got anythin' else to say about my sayin' a prayer?"

Mad Dog held up a hand. "No. Nothin'."

"Damn cars and trucks is all shot to hell anyway,"

Snake said, looking around him. "But Jesus, it's a long walk back to anywhere."

Somebody get a shovel and a pickax," Griz said. "Let's dig some graves and then get the hell out of here."

"That heater feels so good," Jenny said as they drove back toward the highway. "I might be warm by the time we get back to the lodge."

"Somebody is behind the three money men," John said abruptly.

"What?"

"I told you something wasn't adding up. That's it. The bikers don't have enough sense to finance, manufacture, and set up drug distribution. A few outlaw biker groups do go it pretty much alone. That's been established. But not this group."

"All right. I'll agree with that. But they've got Sandoval, Curtis, and Grayson behind them. We know that for a fact."

"But why are they behind them?"

"For money, John."

"They don't need the money, Jenny. They each inherited vast sums of money and they all made more money in legitimate ventures. Then, suddenly, the three richest men in this part of the state are bankrolling outlaw bikers in a drug deal. It doesn't make sense."

They rode in silence for a few miles, Jenny finally saying, "Organized crime?"

"That's what I think."

"The Mafia?"

"Or something close to it."

"Well, in the South they have the Dixie Mafia. What's out here, the Cowboy Mafia?"

"I don't know. But we're going to find out."

"Why would rich people get involved with the Mafia?"

"Oh, it's happened before. For various reasons. Organized crime, as you well know, is into all sorts of legitimate enterprises. And a lot of businesses don't know they're mixed in with organized crime until it's too late. Sometimes they never know."

"Which category do you think Sandoval, Grayson, and Curtis belong in?"

"I don't know, Jenny. But we're sure going to find out. I want all the pieces of this puzzle in place. When we get back to the lodge, call in the rest of the team. The lodge is big enough for all of us. Tell them to get here ASAP."

"It'll be good to see the rest of the gang." She frowned. "Minus one. Seems like it's been a long time."

"Yes, it does. But a lot has happened in a short time."

"John?"

"Yes?"

"I wonder if we'll ever know why Al decided to quit."

"I doubt it. Personally, I think Al was carrying a lot of baggage he somehow slipped by Control. It just finally caught up with him."

"I'll see if I can get the team now," Jenny said, picking up the cell phone from its charger. "Get them moving. They could be here today."

"Good deal."

Jenny talked for a few minutes, then laughed and

punched the off button, setting the phone back in the charger.

"What's so funny?" John asked.

"Most of the team will be here in a few hours."

"Most of the team?"

"Yeah. Chris and Lana won't be able to make it. They're, well, out of service for about a week."

"You want to explain that?"

"They both have chicken pox." Jenny started laughing.

"Are you serious?"

"They interviewed a family whose kids had chicken pox. Seems neither of them ever had the childhood disease. But they do now."

"Chicken pox!" John said. "Incredible."

"Not too incredible," Jenny said. "I never had it either."

The outlaw bikers had buried their dead in unmarked graves, then climbed over the tons of rock and dirt, and were trudging up the road, back to the highway.

"I'm cold," Fireball bitched.

"So what?" Tubby told her. "We all are. Thanks to Barrone and that lousy bitch of his."

"I hate them," Greaseball said. "I wanna kill them both slow. Listen to them holler. I can't wait to do that."

While the others bitched and moaned, Chink asked Griz, "We gonna call Benny when we get to a phone?"

"I already done that," Griz said. "An hour ago. I found a cell phone that wasn't shot all to hell."

"No shit. That's cool, Griz. What'd he say?"

"He said he'd have people waitin' for us at the high-way."

"Why didn't you tell the others?"

"Nobody asked me."

Chink thought about that for a few steps through the muddy snow. "What about our vehicles?"

"Forget them. It'll be days or weeks before anybody discovers this mess. Then it'll take the damn county government more days or weeks to figure out what to do and more days or weeks before they actual do something. By that time we'll long have our asses covered and this crap with Barrone will be over."

"I wanna be the one who kills him and does the bitch."

"You and ever'one else, Chink."

"I reckon so."

"Goddamn snow and slop has leaked through my boots and my feet is fuckin' freezin'."

"Mine, too. How many more miles 'fore we reach the highway?"

"Five or so, I guess."

"We'll all probably catch pneumonia."

Griz ignored that. "Benny is callin' in all the guys from around the state. We gonna have us a full-fledged war, Chink."

"All right! Can I tell the others?"

"Have at it."

"It'll make 'em feel better."

"My ass is burnin' like fire where I was shot," Big Tit called. "I really need to see me a doctor."

"Soon as the poor bastard takes a close look at your funky ass, he'll probably give up medicine," Snake said.

"And women," Big Balls said.

"You know what you can both do with your

mouths?" Big Tit popped right back. "If you don't, I can sure tell you."

"Oh, knock it off!" Griz said. "Save your breath for walking. We've still got a long ways to go."

"My ass hurts!" Big Tit said. "It hurts with every step. I wanna shoot that damn Barrone in his ass and listen to him holler."

"Get in line," Griz told her. "Everybody wants to shoot Barrone."

"Could be it was that bitch with him that shot you," Mean Jeans said. "You ever think about that?"

"I'll shoot her too," Big Tit said.

"Not until after I fuck her," Chink said.

Griz sighed and let them talk. Let them get good and mad, he thought. When the rest of the gang got in from all over the state, they'd get this matter settled.

Once and for all.

TWENTY-TWO

After a hot shower, John fixed a pot of coffee while Jenny was still bathing. He took his coffee into the den and called Control, requesting additional information on Sandoval, Curtis, and Grayson; everything they could dig up, especially on the men's business dealings.

"What have you and that pyrotechnic female been up to now?" Control asked.

John smiled at Control's description of Jenny. "Giving the outlaw bikers a very hard time."

"Disposing of them, I hope."

"We're not hired assassins."

"Semantics, John. This team was not formed to behave as Girl Scouts. Get on with this assignment. We have more work for you."

"I'm sure you do. When do we start on Congress?"

"Very amusing. However, some things are beyond change without a major civil war. That will be up to the citizenry."

"You think that's coming?"

"Of course. The tree of liberty must be refreshed from time to time. But that is not your job. The information you requested will be forthcoming ASAP. For now, good-bye."

Control broke the connection.

"Asshole," John muttered.

"You must have been speaking with Control," Jenny said, walking into the room in time to hear John's comment.

"Who else? You feel better?"

"Much. I'll feel even better after I get a cup of coffee."

"I'm expecting a visit from Sheriff Watson any minute. I can't believe all that gunfire and those explosions went unnoticed."

"We were miles off the beaten path, John. I doubt if anyone heard it." She went into the kitchen, returned with a cup of coffee, and sat down with a sigh.

"I know," John said. "It's been a busy day. It's catching up with me too." He glanced at his watch. "The others should be arriving in a couple of hours."

"You hungry?"

"Not really. But I'll cook something whenever you're ready," he added quickly.

She laughed at the expression on his face. "I can fix bacon and eggs, John."

John heard a car pull into the drive and he pointed toward the front. "Moot point now, Jenny. Here's Sheriff Watson."

"I'll let her in. This should be interesting."

Jimmi strolled in and stood for a moment, looking first at John, then at Jenny. It was not an unfriendly or hostile look . . . more a curious one. "When you folks get going, you really let the hammer down, don't you?"

"What are we supposed to have done now?" John asked.

"Don't play coy with me, John," the sheriff replied. "I started receiving reports of gunfire up on Lost Canyon Road hours ago. I ignored them. Then I took a ride up there about an hour ago. As far as I could go, that is. Jesus, what a mess."

"Have a seat, Sheriff," John said. "Make yourself comfortable."

"Thanks, I will."

"Would you like some coffee?" Jenny asked. "It's good. John made it."

"That would be nice. It's turning colder."

"I'll get it. I remember what you take."

"A bunch of very pissed-off bikers had just hiked out when I was pulling in, John," Jimmi said. "They told me there had been an avalanche. I drove on into the canyon and took a look. Hell of an avalanche."

"Really? They're probably common in this country this time of year. I imagine people have learned to be careful."

"I didn't take a close look on the other side of that huge mound of dirt and rock. The bikers said they didn't lose much."

"Gee, I sure am glad to hear that," Jenny said, walking in with Jimmi's coffee and setting it down on an end table. "They seem like such a nice bunch of people."

Jimmi got a good laugh out of that. "I can just about tell you what's going to happen now."

"Oh?" John questioned.

"There's going to be a war in my county. And that doesn't thrill me very much."

"The bikers are going to fight each other?" Jenny asked.

Jimmi's eyes lost their humor. "No. They're going to fight you two."

"Well, golly," John said. "I hate to hear that. I guess we'd better call in some people to help us."

"I guess you'd better. If you haven't already done so. You can bet the bikers have called in some help."

"You have some intelligence on that, Sheriff?"

"Not yet. But I will have."

"If it happens."

"It'll happen." She took a sip of coffee. "That's good. Hits the spot. How many people do you have coming in, John?"

"Oh, one or two."

Jimmi laughed. "My people are wondering why I don't just run you in and book you or just run you out of the county."

"And you tell them what?"

Jimmi shrugged her shoulders. "I can put them off for a while longer, John. But the D.A. is getting interested now. I can't put him off for much longer. If his office issues warrants, I have to serve them."

"I understand."

"Get this matter settled as quickly as possible and move on. You're running out of time."

"Just who do you work for, Jimmi?" John asked.

"The people." Jimmi looked squarely at him, took another sip of coffee, and smiled.

"Of course you do. How silly of me to ask."

"What can you tell me about Sandoval, Curtis, and Grayson?" Jenny asked.

"They're connected," Jimmi answered. "Do I have to explain that?"

"No. I understand. But how they got connected is something I don't understand. That, and why."

"How and why is easy," Jimmi said. "The three of them began taking in partners in some of their various businesses. The partners began quietly working toward buying controlling interests. A note was sold to this person, bought by another person, and so on, until it ended up in the wrong hands, so to speak." She lifted her coffee cup in a mock salute. "I wondered how long it would take you to fit that piece of the puzzle in place."

"Sandoval, Curtis, and Grayson were clean, so to speak, until the mob came in?"

Jimmi laughed at that. "Clean? Hell, no, they weren't clean. They never have been. They're enormously wealthy men. And don't think for an instant they got that way solely by inheritance. They didn't. They've been involved in shady deals for years. I remember my parents making some pretty sordid remarks about the parents of the Big Three. Like father, like son, I guess, is true in this case. The Big Three, as some refer to them, have cheated the little guy for years. But they're done so legally, if not ethically."

"Nice people," Jenny remarked.

"Salt of the earth," Jimmi said sarcastically.

"Surrounded by a battery of lawyers," John said.

"Oh, you bet. An impenetrable shield of laws, good and bad, all around them. But remember one thing: You'll never connect the bikers to Sandoval, Curtis, or Grayson. Too many people standing in the middle for that."

"And I suppose cops don't bother their kids when they screw up?" Jenny asked.

"Not if the cop has any sense at all. Oh, they might take them to the station and talk to them, but that's about it. The kids are not going to do any hard time. Hassle the kids of those three, and the cops stand a good chance of not just losing their jobs, but of having notes abruptly sold and then called in. They might face inspectors finding all sorts of problems with their homes: zoning laws, wiring, whatever. You know the drill."

"Unfortunately, yes," John said.

Jimmi set her coffee cup on a coaster on the end table and stood up. "I would suggest you people do whatever you came in here to do and get it done quickly."

John thought she chose her words very carefully. "And quietly," he said.

Jimmi smiled. "I doubt that's going to happen. Well, I'd better be going."

"Be sure and tell the folks back around Washington hello, Jimmi," John said.

Jimmi's eyes narrowed just for an instant. She recovered swiftly and smiled. "I don't know many people back in Washington, John."

"Oh? I got the impression you did. Sorry."

She stared at him for a moment, then shook her head. "Now what in the world would give you that impression?"

"Just a thought."

"Well, you two have a safe night. See you around." The sheriff walked out into the late afternoon and was gone.

"There must have been a dozen different thoughts going through her head just then," Jenny said.

"At least. But her reaction didn't leave any room for doubt in my mind about who she works for."

"Nor mine. You pegged her right on the money. And there were a lot of not too subtle warnings being tossed around by Sheriff Watson. Makes me wonder if they didn't originate from Control."

Jenny bumped the rest of the team on the cell phone and asked them to pick up some fast food as soon as they hit town. The remaining members of the team began pulling in an hour after Sheriff Watson left.

Lana and Chris were in isolation at a small hospital in the south central part of the state.

"They'll be discharged in a few days," Don said. "Providing they don't come down with the mumps or something."

"They're both pretty pissed about this," Paul said with a smile. "They're confined in the children's section of the hospital."

"But they get to watch cartoons all day long," Bob added.

John surprised everyone by saying, "Well, that wouldn't be too bad. I like the Tasmanian Devil. He's my favorite."

"You watch cartoons?" Linda asked, astonishment in her voice.

John smiled. "Occasionally."

Don paused for a few seconds while digging into a sack of cheeseburgers. "Roadrunner. That's my favorite." He hauled out a double cheeseburger and asked, "So what did you guys turn up here, John? Bring us up to date."

John and Jenny spent the next fifteen minutes detailing all they had uncovered, their suspicions, and what they had done.

"You two have been busy," Paul said. "What we've done is pretty well establish that right here in this area is the headquarters for the dope operation in the state."

"Cut the head off the snake here and it dies," Linda said, "hopefully."

"For about a week," Mike said. "If that long. What the hell good is one small team of people against thousands of people who are involved nationwide? I think we're spitting into the wind at best."

"I agree with Mike," Don said. "However, if we can save the lives of a few kids, it's worth our efforts."

"If Control thinks that whatever we do here is going to send any kind of long-lasting message to dopers, they're wrong," Paul said.

"You're all correct," John said. "To a degree. But this is where we were sent to do a job, and we're going to do it. So get all your beefs aired, then we'll settle down and finish up."

"Did those biker bastards hurt you in any way, Jenny?" Linda asked. There was a cold fire burning in her eyes. John knew, with Linda's past dealing with outlaw bikers, that if she got half a chance, there would be dead bikers all over this part of the state.

"No. Just pissed me off. But they had big plans. They just didn't have enough time to carry them out."

"So what do we do?" Bob asked. "Do we wait for the dopers to restart the war or do we jump right in and start kicking ass?"

"Let's start kicking ass," Linda suggested. "Right now. Tonight."

"I'm with Linda," Jenny said.

"Settle down," John said. "Let's make some plans."

"Lemmie finish my cheeseburger before we start shooting," Don said. "Anybody gonna eat those onion rings?"

"I wonder what Chris and Lana are having for supper," Paul said.

"You can bet that part of it is skim milk and Jell-O," Mike said, then shuddered at his own words.

Don started on his second container of onion rings.

"Well, we know that Control has eyes and ears watching and listening everywhere," John said. "Don, if you can manage to put aside your food for a moment, bump Control and find out if there has been

any unusual biker movement in this state and surrounding states in the past few hours. I'm betting
there has been."

"And if that's true?" Linda asked.

"We get ready for a war."

TWENTY-THREE

"You son of a bitch!" The shout cut through the cold night air just a few seconds before the air turned hot with gunfire. It was three o'clock in the morning.

All over the lodge, the team members rolled out of their beds grabbing for weapons.

"I think the war has started!" Paul yelled.

"No kidding!" Jenny hollered from the bedroom she was sharing with Linda.

The front windows shattered under the heavy gunfire from automatic weapons, shards of broken glass flying in all directions. Bullets slammed into bookcases and furniture and gouged holes in the walls.

"There go the damn windows again," John muttered. "We're out of here this time for sure."

The gunfire lasted only a few seconds; a few seconds that seemed much longer to those in the lodge. Then the roaring of engines, then silence.

John got to his feet and looked around him in the darkness, which was broken only by a small night-light plugged into a wall socket across the room. "Anybody hit?"

No one was injured.

"Be careful where you step," John cautioned the team members. "We're all barefoot and there's broken glass all over the place. Jenny, you've got Sheriff

Watson's home number. Give her a call and tell her what's happened."

"I'll check the outside," Paul called.

"Carefully," John told him. He glanced at a battery-operated wall clock. It had been stopped dead by a bullet, the hands forever frozen at three o'clock.

"I'll make a pot of coffee," Don said, heading for the kitchen. "I don't think any of us will be going back to bed."

"Keep the lights off," John said. "I think they're gone, but let's make sure before we outline ourselves."

"Well, damn it!" Don said. "There was one cheese-burger left and I was going to heat it up. The sack took a hit. I've got cheeseburger all over the kitchen."

"The man is honest-to-God hungry," Linda said, walking to John's side. "He's incredible. I watched him eat three cheeseburgers, two containers of onion rings, and a huge piece of pie before going to bed."

"And a quart of milk," Mike said, joining them. "I think he's got a tapeworm."

"Sheriff Watson is on her way," Jenny called. "She sounded very unhappy about this shooting."

"I wouldn't say any of us were exactly thrilled about it," John replied.

"The damn fridge took half a dozen hits!" Don yelled. "It's ruined. Shit!"

"How's the coffeepot?" Bob asked.

"There's two of them. Both of them are okay."

"Then quit bitching about food and make some coffee."

"I'll find a broom and start sweeping up this glass," Mike said.

"No," John told him. "Leave everything just the way it is. I want Sheriff Watson to see it."

"Everybody get shoes on then," Mike said. "Or we're going to have some badly cut-up feet."

"It's all clear out here," Paul called from the front of the house. "Lots of brass up by the road."

"Leave it," John said. "Sheriff Watson will want to bag it up for evidence. And check the vehicles while you're out there."

"I did. They're all right. Didn't take a hit that I can see."

"We'll have some coffee in a minute," Don called from the kitchen. "If I can turn on the lights so I can see what I'm doing."

"Turn them on," John said. "No point in stumbling around in the dark. I doubt the shooters will be back tonight."

The place looked even worse with the lights on—those lights that weren't shot to pieces, that is.

Jenny walked over to John and looked at him for a moment. "How much more of this are we going to take before we react in kind? Personally, I've had it. We should have killed them all at the old hippie place."

"You're probably right, Jenny. But do you know for sure the attack tonight was from the bikers?"

"No. You know I don't. But who else could it be, the kids of the money men? Those were automatic weapons being used."

"We'll find us another place to stay and hash this out when we get settled in. Okay?"

"Yes, we sure will, John. You can bet on that. I've had it with these goddamn outlaw bikers." Jenny walked away, into the kitchen.

It's going to come to a head very quickly, John thought as he watched Jenny walk away. *A killing time is fast approaching. But,* he thought, *maybe it's time for that. That seems to be the only thing the bikers understand.*

John stepped out onto the back porch to stand for a moment in the cold early morning air. It was refreshing, at least for as long as he could take it without a jacket—which wasn't very long, only a few minutes. When he reentered the kitchen, he caught the glare of headlights pulling into the driveway.

"Sheriff Jimmi Watson is here," John said.

Jimmi didn't mince words. She nodded at John, and before he could introduce her to the others, said, "You've got to get clear of this place, John. I know a place up in the mountains . . . well, between the foothills and the mountains, sort of. It would be ideal for you."

"Think anyone would rent it to us?"

"Yes, I do. I would. I own it."

Nick Sandoval picked up the phone. Although he didn't want to take the call, he'd been expecting it for several days. "What the hell is going on up there, Nick?" the hard voice demanded.

"I don't know what you mean, Mr. Vergano."

"You know damn well what I mean. Don't give me that crap. Things are out of control."

"I just learned about the problems the bikers are having."

"Who told you?"

Nick hesitated, feeling a bit ashamed. "Ahh . . . from my kids, Mr. Vergano."

"Your kids know more about your damn business than you do? Jesus Christ, Nick. I'm getting heat all the way from L.A. about this and your goddamn kids know more about it than you do?"

"No one told me anything about it, Mr. Vergano."

"*I'm* telling you about it, Nick. And *I'm* telling you to put a stopper in it right now. Do you understand that?"

"Yes, sir. Ahh, sir?"

"What?"

"How do I stop it?"

"I don't care how you do it, just fucking do it!"

"All right, sir. Yes, sir. But I just don't know how. I've never had this kind of trouble before."

"And the bottom line is?"

"Well, I might need some help."

Vergano chuckled. "That's better, Nick. Now you're finally getting some smarts. You want me to send some boys up?"

"I would appreciate that, sir."

"I'll get some boys moving today. They'll be coming out of L.A."

"Yes, sir."

"You don't have to see them. They know what to do. Understood?"

"Yes, sir."

"Fine. You're getting to be a real team player, Nick. I'll talk to you later."

"Yes, sir. Good-bye, sir."

Vergano hung up.

Nick Sandoval exhaled slowly. Talking to Vergano always made him tense. He took several deep breaths, then picked up the phone and punched out a number.

"Dave?"

"Hey, Nick," Dave Curtis said. "What's happening?"

"I just heard from Vergano."

"Oh, shit!"

"Yeah. He's upset about all this trouble."

"Should we be talking about this on the phone?"

"It sure didn't bother Vergano."

"Let's meet. I'll contact Morris."

"All right. Where?"

"Lunch at the club. Noon. I'll make reservations."

"Suits me. This is making me real edgy, Dave."

"Just calm down. We'll talk it out. See you in a few hours."

"How can a local sheriff afford something like this?" Mike asked.

The team was standing in the driveway, watching as Jimmi unlocked the front door of one of the most beautiful houses in the country and waved them in.

"Nice place," John remarked, pausing by the door. "The sheriff must make a lot of money in this county."

"Because of this place?" Jimmi asked. "It was a gift." She smiled faintly. "When I was a deputy just starting out, there was a kidnapping in the county. A young boy was taken and was held for a five-million-dollar ransom. The family is worth about a hundred million. I found the boy and brought him back to his parents, unharmed. It was pure luck; no skill involved. I told the family that. But the father was so grateful he wouldn't take no for an answer. He finally deeded this place to me. I didn't even know about it until his lawyers called me. I almost fainted from shock. The taxes are paid out of a fund he set up." She grinned. "Just the luck of the stupid, I guess."

"Pretty dam lucky."

"I can't sell it. But who would want to."

"I sure wouldn't. It reverts back to the family at your death?"

"Yes."

"The family still live around here?"

"They have a summer house here. I see them every year. Come on in. Believe me, there is plenty of room for everybody, if a couple won't mind the two fold-out couches."

"They won't."

"Okay. You all get settled in and I'll square things about the shot-up lodge with the rental agent. Here is the skinny: You have no neighbors within three miles. Not this time of year. This road dead-ends two miles up. You'll have plenty of privacy."

"Anyone live up toward the road's end?"

"Not in the winter. Several summer places up there. The power is on here and there is plenty of wood in the shed. You'll have to buy your own food," she said with a grin.

"And if this place gets shot up?"

"Whatever the insurance company doesn't cover, you can pay for fixing it. The organization that is financing you can afford it."

"What organization?" John asked.

Jimmi smiled and lifted a hand. "I've got to get back to work. See you, John. You and your people have fun."

"I'd bet a month's pay you're right in your assumption she works for Control," Mike said after listening to the last part of the conversation.

"We'll probably never know for sure," John replied. "Let's get unloaded and settled in. Then we'll talk about our next move."

"Nobody tells me to cool it," Benny said after slamming down the phone and regaining some control over his explosive temper. "Especially some candy-ass like Sandoval."

"What are we supposed to do?" Chink asked. "Just sit back and let Barrone kill us?"

"Sandoval said there's some toughs comin' in from L.A.," Benny said. "They're goin' to take over dealin' with our problem."

"We got enough boys comin' in to handle Barrone and his people," Griz said. "To hell with Sandoval and them others."

"Here's Fussbucket and his boys pullin' in," Hook called. "They're in cars and vans."

"No trailers with their Hogs?" Big Balls asked.

"Nope."

"Fuss has turned soft," Big Balls said.

"Or got smart," Greaseball said. "It's a long ride up here. And it's turned damn cold out there."

"Did they bring their old ladies with them?" Stoneballs asked.

"They's a few cunts gettin' out."

"Where we gonna put all these people?" Nutcutter asked.

"All over the county," Benny said. "We're gonna blanket the area."

"How about the lab?" Griz asked.

"That's your responsibility," Benny told him. "You handle it. You just damn well better do it right."

"I'll handle it. Don't worry 'bout that."

"I worry 'bout ever'thing, Griz," Benny replied. "That's my job."

"Be good to see Valentine again," Tubby said.

"Speak for yourself," Chink said. "I can't stand the bastard."

"I think he's cute," Hot Pants said.

"Who axed you?" Big Train asked. "Shut up."

"Fuck you," Hot Pants told him.

"What are we gonna do about these goons comin' in?" Pinhead asked.

"Let them do their thing. As long as they don't interfere with us."

"And if they do?" Pinhead.

"We'll take care of them," Benny said. "This is our deal. Nobody horns in. Nobody."

TWENTY-FOUR

"This just came in from Control," Don said, walking into the large den waving a printout. "Someone—and we all know who that is—intercepted a phone message from a Mafia boss to another family member in L.A. They passed it on to Control. We've got some muscle coming in."

"Oh, good," Jenny said. "Now the party is really going to get lively."

"Does it say who the mob boss in L.A. is?" Linda asked.

"No. But the call was placed from a New Mexico number belonging to somebody named Vergano."

"Gus Vergano," Jenny said. "He runs the New Mexico operation. He's also suspected of having his fingers in several casinos in Vegas and also some riverboat casinos. The Bureau's been trying to nail him for years. No luck. He's a slick one." She smiled. "But he just may have screwed up big time now."

"You want to pass this on to the Bureau?" John asked, returning her smile.

"Not a chance, Boss."

"I didn't think you would. So, okay. Now, we've got some goons coming in—number unknown—and you can bet the bikers are calling in help from outlaw bikers aligned with them . . . from wherever they can."

"We can take care of the goons," Paul said. "They're going to be city boys in the country. They'll probably stand out."

"Probably. But the sheer number of bikers might be a problem."

"Why?" Linda asked. "God knows we're armed as well as or better than a squad of combat personnel. We can get whatever we want air-shipped into us in a matter of hours. We're just going to have to stay alert."

"Who knows we're living out here?" Bob asked.

"Only Jimmi, so far. But I don't believe it will take the bikers long to find us . . . probably by the end of the day. We'll have to set up guard shifts at night. I think one person can watch front and back. We'll try it that way at first, see how it works out."

"Are we going to be spending much time here at night?" Mike asked.

"Not much. That's the way I see it now."

"So how are we going to be spending our time?" Don asked.

"At war," John told him.

The outlaw bikers from all over the state pulled in, thirty men and ten women. From Fussbucket and his gang in the western part of the state, to Kong and his crew from the extreme southern part of the state.

The muscle from the mob in L.A. were driving in. Three new Cadillacs, three men to a car. "We'll buy us some local clothing when we get to New Mexico," Largo told the others. "We'll blend right in with the natives."

"Do I have to wear those damn stupid cowboy boots?" Big Sal asked.

"Yes."

"Damn things hurt my feet."

"I want one of them big black hats like Lash LaRue wears in them old western movies I like to watch on the TV," Otwell said. "I might get me a whip, too."

Largo sighed. Otwell was not known for his intelligence. Largo figured his I.Q. was just about on a par with an oyster.

"I really don't think you need a whip, Ot," Largo told him. "That might be a bit conspicuous."

"I'm gonna buy one anyways. I want to."

"Whatever," Largo said.

Big Sal, who was driving, cut his eyes to Largo and smiled. "Maybe we'll trade in the cars for some horses."

"Knock it off, Sal," Largo told him.

"Oh, hey!" Ot said from the backseat. "That would really be neat. Ridin' a horse looks real easy. I bet I could do it."

"Ot, you were born in Brooklyn," Largo told him. "The closest you ever came to a horse was steppin' in horseshit after a parade."

"I done that once," Ot admitted. "Smelled really bad."

"This job won't take long," Largo said. "I hope," he added softly.

Big Sal cut his eyes again and smiled at the expression on Largo's face.

The den of the house in the hills resembled a war room. The smell of gun oil was pungent as weapons were being field-stripped and cleaned and magazines loaded up full. John reassembled his weapon and watched as Linda carefully sharpened a thin double-edged dagger.

"You ever used that thing?" he asked.

"Once," the woman said. "It wasn't an approved weapon in the LAPD, so I didn't report it. Besides, I was off duty, jogging up in the hills."

"What happened to the perp?" Mike asked.

"He lived," Linda replied. "After the doctors took about eighty stitches in him." She sheathed the dagger in a holster strapped to the outside of her right leg. "I understand he was a changed man after that experience."

"I damn sure would be," Paul said. "A knife purely scares the crap out of me." He laid his Uzi aside, freshly cleaned and oiled and ready to rock and roll. "We going to go to work tonight, John?"

"We are. We're going to take the fight to the bikers. Benny's place up in the hills. It's on Vista Road. In Morales's county. Jenny, you and I will check it out. We'll leave as soon as you're ready. We'll map out as many avenues of escape as we can find."

"Suits me, Boss."

"Anybody who thinks they might like to grab a nap, do so now. There won't be much time for sleeping tonight"

"Mind if I tag along with you two?" Linda asked.

"Get your coat," John said. "The rest of you stay close. I can assure you, all hell is about to break loose."

A wild whoop startled those in the house. Benny almost spilled his coffee down the front of his shirt. "What the hell is that?"

Griz looked out the window. "It's Kong and his bunch. They got that nutty Ape Man with them."

"Oh, crap!" Chink said. "I hate that goofy bastard. He thinks he's Tarzan."

Another wild whoop cut the cold air.

Benny closed his eyes and shook his head. "Did Kong bring Pig with him?"

"Yeah. I see him. Bit and ugly as ever."

"Don't he have a murder warrant out on him?"

"Yeah," Griz said. "Back in Ohio. Beat some woman to death after he raped her and her kid. The kid escaped."

"I'd rather put up with Pig than with Ape Man," Snake said. "Even if he is the ugliest son of a bitch that ever lived."

"I want that Jenny bitch alive," Chink said. "I want to screw her brains out."

"Will you for Christ sake get pussy off your mind!" Griz said. "I want both of them dead. Them and whoever them others is that was at the lodge this mornin'."

"We gettin' far behind in production," Jimmy Cisco said. "Our outlets is hollerin' about it."

"We can't do ten things at once," Griz told him. "We damn sure can't run no labs with Barrone snoopin' all over the place."

"Hey, the house!" Kong hollered from the porch. "We's here."

"Wonderful," Benny said. "Griz, let 'em in."

John drove up Vista Road and past the house where Benny lived.

"Good God," Linda said. "It looks like a used-car

lot. I count at least a dozen vehicles. I've got a couple of tag numbers."

"Reinforcements have arrived," John said. "That's for sure. Figuring three to a car, we're looking at thirty or so additional people."

Jenny pointed to an approaching intersection. "Left on that road will take us back to the main highway. On up this road another couple of miles is another intersection that will also take us back to the highway."

"Call in those tag numbers now," John said. "We'll drive on for a few minutes and then head back. You can get a few more tag numbers. Give us some indication of what we're up against."

"Scum," Linda said, no small amount of venom in her tone.

"What about the kids of the money men?" Jenny asked.

"What about them?" John said.

"They're involved in this. And we're pretty sure they fired into the lodge the other night. Do we just forget about them?"

"No. But they're not the major players in this. We'll deal with them after we deal with the outlaws and the muscle and the kids' parents. If we have time. If not, we'll let Sheriffs Morales and Watson deal with them."

"A van just pulled out of the driveway of the biker house," Linda said. "Heading straight for us and not being shy about it."

"Good," Jenny said. "Let's get this war started for real."

Linda was studying the occupants of the van through a small pair of binoculars. "Four of them. Ugly bastards too. Uh-oh."

"What?" John asked.

"Weapons. Of the automatic type."

"Hang on. I'm taking this road to the right just up ahead."

"It's only a couple of miles long and then it dead-ends, John," Jenny told him after glancing at a very detailed county map.

"Any homes on it?"

"None that the map points out."

"The van made the turn right behind us," Linda said.

"There's an old falling-down house just ahead on the right," John said. "Good place to make a stand. How about it?"

"Suits me," Jenny said.

"You're driving," Linda said.

John cut into the driveway and slid to a stop at the rear of the old house. The old structure was built of stone. It was now minus part of the roof, and it appeared to have been the victim of a long-ago fire. The trio bailed out, each carrying weapons and a rucksack of ammo, and ran through the opening where the back door to the old house used to be. The trio took up positions: John in the center of the house, the others on either side.

"Jenny," John said, "use your cell phone and call the others. Advise them of our situation and tell them to come on. As stupid-appearing as these outlaws are, we have to assume they've called their friends and help will be arriving in a few minutes."

"We're going to hold them off for forty-five minutes to an hour?" Linda called from John's left.

"If we want to stay alive," John replied with a smile. "Don't worry. I imagine Jenny has some surprises in that rucksack she lugged in."

"You can count on that," Jenny called from the

other side of the old home as she punched out the numbers on her cell phone.

"And there they are," Linda said as the van slid to a halt in front of the house, then quickly backed up, getting out of the line of fire.

"Do we wait for them to open the dance?" Jenny asked.

"Yes," John called.

"I don't know why I ask," Jenny muttered.

Most of the paneling in the old home had been torn out, leaving only the framework and studding in place, enabling the trio to see each other.

"Our people are on the move," Jenny called, clicking off the phone. "It'll probably be at least an hour before they get here."

"It's going to be an interesting hour," Linda said.

"And a cold one," Jenny added.

"There's the fireplace," John said, pointing behind him. "And there's plenty of scrap wood lying around. Help yourself."

"Thanks," Jenny replied. "Unfortunately, most of the roof is gone. But it was a nice suggestion to make."

"Keep your eyes open," John said. "I'm going to get the rest of our equipment out of the SUV."

"Hey, you assholes in the house!" The shout came from a stand of timber in front and slightly to the right of the old house. "I seen you, Barrone. This time your ass and them cunts with you is dead."

"Yeah, we got you now!" another outlaw shouted. "We got lots of help on the way."

"Bring them on, you outlaw prick!" Linda shouted.

"Bitch!" another biker hollered.

"You say that like it's a bad thing!" Linda replied.

"Huh?" the biker called.

"He's not exactly a mental giant," Jenny said.

"And not much of a sense of humor."

John walked back in through the rear of the house, carrying a half-dozen rucksacks of various sizes. He set them down on the floor and straightened up. "How many grenades did you bring, Jenny?"

"Oh, about twenty, I think. Plus some other stuff." She grinned at John. "I'm glad you set them down gently."

Suddenly, bullets started howling and bouncing off the exposed stone walls inside the building. The trio hit the floor and stayed put.

When the firing ceased, Jenny said, "They've come up in the world. They're using sound suppressors."

"Until they blow the baffles out of them," John said. "And that won't take long. Then it's going to get noisy."

Another blast of almost silent gunfire came from the outside, the lead smacking into the walls and bouncing off, creating a deadly whining.

"Do we return the fire now, Boss?" Jenny asked.

"Be my guest," he said.

"It's about time," Linda said, crawling to her knees and peeping outside. She lifted her Uzi. "Hey, you outlaw bastards!" she shouted. "Eat this!"

She squeezed the trigger, spraying the wooded area by the side of the house with lead.

"Jesus Christ!" a biker yelled.

The fight was on.

TWENTY-FIVE

After Linda uncorked a full magazine, there was quiet for several minutes. John used that time to distribute full magazines and grenades to both women. Then he once more took his place in the center of the house.

"We gonna kill you real slow, Barrone!" a biker shouted. "We gonna make you suffer and holler!"

"If these halfwits weren't so damn vicious, I could almost feel sorry for them," John said. "And please bear in mind I said almost. They are so ignorant it's pathetic."

"But John," Jenny said. "Don't you know that they were probably spanked by their parents, or they felt rejected by their peers, or they came from broken homes?"

"Yes," Linda agreed. "Or they had pimples, or the homecoming queen wouldn't date them, or the coach wouldn't let them play. That's why they turned to a life of crime. I thought you knew that!"

"All right, all right, ladies. I said I *almost* felt sorry for them."

"Now you're in for it, you meddlin' bastard and bitches," a biker yelled from timber. "Here comes the boys!"

"Sound like a really bad western, doesn't it?" Jenny asked.

"I want to hump that other broad!" a biker yelled. "Whoever she is!"

"Go hump a stump!" Linda yelled.

"You smart-mouthed bitch! I'll make you pay for that! You'll see! You'll be sorry you talked thataway to ol' Jumbo!"

"God, what names," Linda said.

"You haven't heard anything yet," John told her. "It gets better. I promise you. Or worse. Depending on your point of view."

"Wait until Pisspot gets going," Jenny said.

"Or Big Hurt," John said.

Linda shook her head.

"Hey, Ox!" Jenny called. "Or Ax! You out there, you pair of dumb asses?"

"They're on the way, you bitch!" an outlaw called. "Count on that!"

"I can hardly wait," Jenny said to John and Linda.

"This time we take a prisoner," John said. "Keep that in mind."

"Three of us against maybe twenty or thirty and you're talking about taking prisoners?" Linda asked.

"He's very optimistic," Jenny called.

"I was a Marine," John told them. "We have them outnumbered."

"You folks ready to die?" came the shout.

"That's a scuzzbag called Griz," Jenny said. "I recognize the voice. He's a real winner, believe me."

"You told me Chink was no prize either," John said.

"Lowlife of the first degree."

"Come on out and get us!" a biker shouted.

"This is becoming more and more ridiculous," John said. "They want us to come out of cover and get them."

"I think I now understand why this bunch banded together without much resistance," Jenny said. "They're so stupid the other biker clubs were glad to be rid of them."

"That is certainly something to be considered," John replied.

"It's damn sure the dumbest gang I've run across," Linda called. "But that makes them even more dangerous and unpredictable."

"Barrone?" the shout came from out of the timber. "You want to talk about a deal maybe?"

"A deal?" John asked softly. "What kind of deal?" he shouted.

"You promise to get out of this area and stay out and you live! How about it?"

"Keep them talking, John," Linda said. "Buy us some time."

"How do we know you would keep your word?" John called.

" 'Cause I give you my word, that's why!"

"Who is this?"

"Benny!"

"Ballinger?"

There was a few seconds' pause. "Yeah!"

"Keep him talking long enough for me to centralize his location," Jenny said. "I'll give him a burst."

"This one has some smarts. He's moving around," John said. "And some of the others might be, too. Linda, take the back of the house."

"Will do."

"I wish I had an M-16 with a bloop tube," Jenny said. "We could lob some 40mm grenades into the timber."

"Why don't you wish for an M-60 while you're at it?" John asked.

"How about it, Barrone?" Benny called.

"He's definitely moving around," Jenny said.

"I'm thinking about it!" John shouted.

"Take your time, Barrone! There ain't gonna be no help for you out here! There ain't no neighbors within four/five miles!"

"You promise to dissolve your gang and give us information about your drug network and we'll take you up on your offer!"

There was a long pause, then Benny laughed. "You're kidding, Barrone! You must have a death wish!"

"That's the deal, Benny! Take it or leave it!"

"You 'bout a stupid bastard, Barrone! I'm offerin' you a chance to live and you're makin' counteroffers! What the hell's wrong with you?"

"He's stallin'," Benny," Chink said softly. "Buyin' time is what he's doin'."

"Has Snake give any signal that he's in position behind the house?"

"Nothin' yet."

"What the hell is holdin' him up?"

"He's bein' real careful, that's what."

At the rear of the old house, Linda caught sight of movement and lifted her Uzi. She waited and watched. There it was again. She sighted in and gave the dab of color a burst of 9mm rounds.

"Shit!" Snake hollered, falling facedown on the cold ground as the lead howled all around him.

Linda gave him another burst. The slugs tore up the ground all around the outlaw and spat dirt into the biker's eyes. Snake felt himself slipping. He frantically dug into the earth of the slope with the toes of his boots. But the day had been well above freezing and the earth was slippery due to the melting snow. Snake began a slow slide down the long slope. "Help!" he hollered. "Goddamn it, I'm fallin'. Help!"

"Fallin'?" Chink said. "Fallin' where?"

"Whoooaaa!" Snake yelled as his long, sometimes slick, sometimes rocky and bumpy slide began picking up speed.

"What the hell is happenin' to him?" Griz asked.

"I think he must be slidin' down into a ravine," a biker called Knob said. "Way he's hollerin', it must be a long way down."

"Help!" came the faint cry of Snake. Then . . . silence.

"According to the map that's about a hundred-foot drop back of this place," Jenny said. "You can still see part of the protective chain-link fence out back."

"Yes, I saw that coming in," John replied. "Well, so much for that biker. He's probably hurt and trapped."

"Then we've got our prisoner," Linda called. "Providing we can get him out, that is."

"We've got rope and there's a winch on the front of the SUV. If it comes to that."

"Benny," Mad Dog said, walking up to Griz and Chink and Ballinger. "This ain't been nothin' 'ceptin' one great big fuck-up since Barrone got here. And I personal think it's gonna get worser."

"You might be right," Benny admitted. "But after it gets worse, it's gonna get better. Let's just figure that this here is the worse. Okay?"

"Okay," Mad Dog agreed. "So?"

"So we got Barrone trapped and we're gonna kill him and them cunts with him. That's gonna make it better. See what I'm sayin'?"

"Uhhh. Yeah, I reckon so," Mad Dog said. He walked off shaking his head.

"Now you got me confused," Griz said.

"Don't worry," Benny said. "Have I ever steered you wrong?"

"Not yet, so far."

"Let's split the people up and take that house from all sides. There ain't but three of them. They can't be in four places at once." He looked around. "How many people we got here?"

" 'Bout thirty."

"Well, if thirty people can't handle one old man and two uppity cunts, maybe it's time to pack it in. Get the people spread out, Griz. Tell them to be careful and to wait for my signal before they open fire."

Snake had banged his head several times during his slide down. He had lost both pistol and rifle and ripped the seat out of his pants. His ass was cut and bruised and there were several knots on his head. He sat dazed on the gravel bed of the deep ravine and wondered how in the hell he was going to get out.

"What are those idiots up to now?" John called to Jenny and Linda.

"I can't see any of them," Linda called. "If they're

circling, they're being very careful. But we don't have to worry much about them coming up on the rear of the house. There's no good cover between us and the drop-off."

John hefted a grenade and smiled. "I think I'll give them something to think about," he called.

"Have fun," Jenny replied after chancing a quick look at John.

John pulled the pin and tossed the HE grenade into the timber by the side of the house, then ducked back away from the window and behind the protection of the stone wall, waiting for the explosion.

"What the hell was that?" a biker yelled.

"That's a grenade!" a fellow outlaw yelled, just a half second before the minibomb blew. "Hit the ground!"

The explosion shook the ground and sent loose rocks flying. One of the baseball-size stones clunked a biker on the head and knocked him to the ground, out cold. A large half-rotten limb was jarred loose from a tree and fell on an outlaw, momentarily pinning him to the ground and scaring the crap out of him.

"I'm paralyzed!" the outlaw with the limb across his back and legs yelled. "I can't move my legs. Oh, Lord!"

"This scum is calling on the Lord?" Jenny said aloud. Then she grinned and pulled a grenade from her jacket pocket, jerked out the pin, and tossed it.

"Oh, shit!" a biker hollered, watching the grenade arc toward his position. He jumped to his feet and hauled ass just as the grenade exploded about three feet off the ground. The concussion knocked him sprawling, his ass bleeding from being peppered with hot shrapnel. He lay on the ground, hollering for someone to come help him.

"These must be people from Delta Force," Benny said. "The damn government has sent soldiers in to fight us. That's unconstitutional, by God."

"You wanna call a lawyer and maybe file suit?" Griz asked, no small amount of sarcasm in his tone.

"Go to hell, Griz," Benny told him. "Fire!" he shouted. "Open fire on them damn people. Kill 'em!"

The outlaws cut loose with rifle and pistol fire, most of their rounds bouncing off the stone walls. Those rounds that did make it into the house caused no damage.

Jenny was busy working with a lump of pliable explosive. She slipped in a combination cap/timer and tossed it.

"Watch out!" a biker yelled. "Another grenade."

The plastique bounced off a tree and landed in the timber.

"It's a dud," another biker yelled after a few seconds had passed.

The explosive detonated with a fiery roar about ten feet from an outlaw. Bloody bits and pieces of the biker were splattered for yards around. A severed hand sailed through the cool air and smacked Chink in the face. "Oh, shit!" he hollered, recoiling in horror as the blood from the hand and wrist dripped down his face.

"That's disgustin'!" Pinhead yelled. "Who do that hand belong to anyways?"

"How the fuck do I know?" Chink shouted, frantically wiping his face with a bandanna. "I think I'm gonna puke!"

"Well, don't puke on me!" Pinhead said.

"Kill those people in the house!" Benny screamed, outraged at the sight of the bloody hand. "Charge them and kill them. Go, goddamn it, go! Now!"

Two outlaws jumped up and charged the house from out of the timber. Jenny cut them both down with a short burst, chopping the legs out from under them. They hit the ground and screamed and thrashed in pain.

A biker charged the front of the house, and John stitched him in the belly and chest, knocking him backward and down on the ground, the life abruptly torn from him.

Another outlaw tried to slip up on Linda. He almost made it. He hugged the rear of the house until coming to a window frame. He got one leg in, lost his balance, and a rusty nail gouged him in the ass. He hollered and Linda spun around, giving the biker's exposed leg a short burst of 9mm rounds. He yelled in pain and shock and fell out of the window frame. He began crab-crawling alongside the house until reaching the timber, dragging his ruined left leg, leaving a trail of blood behind him.

"This ain't workin," Benny," Chink called. "We gotta think of somethin' else."

"Well, think of somethin' then!"

"I'm tryin', Benny, I'm tryin'."

"We can't burn 'em out," Griz said. "And we ain't got no dynamite to blow 'em up with. And you can bet they done called them others we seen at the house to come in a hurry. We ain't got a whole lot of time left 'fore they get here."

Benny cussed and nodded his head. "Let's get out of here. We'll regroup and think of something. We gotta get these boys patched up and bury what's left of whoever got blowed up. Griz, you go pick up the pieces of whoever that was. Chink, you get some boys and go gather up the wounded."

"What about Snake?" Chink asked.

"We gotta leave him. He's probably dead or dyin' anyways."

"That don't seem right," Griz said. "He's been with me a long time."

"You wanna stay here with him?"

"Hell, no!"

"Then move!"

"I'm on my way, Benny."

"Chink?" Benny asked.

"I'm gone gatherin' up the guts and stuff. Shit, this is gonna be kinda terrible. I looked at him. Even his head is gone. Shit!"

Benny looked at the stone house. His eyes were cold as a grave. "I'll kill you people," he said softly. "All of you. I swear I will. And I won't never give up till I do it. You're dead. All of you."

Hook limped over to Benny. "Man, I looked down to where Snake fell. I can't even see him. I think he's dead, man. Even if he wasn't, there ain't no way we could get him out of there. That thing is deep."

"We've got to leave him there. We ain't got no choice in the matter."

"Don't make a damn to me. Long as the rest of us get out of here."

"Your loyalty is so touching, Hook."

"Yeah? Well . . . that's the way it goes, man."

"I guess so. Let's move it. We got to get out of here."

John watched and waited for several minutes. Then he heard the sounds of vehicles pulling away.

Jenny looked over at him and smiled. "They're hauling butt, John."

"Sounds like it. We'll give it a few minutes and then start getting that slimeball out of the ravine."

"After we question him, can I shoot him?" Linda asked.

John glanced at her, wondering if what she'd just said was spoken in jest. Somehow he doubted it.

TWENTY-SIX

Linda stayed out in front of the house, near the road, to signal the other team members while John pulled the SUV as close to the drop-off as he dared.

"Can you see him?" John called to Jenny.

"No. It's dark down there. I can't see anything at all."

"Help!" Snake hollered. "Get me out of here, y'all."

"Well, he's alive," Jenny said as John was getting out the rope from the cargo bay of the SUV.

"Your buddies deserted you," Jenny called down into the abyss. "But we'll get you out."

Snake did not reply.

"Did you hear me?" Jenny shouted.

"Yeah, I heard you."

"Your gratitude is overwhelming."

"Fuck you!" Snake called.

"Hell, John," Jenny said, loud enough for the biker to hear, "let's just leave him down there and let him starve to death."

"That's a good idea," John said in a loud voice. "There are mountain lions in this area. They'll take care of him."

"Now, wait just a damn minute!" Snake hollered. "Y'all can't just leave me down here. That ain't de-cent."

"Then watch your mouth," Jenny told him. "You understand that?"

"Yes, ma'am," Snake said. "I sure will. Just get me out of here."

John secured the rope onto the end of the cable and began slowly lowering it.

After a few quiet minutes Snake called, "I got it. Y'all can pull me up now."

"Are you hurt?" John called.

"I'm cut and bruised up some. My ass is awful sore. And the ass-end of my jeans is all tore out."

Jenny and John exchanged smiles, John saying, "We're pulling you up. Hang on."

"Don't you worry 'bout that none. I got me a death grip on this rope. I might need to see me a doctor."

"Oh, we'll take care of you," Jenny assured him. "You can be sure of that."

John started the winch and Snake was slowly lifted up.

As he neared the top, Snake looked up. He saw Jenny standing near the edge of the ravine with an Uzi in her hands, pointing at him.

"I ain't armed!" Snake called. "I lost my guns slidin' down."

Snake was dragged over the top, and John untied the cable and coiled it while Snake lay on the cold ground.

"Get up," Jenny told the still badly shaken biker. "And if you try anything stupid, I'll cut the legs out from under you."

"You 'bout a mean bitch," Snake said. "I ain't never seen no bitch as cold as you. I ain't gonna do nothin'. I give you my word."

"Which is about as much good as tits on an alligator," Jenny replied. "Get up and move into the house."

"I'm movin', I'm movin', lady. But my ass is real cold and sore and my legs is all stiff and hurtin'."

"You're breaking my heart."

"The team is about ten minutes away," Linda shouted from the front. "Everything all right with you guys?"

"Great," Jenny called. "We'll be in the house." In the house, Jenny pointed to a spot in the corner. "Sit," she told Snake. "And don't make any sudden moves."

"Don't you worry. I ain't gonna give you no excuse to shoot me. Whooo!" Snake said as his bare butt touched the floor. "That's cold!"

"You're a tough biker," Jenny told him. "You can take it, can't you?"

"Do I have a choice?"

"None at all."

"That's what I figured."

"So just sit there and be quiet and behave."

"Everybody all right?" Paul asked, stepping into the gutted old house.

"No one hurt here," John said then pointed at Snake. "Except for him."

Paul stopped cold at the sight of Snake and stared for a few seconds. "Who or what the hell is that?"

"He's called Snake," Jenny said. "I remember him from the old hippie place." She glared at the biker. "I think I'll cut your balls off."

"I didn't do nothin' to you back at the hippie house!" Snake hollered. "You ain't got no call to hurt me."

"Let's get him out of here and back to our place," John said. "Tie him, gag him, and toss him in the cargo bay of one of the SUVs." John looked at Snake. "Then he'll start answering some questions."

"I ain't tellin' you nothin'!" Snake said. "Not a god-damn thing. Not now, not ever. Fuck you, Barrone."

"Oh," John said with a smile, "I think you will."

Linda reached down and took her knife from the ankle holster. "I think he will too."

Snake looked first at the knife, then at the expression on Linda's face. He suddenly felt like puking.

In Arizona, in a small town about halfway between L.A. and central New Mexico, the hoods stopped to buy some clothing. "We'll look very rustic," Largo said.

"Or like Lash LaRue," Otwell said.

"Whatever," Largo said. "Let's go get outfitted."

Ot was the last one to emerge from the western store. The others stood in shocked silence and stared at him. He had bought several suits and sport coats. He was now dressed in an electric-blue western-cut suit, with leather trim around all the pockets. He wore a black wide-brimmed ten-gallon hat and new boots with high riding heels.

"You forgot spurs," Sal said, finally finding his voice.

"I can pick them up later if we decide to ride some horses."

"Wonderful," Largo said. "What's in the sack, Ot?"

"A twelve-foot bullwhip. Wanna see it?"

"No! Everybody stow your gear in the cars. Let's roll. We gotta make some time."

The nine men, now all dressed in western clothing, gathered in a group in the parking lot. "When do you tell us who the target is?" Reese asked Largo.

"Some guy named Barrone," Largo replied. "The boss wants him iced."

"And they sent nine of us?" Carlos questioned. "Who the hell is this Barrone? A cousin to Superman?"

"To tell you the truth, I don't know. But I'll brief you all when we get to the town," Largo said. "As soon as we get there, I'm to call some local yokel named Sandoval. He's supposed to know all about Barrone."

"We take orders from this local?" Mabini asked.

"No. He'll bring us up to speed, that's all."

"Nine of us to take out just one dude?" Pizarro questioned. "This has got to be one tough guy."

"Maybe so," Largo said. "We'll know soon enough. Let's roll."

"We can do this easy or hard," John told Snake. "It's all up to you."

Snake was tied to a chair in the basement of the house in the country. And he was scared. It was cool in the basement, but Snake was sweating. He'd been rousted by cops many times in his life, but Barrone and his people were not cops. Snake suspected strongly he was in for a very rough time if he didn't cooperate.

"I don't know nothin' to tell you," Snake said.

"Oh, I think you do," John said. "Let's start with a simple question, all right?"

"Ax me."

"Benny is the gang leader of the bikers, right?"

"That's right."

"And who is second in command?"

"Griz and Chink."

"Who gives Benny his orders?"

Snake sighed. He figured Barrone and his people already knew the answer to that. "You know who. Why you axin' me?"

"Name them, Snake."

"Sandoval, Curtis, and Grayson."

"That's the local people. Who do they take their orders from?"

"Huh? They run the operation, man."

"I don't think so, Snake."

"Well, you wrong, man."

"The labs where the drugs are made, Snake. Where are they?"

"Man, you axin' me questions that could get me killed."

"No. You cooperate and I'll guarantee your safety."

"How?"

"You can walk."

"Walk where? I'd be marked forever."

"You change your lifestyle, your looks. Get a job."

"A job? You mean, like work?"

"Yes."

"Doin' what?"

"That would be up to you."

"I ain't flippin' no damn burgers."

"Would you rather be dead?"

"Well . . . no."

"Then answer my question. Where are the labs?"

"I can't do that, man!"

John looked at Paul and Don. "Get his pants off him; naked from the waist down."

"Now wait a minute. What the hell are you gonna do to me?" Snake shouted, the sweat dripping from his face.

"Get Linda in here," John ordered.

"Whoa!" Snake yelled. "The bitch with the knife?"

"That's her."

"Wait a minute! I'll tell you about the labs. That bitch will cut my nuts off. Her and that damn crazy Jenny. You keep them away from me."

John smiled. "They'll start with your balls, Snake. After that it'll get really unpleasant."

"I said I'll tell you!"

John pulled up a chair and sat down. "That's good, Snake. You're getting smart. Now then, where are the labs?"

"All right," Benny said when all the outlaw bikers were gathered. "Let's count heads and then start figurin' out a plan."

"I done that," Chink said. "They's seventy of us, not countin' the broads."

"You damn well better not leave us out," a biker bitch called Babs said. " 'Cause from now wherever you hard-asses go, we go! You got that?"

"Yeah," a biker babe known as 44 said. Her nickname had nothing to do with a pistol caliber and everything to do with her being rather prominently endowed. "Most of us can fight just as good or better than you guys."

"That's right," Bend Over Betty said. "And so far, you guys ain't done worth a shit in that department."

"You think you can do any better?" Griz demanded.

"We damn sure couldn't do any worse," Fireball popped off.

"All, right!" Benny shouted, stilling the hubbub before it could get started and violent. "The women have by God come up with a pretty good idea, I think. They can do all sorts of stuff: drive and tote ammo and tend the wounded and carry messages and so forth. And fight if need be. Okay. You broads is in. Where we go, you go."

"All right!" the women shouted.

"We're gonna hit them again, real soon."

"But they done moved!" Ax said.

"We'll find out where they moved to," Benny said. "It won't take long. Count on that. I'll meet with our man in Morales's office tonight and find out. If he don't know, our contact in Watson's office will."

"I wanna kill all of Barrone's people," Hammer said. "Make up for what they done to Rammer."

"And don't forget X-Man and all the others," Hot Pants said. "And poor ol' Snake, bless his heart."

"I think I'm gonna cry, thinkin' 'bout Snake," Bouncy said. "I feel really really bad thinkin' 'bout him."

"Well, do it somewheres else," Big Balls said. "Good God, woman, don't tune up and start blubberin' around here. You ugly enough without addin' that awful face."

"Fuck you!" Bouncy said.

"Now?" Big Balls asked. "In front of everybody?"

"Oh, Lord!" Gatepost said. "Not that. I don't want to look at something that awful."

"Well, fuck you too!" Bouncy told him.

"Knock it off, all of you!" Benny said. "We got to start makin' plans. After I make a couple of phone calls. I might get lucky and find out where those bastards and bitches are right now. All of you just hang tight for five minutes."

He was back in one minute, grinning. "I found out where they moved to. Get ready to rumble!"

TWENTY-SEVEN

"Of course you know this tape you made of Snake's confession can't be used in court," Sheriff Watson told the team.

"We know," John said. "But he has agreed to repeat it to you under oath. If you will guarantee his safety."

"I can do that. But not in my jail or in Morales's jail."

"Why not?" Bob asked.

"The bikers have somebody on their payroll in both departments, that's why. And we don't know who it is."

"The bikers or the mob?" Don asked.

"Bikers. But they're really one and the same. The mob has Sandoval, Curtis, and Grayson in their pocket; the Big Three have the bikers in their pockets."

"Where will you hold him then?" Linda asked.

Jimmi shook her head. "I don't know. You want the Feds in on this?"

"No," John said quickly.

"Then we've got a problem. I could call in the state people, but they'd want to know all about you people." She smiled. "And all the dead bodies and mini-wars that have been taking place in this area."

"I'm surprised they haven't come in before now," Jenny said.

"If the shooting ever takes place in a town, you can bet they'll be here in a hurry. But the bikers don't want that any more than you people. Now, I don't gave a damn how many outlaw bikers or mob muscle you kill, but the first civilian who gets hurt or killed means you people are gone from here." She met John's eyes. "Understood?"

"Perfectly. And I understand something else too. Snake's story will never be told in a court of law, right?"

"That's probably very true. Unless you trust him not to tell what he knows about you people. Do you?"

John laughed without a note of humor.

"That's what I thought," Jimmi said.

"So we're basically back to square one," Jenny said. "And that is: what to do with him. Ideas, anyone?"

"Other than shooting him," John said quickly.

"Do what you want to with him," Jimmi said. "Personally, I don't care. But I would rather you not kill him."

"We're not going to do that," John said quickly.

"What about Grayson, Sandoval, and Curtis?" Jimmi asked. "And their damn sorry-assed punk kids?"

"We'll handle them," John told her. "I can promise you that. When the time is right."

"All right," Jimmi said, standing up. "I'll leave them up to you people. I don't care what you do with them either." She glanced at her watch. "I'm out of here." She turned and started toward the door.

"Hey, up there! I wanna talk to the sheriff!" Snake hollered from the basement. "Sheriff, I want some protection from these crazy people. Sheriff Watson, they threatened to cut my pecker and nuts off. You gotta help me. I know you're up there, Sheriff. I done heard you. You better talk to me."

"You want to talk to him?" John asked.

Jimmi nodded. "Might as well. He knows I'm here."

"A couple of you go down there and bring him up here," John said. "I don't blame him for hollering. It's damn cold down in that basement."

"We'll do it," Don said, looking at Paul. They started after Snake, who was still hollering for somebody to come get him.

"At least that might quiet him down," Paul said.

Snake was led up the stairs to the main floor. As soon as he spotted Jimmi, standing next to John, he blurted out, "You gotta get me away from these folks, Sheriff. I mean, you got to. It's a matter of life and death. And I ain't kiddin'. They made me tell them all sorts of stuff that ain't true. I made up a whole bunch of shit to keep them from torturin' me. They was threatenin' to do all kinds of vile and horrible and disgustin' things to me. You wouldn't believe all the nasty things they was threatenin' to do to me."

"I'm sure I wouldn't," Jimmi said, the sarcasm thick in her tone.

"It's Academy Awards time, gang," Jenny said.

"And she's the worser of them all," Snake said, looking at Jenny. "She's the most horriblest of them all. She's plumb crazy."

"That's me," Jenny said brightly. "My next suggestion was to find a big pot and cook and eat him. Anybody got any ketchup?"

"See what I mean?" Snake hollered. "She's disgustin'!"

"I would prefer roasting him," Linda said. "Slowly. The fire place is large enough if we cut off his legs, say, at the knees. He'd fit if we did."

"Oh, shit!" Snake hollered. "They's gettin' worser and worser, Sheriff." He looked at Paul. "And I don't trust that nigger there at all. I think he's the meanest of them all."

"Do you sing and dance too," Don asked, looking at Paul.

"Oh, I have rhythm like you wouldn't believe," Paul said with a straight face. "And I can sing 'Mammy' in a way that'll bring tears to your eyes."

"That's probably quite true," Mike said. "So spare us all your rendition."

"Now my feelings are hurt," Paul said. "You have crushed my artistic whatever."

"Good," Bob said.

"See what I mean?" Snake hollered. "They's all crazier than a bessie bug."

"Well, let's see," Jimmi said. "I believe, after speaking with Sheriff Morales, that I have enough evidence to charge you with the torture/murder of Maria Sanchez. How about that?"

"Huh? Hey, I didn't have nothin' to do with that spic chick. And that's the truth. That was Griz and Chink and them others. Not me."

"You would swear to that in a court of law?" Jimmi asked.

"You bet I will."

"You were there? You saw it?"

"Yeah, yeah. But I didn't have nothin' to do with it."

"Did you try to stop it?"

"I told 'em it was wrong, what they was doin', yeah."

"Maybe we can work something out," Jimmi told him.

"You'll get me away from these crazy people

"Perhaps. But you'll have to tell me a lot

about what happened to Maria. Are you prepared to do that?"

"You bet!"

The sheriff glanced at John. "Get a tape recorder, John. Will you?"

Half a dozen automatic weapons opened up from the rear of the house. The back windows were blown out and glass was sprayed all over the dining room. Sheriff Watson and the team hit the floor and bellied down. Snake was a half second slower, and his hesitation cost him his life. Snake got stitched across the chest by high-powered slugs from an AK-47, and was dead when he hit the floor.

Those inside the house could do nothing but hug the floor and hope for the best for what seemed like an eternity, but actually was only a few seconds. When the shooters paused to change magazines, the team grabbed for their own weapons.

"Did anyone get hit?" John called.

"Only Snake," Bob said. "I think he's dead."

"If he is, that solves that problem," Jenny said.

The team crawled to the rear of the house and went on the offensive.

"Don, you take the left side of the house," John said. "Paul, you take the right. Bob, you take the front. The rest of us will cover the rear."

Jimmi was cussing a blue streak as she crawled toward the rear of the house. All of them were trying to avoid all the broken glass that littered the floor.

Linda was the first to get into position, and she cut loose with her Uzi, spraying the backyard with lead. Someone in the timber began screaming.

"I'm hit! Oh, Jesus, they shot me in the belly! Come help me, someone, I'm hit bad!"

"One out of it," Jimmi said, blasting the timber with her 9mm.

Those in the rear of the house joined in with automatic-weapons fire, filling the backyard with lead.

"Pour it in there!" Benny shouted. "Keep them pinned down! Somebody get that dynamite ready!"

"Oh, hell!" Jimmi said.

"Keep up the fire!" John called. "Make them stay down!"

John saw a man jump up from cover just at the edge of the timber in the rear of the house, a sputtering bundle of explosives in his hand. He drew back his hand to throw the explosives just as John gave him a burst of 9mm lead. The rounds took the man in the chest, knocking the outlaw back. He stumbled a couple of times, then sank slowly to the ground, losing his dying grip on the dynamite.

"Oh, shit!" a biker yelled. "Spike's hit and he dropped the dynamite! Run, damn it, get the hell out of here!"

The fuse was either cut too short, or it was a flash fuse and the outlaws had not realized it. The bundle of dynamite exploded. In addition to bringing down several trees, the blast tore apart several outlaws. Various body parts went flying in all directions. A severed arm landed on the rear deck of the house, about two feet away from Jimmi.

"Oh, gross-out!" the sheriff said.

"Scratch at least a couple of assholes," Jenny said, eyeballing the bloody stump of arm. "That's what they get for playing with dynamite."

"Spike and C.B. and Sandy is all blown to hell!" a biker shouted.

"Back off!" Benny yelled. "Get out of here! Move!"

"Let's finish it!" Griz yelled.

"No!" Benny said. "Later! Move it!"

Those in the house waited a few minutes. No more shouted threats or gunfire came from the timber.

"I think they quit," Jimmi said, looking around. "Jesus, what a mess."

"I'll check it out," Paul said. "Hold your positions." A few more minutes passed in silence before Paul yelled, "All clear. They're gone."

"Let's check it out," Jimmi said. "Then you folks have got to get out of here. Pick up all your brass and pack up everything you brought in. Don't leave a trace of anything. We'll pick up the pieces of the bikers and dispose of them."

"You going to call this in?" John asked.

Jimmi shook her head. "I don't think so. You can bet the bikers aren't going to report it."

"Come on, Don," Mike said. "Let's go find the body parts."

"I'll get a garbage bag," Don said.

"You know a carpenter who can keep his mouth shut?" Jenny asked the sheriff.

"Oh, yeah. There's a couple of contractors in this area who owe me big time. I'll give them a call as soon as you folks get clear."

"Where to now?" Bob tossed out.

"For sure out of this county," John said. "Where? I don't know. We might just drive down to Albuquerque, get some motel rooms, and operate out of there." He paused for a few seconds. "I think that's what we will do. Right now, let's get this brass picked up and then we'll pack up and get out of here."

"And dispose of the body parts," Jenny said.

"That, too."

"Sheriff" Mike called. "We've got one alive out here."

John and Jimmi knelt down beside the badly injured outlaw. A tree had fallen across his mangled body and he was not long for this world. John told him so.

"I know it," the biker said. "Better than you."

"You have anyone who would be at all interested in placing flowers on your grave?" John asked.

"Shit, no! And I don't care where you plant me. But you better be thinkin' about flowers for yourself, Barrone."

"Oh?"

"Yeah. Some hoods is comin' in from L.A. to settle your hash."

"Is that right?"

"Yeah." The outlaw coughed up blood.

"What's your name?" Jimmi asked.

"What difference does that make?"

"None to us if that's the way you want it."

"I do. So fuck you both!"

"You're about to meet your Maker," John said. "I don't think I would want to go out with a curse on my lips."

"Who the hell asked you?"

John shrugged his shoulders.

"Tell us about your gang," Jimmi asked.

"Oh, you know I'm gonna do that, bitch!" Then he cursed her until he was out of breath and again coughing up blood.

"Thanks for the information," Jimmi said. "You've been real helpful. Anything else you'd like to add to that?"

The biker laughed and spat out a mouthful of blood. "You're a damn randy bitch, I'll give you that. And I'll bet you'd be a good hump too."

Jimmi had no reply to that.

The biker cut his eyes to John. "Your turn, Barrone."

"What is it?"

"How many of my people bought it this day?"

"Four or five. We haven't tallied it up yet."

"The whole damn bunch of you candy-asses ain't worth one of my people."

Neither Jimmi nor John offered any reply. They waited in silence. The biker was tough and hanging on, defiant to the end.

"How many members in your gang?" Jimmi asked.

"Enough to handle you people." The biker suddenly stiffened as waves of pain hit him. A groan was forced past his lips. "I'm just sorry I won't be there to see the end of you meddlin' bastards and bitches."

John and Jimmi exchanged glances and stood up. "We'll take you to a hospital," Jimmi said.

"Why?" the biker asked. "No point in wastin' your time or mine. I'm tore all to pieces. Hell, I can see that. My guts is hangin' out. And my back is broken. I can't move my legs or feel nothin' from the waist down. Go ahead and shoot me. You'd do that much for a horse or a dog, wouldn't you?"

John and Jimmi looked at one another. John opened his mouth to speak, then thought better of it and remained silent.

The outlaw's eyes were on him and he laughed. "You can't understand me, can you, Barrone?"

"I have to say I don't," John said.

"If you're waitin' on me to beg for forgiveness and accept the Lord and all that shit, forget it. It ain't gonna happen."

"Tough to the end, right?" Jimmi asked as members

of the team gathered around to listen and stare at the dying outlaw biker.

"You bet your ass I am, bitch."

"Then hurry up and die," Linda told him. "We've got things to do."

The biker cut his eyes to look at her. He then cursed the former LAPD member, each word and breath spraying blood. His hands dug into the cold ground and his eyes began losing light. His head lolled to one side and he fell still and silent.

John squatted down and felt for a pulse. There was none. "He's had it." He stood up and looked at Jimmi. "What do you want to do with him?"

"Dump him somewhere," the sheriff said. "A long way from here."

"We'll get the tree off him," Paul said.

"Tough son of a bitch." Mike said, offering a left-handed compliment to the dead outlaw.

"That's as good a eulogy as he's going to get, I suppose," John said.

TWENTY-EIGHT

"So where do we find this Barrone and his people?" Pizarro asked.

The mob toughs had checked into a motel in Albuquerque and then gathered in Largo's suite.

"I got a number to call," Largo said. "I'll get further instructions." He looked over at Otwell, dressed in his electric-blue suit. "You look stupid," he told him. "You stand out like a boil on a nose."

"This is cowboy country, ain't it?" Ot said. "I'm dressed like a cowboy. So what's your beef?"

"Oh, hell, forget it," Largo said, digging into his briefcase for a small address book. "Let me call this number and get this show on the road. The sooner it's done the sooner we can get back to the city."

"I like it here," Ot said.

"Then you can stay right here far as I'm concerned," Sal said.

Mills jerked open the door and said, "That damn Barrone and his crew is right here in this motel, Largo!"

"What?"

"It's true. I was in the lobby getting a paper when they come in and registered. I heard him call his name. John Barrone. Older guy with a lot of gray in his hair. But he looks to be in real good shape."

"How many?"

"Six or seven of them. Couple of them women. All of them got kind of a hard look about them."

"Keep an eye on them, Mills," Largo ordered. "See what rooms they get. When they leave, we go after them and take them out. This is gonna be just too easy."

"Maybe too damn easy," Mabini said.

"What do you mean?"

"Just that, Largo."

"You worry too much. It's just coincidence, that's all."

Mabini gave Largo an odd look, then shrugged his shoulders.

"Check your weapons," Largo ordered. "I want everything ready to go. Let's make this real smooth."

"This is a real nice place," Jenny said, looking around the two rooms. "I like these suite-type motels."

She and Linda were bunking together. Linda said, "Yes. But this is the fifth motel we've checked into since leaving the lodge."

"John wants lots of hidey-holes, I guess."

Linda sat down on one of the beds and smiled. "You and John getting close?"

Jenny shook her head. "Nope. He's friendly, but that's all. He's a hundred percent business. I guess that's best."

"I'd get friendly with him in a heartbeat," Linda said, leaning back on the bed. Her remark came as no surprise to Jenny. "But I don't think he's going to let anyone get too close," Linda acknowledged.

Jenny was not surprised at her friend's remark. "He

can be a lot of fun at times. But John's kind of old-fashioned in a nice sort of way."

"What did he have to say about Al?"

"He was surprised. Said Al must have had a lot of personal baggage that Control didn't pick up on during the initial interviews."

"Yeah, that's the way I figure it."

"You hungry?"

"I could eat." She sat up on the bed. "And we'd better eat now. I think John's going to have us rambling all night. I'll go check on the others."

Linda noticed Mills within seconds of stepping out of the motel room. She knocked on John's door, and after closing the door behind her said, "We're being watched, John. Some clown dressed in new western garb. He looks totally out of place."

"Biker?"

"No. My first guess would be big-city muscle. The clothes he's wearing still have the hanger and fold creases on them."

John pointed to the phone. "Call the others. Tell them to join us in the dining room. Let's see how this plays out."

Linda moved toward the phone. "I'm sure ready for something to eat. It's been a long day . . . and part of the night."

"We'll all have a nice leisurely dinner," John assured. "If the dining room is still open, that is. And then we'll see about meeting with the muscle."

"Meeting with them?"

"So to speak," John said with a smile.

Linda called the others and briefed them. A few minutes later they met on the open walkway in front of the rooms. Mills had disappeared.

"We walk to the dining room," John said, checking

his watch. "Although I doubt it's going to be open. It's after ten."

"A couple of cheeseburgers, a double order of fries, and a large Coke would suit me just fine," Don said.

"Now what?" Paul asked.

"We find a hamburger joint?" Don suggested.

"We get to our vehicles and convoy out of here," John said. "Let's see if the muscle—if that's who they are—follows us."

"And if they do?" Linda asked.

"We'll know for sure."

"And then?" she asked.

"We find a good spot and press the issue."

"Interesting way of saying we start a war," Bob said, smiling.

"You got it," John told him.

"Do we maybe find a hamburger joint on the way out of town?" Don asked, a hopeful note in his voice.

"No," John told him. "We'll eat later."

Three SUVs pulled out of the motel parking lot, heading north. Three Cadillacs pulled out right behind them.

"Now we know," John said behind the wheel of the lead SUV.

Jenny was in the backseat, studying a detailed map of the county. "About ten miles ahead turn west," she said. "That'll take us out into the flats, I think. Whatever it is, and I can't really tell about the terrain from this map, it'll be sparsely populated."

"Good place for a shoot-out," John said. "That's what we're looking for."

* * *

"Where's them bastards going?"' Sal asked. "Hell, it's the middle of the night and according to this map there ain't jack-shit out here." He studied the map for a few seconds. "Some damn Indian reservation over to the west."

"They got a place in mind," Largo said. "We'll just follow them and find out."

"Indian reservation?" Otwell said from the back-seat. "Real redskins?"

"Shit!" Largo said softly. "Now you've done it."

"Apaches?" Otwell asked.

"No," Sal told him. "I never heard of this tribe."

"Drop the subject," Largo said. "I don't want hear any more about a bunch of goddamn Indians."

"Largo, we've got people following us," Reese said, calling from the rear vehicle on his cell phone.

"Following us?" Largo questioned. "That's impossible. No one knows we're here. Are you sure?"

"Yes. Half a dozen cars and pickup trucks and vans. They're sticking close."

"I think maybe it's just normal traffic," Largo said. "This is a busy interstate. Keep your eyes open."

"There's a whole line of traffic behind us," Bob called from the team's rear SUV. "It's a damn convoy."

"I see them." Jenny said. "It's a regular parade."

"The bikers found us already?" Linda asked. "What kind of intelligence network do they have, for Christ sake?"

"If it is the bikers," John said. "They obviously have a very good intel system. But that shouldn't surprise anyone. Your larger and better known outlaw biker clubs certainly do. These bikers were sure to have brought some of those sources with them."

"Good God!" John said. "The line of traffic is a half mile long."

"Just a few more miles and we exit," Jenny said. She told him the number of the exit. "I wish I knew exactly what kind of terrain we're going to be getting into."

"But you did say it was sparsely populated."

"Oh, yes. Except for an Indian reservation to the south of where we're going."

"How far to the south?"

"A few miles."

Linda laughed aloud and John cut his eyes to her, wondering what she found so funny about the situation.

Jenny met his eyes and said, "The goons from the city right behind us, those half-wit bikers tagging along behind them. This promises to be one hell of a night."

John cut his eyes to the rearview mirror. Jenny was grinning at him.

"The two of you find this situation amusing?" he asked.

"Not funny ha-ha," Jenny told him. "Just that it promises to be very interesting, that's all."

"I can but assume you brought some explosives with you?"

"You bet I did. A great big box of things that go boom. All different types. I can hardly wait to get this started."

John smiled. "You both sound as though you want to end this operation tonight."

"I want to put an end to some trashy damned outlaw bikers," Linda said. There was not even a tiny hint of humor in her voice.

"I suspect we'll knock some of the spirit out of them," John replied.

"Found it!" Jenny exclaimed. "I knew I had it."

"Found what?" John asked.

"A better map. There's a whole pile in this case. When we exit just up ahead, stay on the county road heading west. After about five miles we run out of houses. It's mountain desert, according to the map."

"Mountains?" Linda asked.

"They're off to the west. But we'll be heading into the flats for our showdown," Jenny said quickly.

John glanced in the rearview at the long line of headlights and muttered, "This is getting worse than the Keystone Cops."

A few minutes later John pulled onto the exit ramp and headed west. The muscle from L.A. and the bikers stayed with him, maintaining their distance.

"I bet we could get those goons from L.A. lost if we tried," Jenny said.

"I bet we could get ourselves lost without too much trouble," John replied.

"There is only this one road, John," Jenny told him. "Of course, it does sort of peter out in about a mile further on."

"Sort of peter out?"

"Narrows down to one lane and becomes dirt and gravel . . . mostly dirt, I think."

"Thanks for telling me."

"You're certainly welcome. By the way, see the lights just up ahead?"

"Yes."

"That row of houses is the last of the houses that's shown on the map."

A moment later they drove past the dark shapes of the houses, which showed no signs of life of any kind, and the bumpy old paved road turned to dirt.

"After this," Jenny said, "nothing. And I mean nothing."

"What does the map show about the terrain?"

"Rocks and desert and cactus and ravines and isolation."

"Sounds delightful," Linda said.

"Where in the hell is them fools taking us?" Sal asked. "There ain't nothing out here."

"Where are the Indians?" Otwell asked. "I ain't seen no Indians."

"This road is shit," Largo said. "It's gonna beat this car to pieces. This is awful."

"Them assholes is still behind us," Sal said. "Whoever the hell they are, they're beginning to bug me."

"We'll deal with them when we finally get to wherever we're going," Largo told him.

"Wherever the hell that might be," Sal said.

"I think I'll take my whip," Ot said. "When we capture them no-goods, I'll give them a good horsewhippin'."

"That's great, Ot," Largo said. "But the idea is to kill them."

"Oh, we can do that after I whip them."

"Wonderful," Largo replied.

Sal grimaced and shook his head.

"They're slowing down!" Largo said. "Pulling over. It's show time, boys."

TWENTY-NINE

"Over there," Linda said. "Just ahead and to your right. The outline of buildings."

"I see them," John said. "The buildings appear to be falling down. That's as good a place as we're likely to find for a stand. Here we go." He slowed and made the turn, the team SUVs right behind him.

The muscle from Los Angeles did not immediately follow the team. They stopped on the road, the line of outlaw bikers in their cars and pickups and vans stopping some distance behind the goons.

John and his team pulled around behind the old buildings and bailed out of the SUVs, carrying weapons and heavy equipment bags, filled with grenades and full magazines. John did not have to tell them to stay low and spread out. Within seconds the team had formed a defense line and was waiting for the attack to begin.

Largo stepped out of the lead Cadillac. The bikers behind him had cut their headlights.

"You're takin' a chance," Sal said. "We don't know who those assholes behind us are. They might be the cops."

"Naw," Largo said. "They're the doper bikers. Bet on it."

"How come they ain't ridin' motorcycles?" Ot asked.

Largo ignored the question and stood by the darkened vehicle, waiting. The other goons got out of their Cadillacs, weapons in hand.

"You guys from L.A.?" Benny shouted. "Who are you?"

"No, we're from Mars," Largo yelled. "Who the fuck are you?"

"We axed you first!" Chink hollered.

"They're bikers," Largo said.

Apeman stepped out of his van, beat on his chest, and let out a jungle call, piercing the night.

"That's Tarzan," Ot said.

"That's an idiot," Largo told him. "The boss said a lot of these guys were off in the head. I believe him now."

"What in the hell was that?" Jenny asked.

"Sounded like Tarzan," Linda replied.

"I have been involved with some strange people during my years with the Company," John said, "but this bunch has got to take the prize."

"Shut up, Tarzan," Benny told the biker. "We got to work somethin' out here."

"We need to talk," Largo yelled.

"So talk, man," Benny called.

"Face-to-face."

"So come on. I'll meet you halfway."

"Barrone and his people might be callin' the cops right now, Largo," Sal said.

"Naw. The boss said these people were independent

operators. They don't want the cops in this any more than we do. Hang tight. I'm gonna talk with this biker asshole."

John had been looking through night lenses. He laid the binoculars aside and said, "The goons and the bikers are meeting."

"It should pop any moment then," Linda said.

"What in the hell was all that yelling a minute ago?" Paul asked. "Sounded like something out of a Tarzan movie."

"Your guess is as good as mine," John said.

Largo walked back to his crew. "We got a damn army here, boys. The bikers all got automatic weapons and plenty of ammo. There ain't nobody lives within miles of here. So we got it made."

"What's the drill?" Sal asked.

"We attack," Largo said simply. "They's five men and two cunts over there. This is gonna be a piece of cake."

Sal jacked a round into the chamber of his M-16. "So let's do it."

"The bikers also got about a dozen cunts with them," Largo said.

"Why'd they bring them?"

"Who the hell knows? But they're all armed and they look like they know how to use the weapons."

"We'll see. You ready to get this goin'?"

"Soon as the bikers get geared up and in place. Won't be long." Largo looked around him. "Where's Pizarro?"

"Checkin' out the terrain."

"Okay. You see to getting the cars out of here. I don't want them all shot up and we have to walk out."

"Good idea. That would be a long walk."

"They're backing the cars out, John," Don called.

"I see them. Let them go. I want them to start this war, not us."

The team waited in the quiet darkness, the silence broken only by the sounds of engines as the pickups and vans and cars were backed away.

John was watching the moves of the goons and the bikers through night lenses. "They're forming a rough semicircle around us," he said. "Pass the word. I think they're about ready to get this started."

"I wish they'd come on and get it going," Don called. "I'm hungry."

"I brought some emergency rations," Mike told him.

"What kind of rations?"

"Good to eat, hot or cold. Those wonderful MREs."

Don made a horrible gagging sound. "I'll pass. Thanks just the same."

John glanced up. "Well, at least we have part of the roof above us, in case the weather turns bad."

"The forecast did call for rain," Jenny said.

Apeman gave another Tarzan call, splitting the night.

"Somebody shut that son of a bitch up!" Yard Dog yelled.

"You want me to shoot him?" Pig called. "I'll be more than happy to do just that!"

Yard Dog did not reply.

Apeman did his Tarzan bit again.

"Nice people," Mike said after listening to the short exchange. "Good-quality folks."

Linda glanced in his direction and spat on the ground. "I intend to make several of them very nice before this night is over," she said. "The only good outlaw biker is a dead one."

"Such hostility," Mike called.

"Let's kill those bastards!" Benny yelled. "Open fire! Now!"

John and his team hit the ground as the bikers opened up with automatic-weapons fire and lead began buzzing and whining all around them.

Big Train hurled several sticks of taped-together dynamite that fell about fifty feet short of the ruins of the old home.

The dynamite blew and sent a shower of dirt and stones flying.

Paul jumped to his feet and cut loose with his Uzi.

"Whoa, shit!" Big Train yelled, and went belly-down on the cold ground just in time to avoid being stitched by 9mm rounds as Paul swung the muzzle of the Uzi.

"It's too far for a good throw, Big Train!" Chink yelled. "Forget the dynamite until we can get closer!"

"Everybody pour on the lead!" Largo yelled. "Maybe we'll get lucky and they'll catch some ricochets!"

For the next ten minutes both sides exchanged gunfire, the bikers and the goons burning a lot of lead and hitting nothing that bled. John and his team were cautious with their ammo, firing only occasionally.

"This ain't worth a damn," Sal said, easing over to Largo. "They got good cover and all we're doin' is wastin' lead."

"I know it. But those crazy damn bikers won't let

up. I already told that Benny to cool it. He said he don't take orders from me and to fuck off."

"You want me to go shoot him?"

"Naw. Hell, we'd only end up fighting each other and they got us outnumbered about five to one."

Gradually, the bikers ceased fire. Benny walked over to Largo and Sal. "This ain't no damn good, guys."

"I believe I said that about five minutes ago," Largo said.

"Yeah? Well . . . I changed my mind. You got any suggestions?"

Largo shook his head, then realized the biker could not see the gesture in the dark. "Not really. Barrone and his people have the best position and a clear field of fire."

"Hell, I know that," Benny replied. "I thought you might have a good plan. Guess I was wrong."

"Maybe I do," Largo said. "Can you work some of your people behind them?"

"Probably. What then?"

"Then we'll have them surrounded," Largo said patiently. "We can disable their vehicles."

"Yeah?" Benny questioned. "And then what? We wait them out?"

"If we have to. But I think they might panic and do something stupid."

"All right," Benny said after a few seconds of thought. "We'll try it. Give me a few minutes to pick some boys. I'll holler when I got them ready to move."

"Do that," Largo replied.

"What an idiot," Sal said when Benny had walked away.

"Cannon fodder," Largo told him. "We use them as shock troops while we keep our heads down."

"Then after we deal with Barrone, we kill what's left of the bikers?"

"That's what I have in mind."

"Then who runs the dope operation?"

"Maybe the boss sends some people in to take over. Hell, I don't know. Or he shuts it all down. Whatever. He's tired of all the worry connected with this operation anyway."

"He told you that?"

"Yes. The Feds are starting to breath down his neck and this operation is not profitable enough for all the worry. Everybody has to go, if you get my drift."

"The New Mexico boss?"

"Him too."

"Well, I'll be damned. Okay. So why then are we screwin' around with Barrone and his bunch?"

"First things first, Sal. Barrone is financed by a private group. The boss got that word straight. Barrone is on a . . . well, a mission, I guess you could call it. He operates outside the law. But he works against the criminals."

"Sort of like in the movies?"

"Yeah."

"Well, I'll be damned. I didn't think things like that really happened."

"Hey!" Benny called. "We're ready!"

"Give it hell, Benny!" Largo shouted. "We'll back you all the way!"

"Something is about to happen," Jenny said.

"You and Paul take the rear of the house, Jenny," John said. "And take along your sack of grenades."

"I never leave home without them," Jenny said. "Come on, Paul."

"People are slipping around to the back," Don called. "I catch a glimpse of a shadow occasionally. It's about to get real interesting, I think."

"I wondered when they'd try that," John said. "Everybody in their body armor?"

"Everybody is sittin' on ready," Mike called. "I just hope these newfangled vests work."

"We'll sure find out soon enough," Bob said. "Although I'm not looking forward to taking a hit."

"Now!" The shout came from the rear of the ruins. "Let 'em have it!"

The night exploded in gunfire and several bikers charged the house from the rear. Paul and Jenny cut them down. Jenny knocked the legs out from under one, and Paul stitched another across the belly and chest. The third biker threw himself belly-down on the rocky ground and hugged the earth close.

Dark shapes charged the house from both sides, and they met a hail of 9mm rounds from automatic weapons. Two were down and did not move. Two more went down, wounded, and began slowly, painfully, crawling away into the darkness.

"Don't nobody else try it!" Benny yelled. "This ain't workin' out worth a shit!"

"I rather liked it!" Linda shouted. "Send some more of your assholes, you asshole!"

"I'm gonna get you, bitch!" a biker called Stinky yelled. "You gonna be sorry for havin' a hand in this!"

"I can hardly wait!" Linda shouted. "Why don't you come on and try it yourself? What's the matter, you lost your guts? You chickenshit!"

Stinky cussed Linda, loud and long, telling her in great and profane detail what he was going to do to her when he got his hands on her.

Linda laughed at him. "Don't tell me about it, you

prick!" she shouted. "Come do it, if you've got the balls!"

Stinky jumped to his feet, and a biker jerked him back down. "Don't be stupid," Pretty Boy said. "Showin' yourself is what she wants."

"I'll kill that smart-mouthed bitch!"

"Later," Pretty Boy said. "But not now, not this way."

"It's over here," Largo said. "We all blew it. Best thing we can do is get out of here and try to take them another place, another time."

"What about the bikers?" Sal asked.

"Hell with them. If the bikers stay here tonight, more are going to die. And that will mean the fewer we have to deal with."

"So we're leavin'?"

"Right now. Get the boys back to the cars."

The muscle from L.A. quietly pulled out, backing their cars around and heading out without saying a word to the outlaw bikers.

"Them chickenshits is leavin,' Benny!" Chink said.

"I see them. Hell with them. Let them go, we don't need them."

"The goons aren't stupid," Mike said. "They're pulling out."

"We'll deal with them later," John told him. "The bikers haven't given up, though."

"How many people did we lose?" Benny asked as he squatted in the darkness about fifty yards from the ruins.

"Four dead, a couple more wounded," Chink told him. "That I know of for sure. There might be more than that."

Benny mentally chewed on that for a few seconds. Then he shook his head. "We don't have the equipment or the time to dig those people out."

"But we got the people," Chink protested.

"And if we keep up this fight we're gonna lose more and more. Hell, there's always another day."

"The muscle from L.A., Benny. Why are they really here, you reckon?"

"What do you mean?"

"I mean, I think they might be here for more than just Barrone and his people."

"Us?"

"Maybe."

Benny chewed on that for a moment. "Why do you figure that, Chink?"

"Well, me and Griz was talkin' a few minutes ago. He feels the same way I do 'bout them goons."

"You didn't answer my question."

"I just feel that way, that's all."

Benny was silent for a moment. "Get our people out of here," he finally said. "I ain't gonna lose no more this night."

"Let's go deal with the L.A crowd, Benny," Chink urged.

"You show me some proof that they're here to ace us and we will. But not until then."

"I ain't got no proof. Just a feelin', that's all."

"We're out of here, Chink. Let's go."

Jenny rejoined John at the front of the house. They stood and watched as the bikers pulled out. "Now what?" she asked.

"We switch to another motel and get some sleep."

"And something to eat," Don said, walking up. "I'm starving."

"Of course you are," John said. "It's been at least six hours since you ate enough for all of us. Let's get out of here before you faint from hunger."

THIRTY

John arranged for different vehicles, and then split up his people and assigned the various teams to watching the bikers. "We go after the labs," he told them. He looked at Jenny. "Once we find the labs, you can play with your explosives."

She grinned at him.

"Let's go to work," John told his people. "Stay in touch."

A couple of hours later, Bob used his cell phone to call in. "I think we've hit paydirt," he said. He gave his location. It was just inside Sheriff Morales's country.

"Nice house," Jenny said later as she and John drove by. "I wonder who owns it."

"Sandoval, Curtis, or Grayson," John said.

"They're going to own nothing but a pile of stones when I get through," Jenny said. "When do we go in?"

"How about right now?"

"With just Bob and Paul as backup?"

"Why not?"

"Suits me."

Ten minutes later the four of them had parked about a half mile from the house, and were walking up through the timber toward the rear of the stone home. John, Jenny, and Bob paused on the far side of a small ridge while Paul went on ahead to check out the rear of the house. He was back in five minutes.

"Four vehicles parked in the rear of the house," Paul said. "No guards visible. At least not in the back of the place."

"Surely they're not that stupid," Bob said, shaking his head. "They must be watching from inside."

"Wait a minute," Jenny said, chancing a quick look. "There's a low ridge over to our left. We can make it most of the way using the ridge for cover. I'd say it was about fifty feet from the ridge to the house."

"Let's go for the ridge," John said. "Make sure your sound suppressors are secured properly and stay low."

The team made the ridge that ran along the side of the house without being seen—at least no one took a shot at them—and paused for a moment to catch their breath.

"There are neighbors about a mile away," John reminded the team. "Up and down the road and on both sides of the road. Jenny's got one tear gas grenade, so she's got to make that count."

"It's a lulu," Jenny said. "New type developed by the lab that thinks up all the goodies for Delta Force. But there's a chance it might ignite the chemicals in that house. If so, there's gonna be one hell of a big boom."

"And no survivors," Paul added. "At least not inside the house."

"How unfortunate," John said.

"I can tell you're all torn up about it," Jenny said.

"Positively heartbroken," John replied.

"Who tosses the grenade?" Bob asked.

"I'm the fastest runner," Paul said. "I proved that doing sprints back in Texas. So I'm elected."

"It's a five-second fuse," Jenny told him. "As soon as you pop the pin, toss it and kick in the afterburners to get clear."

"The chemicals used to make speed and all that other crap are highly volatile," Bob warned him. "If they go up, it's going to be one hell of a bang."

"I can make that concrete-block building in the rear of the house," Paul said, checking the rear of the house. "As long as a piano or a commode doesn't land directly on top of me, I'll be all right behind that building."

"If the chemicals don't go up," John said. "The three of us will storm the house. Join us when you've caught your breath."

"Will do," Paul said, taking the grenade Jenny handed him. He smiled. "See y'all in a few minutes." Then he was up and running toward the house.

When Paul neared the house he tossed the grenade through a window and cut to his left, picking up speed as he raced toward the small concrete-block building at the rear of the house. Paul slid behind the building just as the grenade blew, spewing clouds of tear gas throughout the house. Shouts of panic and profanity came from the tear–gas–filled house, followed by coughing as the gas went to work.

Then the house exploded.

The roof actually lifted off a few feet as the windows blew out, sending broken shards of glass flying in all directions. The roof settled back for a few seconds before a second explosion tore the structure apart.

"Holy shit!" Bob said as the house disintegrated.

Huge chunks of the house were blown high into the air and in all directions close to the ground as the walls came apart. Parts of human bodies were mixed in with bits and pieces of wood and stone. A severed leg landed a few yards from John, and bounced several times before settling just inches from where he lay on the cold, rocky ground. The boot was still attached to the foot. Nerves in the severed leg caused the muscles to twitch a couple of times. John noticed the sole of the boot was badly worn.

There was a brief fire among the rubble that quickly died out when the flames failed to find anything to ignite.

"Jesus!" Jenny said. "I don't know exactly what chemicals were stored in that house, but every room must have been filled with drums of the stuff."

"Let's get out of here," John said. "Quickly."

Within minutes the quartet was driving away. Behind them, coming up the main highway, fire trucks were wailing toward the smoking rubble of the dope house.

"What the fuck happened over there?" the voice yelled into Largo's ear.

"What are you talking about?" Largo asked.

"Haven't you watched the TV news or read a newspaper?"

"Ah . . . actually, no, I haven't. We've been trying to track down Barrone and his bunch. They've switched locations on us."

"Well, let me bring you up to date . . ."

Largo listened, his face changing expressions several times as his boss from Los Angeles spoke.

Just before the mob boss in L.A. hung up, he said, "I'm sending a few boys to finish Vergano. You just take care of the situation where you are. Understood?"

"Yes, sir."

The boss hung up.

"Trouble?" Reese asked.

"Turn on the TV and find some news," Largo told him. He looked at Pizarro. "You go get us a couple of newspapers. Barrone's been busy and we're behind the times."

"The boss is pissed?"

"I think you'd be safe in saying that. Move!"

Sheriff Morales located Barrone and paid the team a visit. The sheriff was somewhat irritated. "Goddamn it, John!" he raged. "Why didn't you tell me about the lab? I could have dealt with it legally."

"Lab? What lab?" John asked innocently. "What in the world are you talking about, Sheriff?"

"Don't play cute with me, Barrone! You know damn well what I'm talking about."

"I'm afraid I don't, Sheriff. You want to tell me about it?"

Morales sat down in a chair in the motel suite and stared at John. "Do you know how many people were killed in that explosion at the biker lab, John?"

"What explosion, Sheriff? Lab? What sort of lab?"

Morales sighed. "There were either six or eight outlaws in that house when it blew up, John. We're not sure exactly how many were in there. My people are still finding bits and pieces of some of them. It's a real mess."

"I can't say I'm sorry to hear of it."

"Well, you might be sorry to hear this: We've got the Feds in here now."

"That's going to slow any investigation you have going down to a crawl. Believe me, I know how they work."

"Unfortunately, so do I."

"Any leaders of the outlaw bikers killed?"

"Who the hell knows? We can't find all the pieces of them. It appears the walls contained the first blast and the concussion probably killed most of them, then the second blast ripped them to bloody bits. That's what the Feds are saying probably happened." Morales shook his head. "I've never seen so many eyeballs and other assorted crap in my life."

"Must have been a lot of highly combustible chemicals in the lab."

"Fifty-five-gallon drums of it. The exploding drums turned into bombs when they blew, sending shrapnel flying all over the place."

John said nothing.

Morales stared at him for a minute, then heaved himself out of the chair and walked to the door. He paused, one hand on the doorknob, then turned around and said, "The Feds know you're here, John. You're the first person they asked about. They want to talk to you."

"If they want to talk to me badly enough, they'll find me."

"Be assured of that." The sheriff walked out of the suite without another word.

"I think it's time for us to take a vacation," Sandoval said. "We're right in the middle of a war."

"I thought Vergano was sending some muscle in to take care of . . . these people?" Curtis said.

"Vergano is on the run," Sandoval told him.

"What the hell are you talking about? On the run?" Grayson asked.

"His girlfriend called me about an hour ago. Right

before I called you guys. She's in a panic. Some muscle came in from L.A. early this morning and when they couldn't find Vergano, they came to see her and roughed her up a little bit. She doesn't know where Vergano is. Only that he's gone. Left town in a hurry."

"He's on the run?" Curtis asked.

"Until they catch him," Sandoval said grimly. "And they will."

"Suddenly, I'm scared," Grayson said in a low voice.

"I've been about to piss all over myself since I heard about it," Sandoval said.

"I wonder what Vergano did," Curtis said.

"Who knows? But he's a dead man, you can bet on that. Nobody gets sideways with the mob and lives for very long."

"I wonder if we're in trouble with . . . those people?" Grayson said.

"Who knows. I would say yes, we are."

"How come?" Curtis blurted out, a sudden shrillness to his voice.

"I don't know. Except that Vergono's girlfriend told me that the big man in L.A. is tired of the bikers and the whole dope business in this area. And I guess that includes us."

"Damn!" Curtis said. "Hell, we can't go on the run. I mean . . ."

Sandoval waved him silent. "I know that. Running is impossible for us. We've got too many businesses to run."

"So what do we do?" Grayson asked.

"Right now, I'm going to have another drink," Curtis said, waving the waiter over.

"Good idea," Grayson said.

The men each ordered a double martini, straight up.

"Keep them coming," Sandoval told the waiter. "And bring us something to munch on too. I'm a little bit hungry."

After their second double martini, Sandoval said, "I've got an idea, if you guys are game for it."

"Let's have it."

"We could really get in good graces with the big boys in L.A. if we took care of the damn bikers, right?"

"You bet!" Curtis said.

"And how about those other people who are snooping around causing trouble? You know, that Barrone bastard our snitch at the sheriff's office told us about? They're the ones who really started all this crap."

"Yeah," Sandoval said. "Them too."

"How do we do it?" Grayson asked.

"Hell," Sandoval said. "We know what to do. We've all got military experience and we've all got guns."

"We all enlisted in the National Guard," Curtis reminded him. "I was a clerk typist, Grayson was a cook, and you broke your foot during the second week of basic and never finished. What military experience?"

"Well, hell," Sandoval said. "We're all good shots, aren't we?"

"Pretty good," the other two admitted.

They all ordered another round of martinis.

Sandoval said, "We finish these drinks and head for home. We change into hunting gear and get our weapons."

The booze was filling them all with false courage. They were getting braver and braver with each sip.

"And then?" Curtis asked.

"We meet down at that old filling station where we used to hang out as kids and go settle this matter, once and for all."

"We shoot the bastards, all of them," Grayson said.
Curtis nodded his head. "Damn right."
Sandoval pushed back his chair and stood up. "Let's do it, boys."

THIRTY-ONE

"Our people intercepted a message from the DEA," Don said. "The mob boss out of L.A. has put a contract out on the New Mexico boss."

"Vergano?" Linda asked.

"Yes. He's on the run."

"He won't get far," John said. "They never do, unless they go to the Feds and roll over, requesting protection."

"Vergano wouldn't last a day in prison," Linda stated. "The Feds would have to put him under the witness protection program."

"Is he important enough for them to do that?" Paul asked.

"Probably," Linda replied.

The team had gathered in John's suite, drinking coffee and talking. The motel they had just checked into was in Morales's county. And the team's presence did not make the sheriff terribly happy.

"So what's on the agenda for this afternoon, John?" Paul asked.

"We wait."

"For what?" Jenny asked.

"Several things. To see what the muscle from L.A. does, for one, as well as what the bikers might decide to do. And then there are the three money men in this county."

"What about them?" Paul asked.

John looked at Bob and returned the ex-NSA man's smile. "It will be interesting to see what they do when they learn about Vergano being on the run."

"Ahh!" Don said. "You think they might get nervous when they learn about Vergano?"

"If you were in their shoes, wouldn't you get nervous?"

"Indeed I would."

Mike stood up and reached for his coat. "I think I'll go cruise by the homes of our money men and see if they're up to anything."

"Good idea," John said.

"Anybody want to come along?" Mike offered.

"Me," Linda said.

"And me," Paul said. "You two might get into trouble and you'll need someone to bail you out."

"I welcome your company, folks," Mike said. "Let's go."

The door had just closed behind the trio when John said to the others, "Anybody want to go with me and see if we can stir up something?"

"You're a troublemaker, John," Jenny said. "But I'm game."

"We'll take two vehicles," Don said. "Maybe we can get something to eat on the way. I'm hungry."

Muttering about Don having a massive tapeworm, Jenny grabbed her coat and followed John out the door.

Sheriff Morales was parked across the street, sitting in an unmarked car in the middle of a used-car lot. He had watched as Mike pulled out, Paul in the front seat, Linda in the second seat. Morales had let them go. He wanted to see if John Barrone would follow. He smiled as John walked out the door a couple of minutes later, Jenny getting in the vehicle with him, Don and Bob getting in another vehicle.

"Now we're getting someplace," Morales said, cranking the engine. He pulled out, staying a full block behind John's SUV, several vehicles between them.

"You have a destination in mind?" Jenny asked in the SUV.

"Not really," John replied. "Maybe we'll get lucky and the bikers will spot us and start some trouble. Or the muscle. We'll just wander and see what happens."

"Looking for trouble," she said with a smile.

"Beats sitting around the motel."

The muscle from L.A. fell in behind Morales's car, staying well back. They had been loosely following the sheriff since the biker lab explosion.

"I told you Morales would lead us to Barrone," Largo said, smiling.

"But what the hell can we do with the sheriff between us and them?" Carlos asked.

"So we'll take out the sheriff, too," Largo replied.

"Kill a cop? Shit, man! That's asking for a lot of trouble."

"He isn't anyone special. Just a hick county sheriff, that's all. We'll ice the bunch of them and get gone. It's no big deal. We'll be out of state and in other vehicles before their bodies are found."

"Back to L.A.?"

"No. We'll head for Vegas. Relax some until the heat dies down."

"You got the okay to ice a sheriff?" Sal asked from the backseat.

"This is my show," Largo said. "It's open-ended. The word I got is that I can play it any way I see fit."

"I don't like it, man."

"You don't have to like it. Just do it."

"Okay, Largo. Okay. Don't get in a sweat. I'm just voicing an opinion, that's all."

"This is why we ain't checked into no motel yet today, right?" Carlos asked.

"Now you're using your head. Yeah. That's right."

"Largo, we can't follow the sheriff around all the rest of the damn day," Sal said. "We'll be spotted for sure."

"We got three cars and cell phones," Largo patiently explained. "In a few minutes we'll fall back and Lucas can take the lead. Then Mills. But I got a hunch we'll have the job done and be gone in less time than you think."

"I hope," Carlos said.

The cars that were between Sheriff Morales and the team's SUVs turned off before John reached the city-limit sign and the street became a state highway. Morales eased back about a hundred yards, hoping the Cadillac behind him would pass.

"We got to pass this asshole," Largo said. "He's slowing down. Damn!"

Three Cadillacs passed the sheriff. Cadillacs with California plates, Morales noted. Each Caddy had three men in it. Then it hit him.

"Shit!" Morales said. "That's the muscle from L.A. I'd bet a hundred dollars it is." Then Morales noticed a line of cars behind him, stretching out for half a mile. "Now who in the hell is that?" he muttered.

The FBI, the DEA, investigators from the New Mexico attorney general's office, and several unmarked cars carrying plainclothes New Mexico state police.

"We've got the L.A. mob boys behind us," Jenny said.

"I noticed," John said. "But who is all that behind them?"

Jenny adjusted her binoculars. "When you reach the top of this hill I'll be able to see the drivers. I think." She lifted the long lenses to her eyes and said, "It's Sheriff Morales in the fifth car."

"How about the other vehicles?"

"I don't know. But the ones I can see are all wearing suits."

"Feds," John said. "But in all those cars?"

"Getting crowded, isn't it?" Jenny remarked.

"Tell Don to pull over and get behind the line," John told her. "To stay there and follow."

"It's going to be a mess," Jenny said, punching out the number. "We're all going to be falling all over each other."

"Or shooting each other," John added. "We've got a long stretch of road that's clear. Any of the cars behind Morales passing him?"

"No," Jenny said. She passed the instructions to Don.

"It's a damn parade," John said. "The muscle is following us. Morales is either following us or the muscle, and the Feds are following the muscle. Now all we need are the bikers and Sandoval, Grayson, and Curtis."

Paul called from the cell phone in his SUV.

"What is it?' John asked him.

"Just got a call from Control. The money men have been found. They're a couple miles ahead of us, on this highway. They're all dressed in camo hunting gear and loaded down with guns. They also appear to be drinking heavily."

"Where are the bikers?" John asked.

"No sign of them. Wait a minute." Paul listened for

a few seconds. "The money men are pulling out in a green Explorer."

"We'll let them go," John said. "Jenny, look at the map and tell me where the next intersection is. Never mind, I see it just up ahead. Hell with it. Who cares where it goes? We'll take it." John smiled.

"You thinking the money men might help bring this mess to a head?" Paul asked.

"They might also get themselves killed," Jenny said.

"Wouldn't that be a terrible blow to society," John replied.

"Just awful," Paul said, then broke the connection.

The cell phone rang again. Jenny answered and listened. "Don wants to know what the hell is going on," she told John.

"Tell him we're at the head of a parade."

"He says he's hungry."

"What else is new? Tell him I'll buy him a steak dinner this evening."

"He says we might not be alive this evening."

"There is that to consider."

Sandoval headed for one of the bikers' known addresses. "We'll get out and start shooting," he told his friends. "No talk, just bullets."

"They got guns, too," Curtis told him.

"Our guns are better."

"Yeah," Grayson said. "I paid a thousand dollars for this shotgun."

"Nick?" Curtis asked.

"Yeah?"

"You doin' this on 'count of what happened to your brother Dennis?"

"No. Dennis was a fool. I told you before he was

skimming. Him and those others with him. No telling how much money they screwed us out of."

"He's still dead," Curtis said. "And the bikers just might be partly responsible for that. They were all in the wrong spot at the right time."

"I never liked him anyway," Sandoval said. "But you're right about the bikers. I never looked at it like that."

"One more reason for us to wipe the bastards out," Grayson said from the backseat. "I'm kind of looking forward to it."

"Yeah, me too," Curtis said. "I think that maybe we all need some action to keep us on our toes."

"We'll drive by the house real slow. Look the situation over. Hey, were you guys' wives at home?"

"Mine wasn't," Curtis said. "I don't know where she is."

"Mine neither," Grayson said. "She left me a note. Said she was out with you guys' wives for the afternoon."

"No telling where they are," Sandoval said. "Hell, they might have gone to Sante Fe. Who gives a shit."

"I don't," Grayson and Curtis said as one. Curtis grimaced and said, "Angie hasn't give me any in weeks. Cut me off cold."

"But I do wonder what she did with the kids," Grayson said.

"They're all old enough to take care of themselves," Curtis said.

"Let me rephrase that," Grayson said. "I'm just wondering if the kids are out somewhere fucking up."

"Probably fucking somebody is more like it," Curtis said. "Davy would screw a snake if it would hold still."

"You think she's got her a boyfriend?" Grayson asked.

"I don't know. The thought has crossed my mind a time or two. I wish I could catch them. I'd shoot both of them."

"Don't be stupid," Sandoval said. "All that would get you is a lot of years in prison. I don't think you'd like prison."

"My Honey would never even think of a boyfriend," Grayson said. "She's too goddamn stupid."

"But she's a good-lookin' woman," Sandoval told him. "One of those quiet types. Those are the kind you have to watch."

"I never worry about her," Grayson said. "She's scared of me anyway."

"Honey is scared of you?" Curtis questioned.

"Tell us about it," Sandoval said.

"Yeah. I gave her a good ass-whippin' one time. I mean, I beat the livin' shit outta her. She got all up in my face about a personal matter and I knocked her down about ten times. I thought I'd killed her."

"That personal matter," Sandoval said with a smile. "It didn't involve a little piece of nooky named Grace, did it?"

Grayson laughed. "A man is entitled to some strange ass every now and then. It's just part of bein' a man."

"Damn right," Curtis said. "And when we get done dealing with the bikers, let's us all go out and get some pussy."

"Good idea!" Sandoval said. "Crack open that other bottle, will you? No sense in lettin' any go to waste. We got us a few more miles to go."

" 'Bout ten, I think," Grayson said.

Morales smiled when he realized that John was intentionally leading the line of cars somewhere. He wasn't sure just who was in all the cars that were doggedly staying on his tail, but whoever they were they were certainly persistent.

"Well, I've got all afternoon," he muttered. "And it's a pleasant day for a drive."

The sky was blue and cloudless, the temperature mild, and the highway clear.

"What the hell is all them cars doin' behind us?" Mabini asked, using his cell phone to call Largo.

"How the hell should I know?" Largo told him.

"They're wearin' suits."

Largo gave that a few seconds' thought. "Cops," he said. "Probably state and federal. Shit!"

"They've made us," Sal said. "Let's get the hell out of here."

"And go where?" Largo asked. "If we pulled out now, that would put the spotlight on us. We ain't done nothing so far. We're just driving around. We're looking for property to buy. Tell the other boys that's the story and if we're stopped to stick with it. The cops don't know who we are."

"We got a hell of a lot of guns, man. We get caught with those, we're a long time in the bucket."

"Then we won't get caught. Is that simple enough?"

"Jesus, Largo! They's a line of cars filled with cops stretchin' out a fuckin' half mile behind us. We're caught!"

"Relax," Largo said. "Just calm down."

"I hate this fuckin' country," Carlos said. "I hate this fuckin' job."

Largo cut his eyes and laughed at the expression on his friend's face. "Just think how nice it will be to get back to the city."

"We're screwed," Sal said. "Caught. I just know it."

"We're just driving around," Largo said. "That's all
So relax."

"Paul says they're way to hell and gone out in the
country and wants to know what they should do if our
money men figure out where they're going and get
there," Jenny said.

"Interesting way of phrasing it," John said
"Well . . . tell him to just keep an eye on them. We're
playing this by ear."

Jenny passed along the instructions and then began
studying a map. "John, I think I know where Sandoval
and his buddies are going."

"Oh?"

"The bikers have a house near where Paul called
in."

"And the money men are all carrying weapons?"

"Yes, and drinking heavily."

"Tell Paul not to interfere with whatever happens
This just might prove to be very interesting."

"Do we lead these cars behind us over toward the
biker house and Sandoval and his friends?" Jenny
asked.

"No. We lead them away from that area."

Jenny glanced at him and then smiled. "You have
a mean streak in you, John."

"Oh?"

"Yes, you do. You're hoping for a shoot-out between
the bikers and Sandoval and his buddies, aren't you?'

"That wouldn't break my heart."

"But why would they turn on one another?"

"I don't know. Maybe that isn't the reason Sandoval
is heading over that way. We'll just have to see what
happens."

"I'll tell Don what's shaking."

"Okay." John started chuckling at the possibility of a showdown between the bikers and the money men.

"Mean streak," Jenny said, punching out the numbers on her cell phone. "I love it!"

THIRTY-TWO

"There's the biker house just up ahead!" Curtis said. "Sure a bunch of vehicles parked around th place. Hey! Isn't that your wife's car, Nick?"

"Naw," Sandoval replied. "Just one that looks lik hers. What the hell would she be doing out here wit a bunch of crummy bikers?"

The trio drove slowly past the biker house, and Nic Sandoval's lips tightened and a flush rose slowly u his face as he looked at the license plates on the Lir coln Town Car parked by the side of the house.

"Uh . . . Nick," Grayson said.

"I see it," Sandoval said tersely. "That miserabl bitch. That no-good cunt. I give her everything sh wants and she repays me by screwing bikers." He be gan wildly cursing his wife, beating the palm of hi hand on the steering wheel.

Dave Curtis and Morris Grayson sat quietly and sai nothing while Sandoval vented his rage.

While you've been gettin' some strange ass," Curti said, "your Sugar's been gettin' herself some strang dick."

Sandoval continued his wild cussing, pretending no to hear his friend's ill-thought-out comments.

"You're forgetting one thing, Dave," Grayson said "Oh? What's that?"

"Our wives are in there too."

Dave's mouth dropped open. When he finally found his voice, he said, "Oh, no way, man. Not my wife. She's scared to death of bikers."

"So she tells you," Grayson said, a nasty edge to his voice. "And all the time she's been bumpin' uglies with outlaw bikers."

"Yeah?" Dave flared. "Well, Morris, here's something for you to think about: Your wife is in there with her round heels up in the air too."

"Not my Honey. She's too scared of me to step around behind my back. I'd bet a thousand dollars on that."

"You're on with that bet, Morris," Sandoval said. "How about it, Dave? You want a piece of it too?"

"Sure I do. Honey's in there with the others, humpin' and bumpin' and gettin' her jollies off."

"No way!"

"We'll soon see," Sandoval said. "We'll pull over at this intersection just up ahead and plan out what we're going to do."

The team members following them had pulled over about a hundred yards from the biker house and were all watching through long lenses. Paul got on the horn to Jenny.

"Are the money men doing anything?" Jenny asked.

"Not yet."

"John says to keep an eye on them and don't get involved with anything that happens."

"Will do."

Sandoval pulled over on the shoulder of the road and twisted in the seat. "This is what we're going to do, boys. We're going to park a couple hundred yards

from the house and come in from the back. And we're
going to hit them hard and fast."

"What if our wives get in the way?" Curtis asked.

"You really give a shit if they do?" Grayson said.
"After they all been slick-dickin' those damn greasy
bikers?"

"I guess not. Not since you put it that way. Sorta
makes me sick at my stomach to think about it."

"I wonder how long this mess has been goin' on,"
Grayson said.

"Our wives have been going out for the afternoon
twice a week for several months," Sandoval said. "So
I guess it's been going on for that long."

"I'm gonna go see a doctor as soon as this is over
with," Curtis said. "No tellin' what sorts of awful dis-
eases those bitches gave us."

"I hadn't thought about that," Grayson said. "God!
We've probably all got the Hong Kong rot."

"Enough talk," Sandoval said. "Let's finish that
open half-pint of booze and then get going."

"I'll save us a full pint for when we get back," Curtis
said. "I think we're probably gonna need it."

"You bet," Grayson said. "Then we'll all go out and
get laid."

"Damn right," Sandoval replied. "Maybe we'll drag
our wives with us and make them watch us hump."

"That's a damn good idea, Nick," Curtis said with
a slightly drunken laugh. "Boy, that would be a hoot,
wouldn't it?"

Sandoval stepped out of the SUV and got his shotgun. He loaded it up and slung a small rucksack filled
with shells over one shoulder. "Let's go kill some bikers, boys. Then we'll beat the shit out of some wives."

"Damn right," Grayson said, almost losing his balance as he stepped out of the vehicle. He leaned

against the SUV for a moment. "This time I'm gonna teach my old lady her place once and for all."

"You got that right," Curtis said. "Spare the rod and spoil the bitch."

The trio thought that remark was hysterically amusing. After they cackled and howled, they picked up their weapons and moved out, staggering slightly as they walked.

Mike had taken binoculars and slipped up on a wooded ridge, scanning the terrain. He spotted the trio of drunks as they came staggering along, approaching the rear of the biker house. He called in to Paul and Linda.

"If the number of vehicles parked around the place means anything," Mike said, "there must be at least fifteen or twenty bikers in that house. But I can't figure who belongs to that Lincoln Town Car."

"Are the money men armed?" Linda asked.

"Heavily. Shotguns and pistols and lots of ammo, looks like."

Linda smiled as a thought popped into her mind. "Can you get a tag number on the Lincoln?"

"Not from where I'm located," Mike said.

"What are you thinking, Linda?" Paul asked.

"That Lincoln just might belong to one of the men's wives."

Paul grinned. "Now that would be interesting."

"Wouldn't it, though?"

Linda used another cell phone to call John and bring him up to speed.

"What model car is it?" John asked.

"Lincoln Town Car."

"Nick Sandoval's wife drives a Lincoln," John said. "Morales gave us that information, remember?"

"A black one?"

"Yes."

"Oh, boy!" Linda said. "This is about to get lively, I'm thinking."

John laughed. "Don't interfere. Stay clear and keep me informed. I wish I could be there to see it."

"Don't worry, John. We're clear and plan to stay that way."

"Jenny," John said, "you have Morales's cell phone number?"

"Yes. It's programmed in."

"We might want to call him a bit later on."

Jenny laughed. "I'll say it again, John. You have a mean streak in you."

"I think you're right, Jenny."

THIRTY-THREE

The smell of marijuana was strong in the nostrils of the three men as they approached the house in the country. All three of the men used marijuana often, and all three knew the stuff they were smelling was high-grade and powerful.

"Great stuff they're smokin' in there," Curtis said.

"Might be some of that Canadian stuff I've been hearin' about," Grayson said. "I'd like to get my hands on some of that."

"Well, they apparently got plenty in there," Sandoval said. "So we'll grab us a bag full when this is over."

"Then it'll really be party time," Curtis whispered.

The back door suddenly opened and the three men pressed up against the house, Sandoval and Curtis on one side of the door, Grayson on the other side. A biker staggered out, bringing with him the nearly overpowering odor of marijuana, booze, and sex.

The biker closed the door behind him, then stood for a moment, trying to get his glassy eyes to focus. He never made it. Grayson stepped away from the house and popped the biker on the back of the head with the butt of his shotgun. The big biker went down and Sandoval and Curtis grabbed him, dragging him to one side and dumping him on the ground face-down.

"I think you might have busted his skull, Morris," Curtis said, looking down at the unconscious biker.

"So who gives a big rat's ass?" Grayson asked.

"Not me," Curtis acknowledged. "Screw 'im."

"I definitely heard a cracking sound," Sandoval said. "I personally hope you killed the bastard."

"He's still breathin'," Grayson said, looking down at the biker. "Forget him. Now what, Nick?"

"We go in the house and get our wives."

"What do we do with them when we get them?" Curtis said, momentarily forgetting what the three men had decided to do.

"We beat the shit out of them!"

"Yeah!" Curtis said. "That's right. I forgot."

"You're drunk," Sandoval said.

"And you're not?" Curtis challenged.

Sandoval laughed softly. "Maybe a little bit," he admitted.

"Enough talk," Grayson said, stepping in front of the closed door. "Let's do it, boys. It's what real men would do."

"That's us," Curtis said. "Open the door."

"What's happening over there?" Jenny asked.

"Mike just called to say they're going into the biker house," Linda reported.

"Okay. Stay clear of any trouble. John says when the shooting starts, if it does, you three haul ass out of there."

"Will do."

* * *

Grayson slammed open the door, and the smell almost caused the three men to stagger back in shock. They shook their heads and ran into the house, then into the kitchen. A man seemed to be passed out at the kitchen table, his head on the table. He suddenly raised his head and looked at the three men.

"Whutthefuckyouwant?" he mumbled.

"Shut up, you piece of shit!" Sandoval told him.

The biker reached into his pocket and pulled out a pistol.

Sandoval shot him in the face at nearly point-blank range. The double-aught buckshot blew the biker's head apart, sending teeth, bits of bone, brain, and eyeballs splattering all over the counter behind him.

"Oh, gross!" Curtis said. "I think I'm gonna be sick."

"What the hell is goin' on in there?" a man shouted from another room.

"Fuck you too!" Sandoval shouted.

Curtis suddenly bent over and puked on the floor.

"Shit, Dave!" Grayson said. "You puked on my shoe, damn it."

"Who's that tellin' me to get fucked?" the biker shouted.

"Who farred that gun?" another biker called. "Damn near deefened me."

Sandoval pumped another round into his shotgun. But he did not know that when he dumped the extra shells into his rucksack, he was dumping in very light loads of birdshot. He had fired his only buckshot round. The others had also unintentionally loaded up with light loads.

"I did, you asshole!" Sandoval shouted out in answer to the biker's question.

"Asshole! Is that you, Swede? You prick!"

"No!" Sandoval shouted. "It's Mr. Sandoval, you bastard! I've come to get my wife." Sandoval leveled his shotgun and blew a hole in the door.

"Jesus Humpin' Christ!" a biker yelled.

"Here!" Grayson yelled. "Have another one." He blew off a couple of rounds, as fast as he could pump.

"Is that really you, Nick?" a woman yelled. "Oh, darling, I'm so glad you came. This band of horrible people kidnapped us and forced us to come out here. We've been forced to do all sorts of disgusting things." She suddenly belched very loudly.

"Morris?" another woman yelled. "Oh, thank heavens you're here, darling."

"You lyin' bitch!" Grayson yelled, and triggered off two more rounds, then paused to reload.

"Shit!" a biker yelled. "Git your guns, boys. Them's some pissed-off husbands."

"Let's go, guys!" Sandoval yelled, and began his run into the next room. He got halfway in the room before he lost his balance and went to the floor in a tangle of arms and legs. Sandoval lost his grip on his shotgun and it hit the floor and discharged, the shot blowing out a window and sending bikers—in various stages of undress, some of them naked—running in all directions.

Curtis lined up a biker and pulled the trigger, most of the birdshot missing the naked biker, but a few tiny shots catching the doped-up biker in his ass.

"Whoooooeee!"the biker known as Knob hollered as he picked up speed. "I'm hit, boys. My ass is on fire!"

Knob headed for the front door and ran out into the yard, forgetting he was stark naked.

* * *

"The shooting has started!" Mike said from his position on the ridge.

"Get out of there!" Linda told him. "Let's go!"

"There's a man just ran out of the house holding his ass. Good God!" Mike said. "He's totally naked."

"Come on, Mike," Linda urged. "Move it!"

Mike reluctantly left his position and headed for the SUV. Linda was on another cell phone, talking with Jenny.

"Naked?" Jenny asked.

"That's what Mike just said. And he was holding his ass."

Jenny started laughing so hard she couldn't speak.

Grayson let his shotgun bang as fast as he could pump it. The first shot blew a lamp into a hundred pieces and sent a biker jumping behind a worn couch. The next blast peppered a biker's ass. The biker hollered and ran out the front door, just as naked as his friend, who was sitting down in a muddy puddle, trying to put out the fire in his butt.

Grayson's third shot went into the ceiling as a biker slammed into him, knocking him to the floor. Sandoval had crawled to his knees and found his shotgun, and popped the biker on the noggin with the butt of the weapon. The biker's eyes rolled back and he hit the floor, unconscious. He landed on top of Grayson.

"Where's my goddamn pants!" Sandoval's wife, Sugar, screamed as Curtis's shotgun boomed in the other room.

"Hell with your goddamn pants!" Angie squalled. "I can't find *any* of my clothes."

Grayson rolled free of the unconscious biker and found his shotgun, pointing it at a biker who was heading his way, a baseball bat in his hand and a very mean look in his eyes. Grayson pulled the trigger and the biker's legs caught the full load of birdshot. The biker staggered back, yelling that he'd been mortally wounded. He sat down hard on the floor and stayed there, hollering about not being able to move his legs.

Honey Grayson ran naked into the gunsmoke-filled living room, and tripped over a biker who was out of it from too much booze and dope. The woman went sprawling onto the floor.

"You rotten bitch!" Grayson yelled. "Whore!"

"Oh, fuck you!" Honey screamed at her husband.

"I wouldn't stick Castro's dick in you after this day!" Grayson yelled. He lifted his shotgun, aiming at his naked wife, who was just crawling to her knees.

Honey screamed and hit the floor just as her husband pulled the trigger and just as a biker ran into the room. The shot meant for Honey hit the biker's legs and private parts and set him down on the floor.

"I'm ruint!" the biker hollered. "He shot my dick off! Oh, Lord!"

The three irate and very drunk husbands reloaded and started blasting away in all directions. Half-naked bikers went out doors and windows in an effort to escape the gunfire. Women were screaming in rage and terror.

"Get your whoring asses outside, all you bitches!" Curtis yelled at the three women. "Out the back door, goddamn you!" He tried to kick his wife on the ass, lost his balance, and fell backward, landing on his butt on the floor. The shotgun went off, blowing a hole in the ceiling.

"You drunk son of a bitch!" Angie yelled. "Hell with you, you bastard!" She picked up what was left of a lamp and hurled it at him. The lamp hit Grayson on the head and knocked him to the floor.

Sandoval blew a load of birdshot at a biker who was only trying to escape out the front door. The shot caught him on his jeans-clad butt and really put some pep in his step. He went hollering and squalling out into the yard, his ass filled with birdshot.

"Get out of here and let these crazy bastards have it!" a biker yelled. "Get gone, boys, 'fore the cops get here."

Those few bikers who had not already exited the house promptly did so, most of them climbing out of windows. They jumped into cars and trucks and vans and roared away. They left behind two bikers, one in the kitchen with his head missing, and another unconscious in the backyard. The biker in the backyard would die within hours from massive head injuries.

"Get up," Sandoval told his wife, pointing his shotgun menacingly. "And get those other bitches you brought with you. Move, you damned whore!"

"Now wait a minute. What are you gonna do, Nick?" she asked, her anger vanishing and fear taking its place.

"I don't know, Sugar. Except give you a damn good ass-whipping. I know for sure I'm gonna do that."

The three men had sobered up considerably. But the wives were still stoned, glassy-eyed, and somewhat unsteady on their feet.

"You're not whippin' my ass, Dave Curtis," Angie said.

"The hell I'm not, you bitch!"

"Try it, you bastard!"

Dave stepped forward and Angie, clad only in panties and tennis shoes, lashed out with one foot and kicked her husband solidly in the nuts.

Dave faded like the last rose of summer. He turned pale and slumped to the floor, dropping his shotgun, which was empty, fortunately for all concerned. He knelt on the floor, both hands holding his crotch.

"Angie," Grayson said, "that was really uncalled for."

"Fuck you!" Angie told him.

"You watch your filthy mouth, bitch!" Sandoval said.

"Fuck you too!" Angie told him.

"Oh, my balls hurt," Dave groaned.

"Good," Angie said. "I hope they rot and fall off."

"You bitch!" Dave said.

"There's a man out here in the kitchen with his head missing!" Honey screamed. "Oh, God, I'm going to be sick."

"Did you fuck him, too?" her husband called.

"Hell, I don't know," Honey replied. "His head's gone. I can't tell who he is."

"Look at his dick, Honey," Angie called. "You got real close to that."

Sandoval stepped forward and backhanded the woman hard, almost knocking her off her feet. A thin line of blood trickled from her mouth.

"Don't hit my wife," Dave said from his kneeling position on the floor. "If she needs hitting, I'll do that."

"From the floor?" Sandoval questioned. "Hell, you can't even stand up."

Dave struggled to his feet, both hands still cupping his groin. "I'm hurt bad," he said.

"Good," Angie said.

"I'm gonna stomp your face in when I get you home," Dave told her.

The sounds of Honey's retching in the kitchen drifted out to the living room.

"Your wife is ill, Morris," Angie told him.

"She's gonna be a lot sicker when I get her home."

"Big brave men," Sugar said. "You all make me sick. Come on, Angie, you go find your clothes while I get Honey. Then we'll all go home and pack."

"Are we going on a trip?" Angie asked.

Sugar laughed. "You bet we are. First to a motel and then to a lawyer."

"Now wait a damn minute!" Sandoval said.

"You going to kill us too?" Sugar asked, defiance in her voice. " 'Cause that's the only way you're going to stop us."

Nick stared at his wife for a moment, then slowly shook his head, stepped aside, and waved her to pass. He was sobering up very quickly. "Go on. I won't try to stop you. I'll just be damn glad to be rid of you."

"You won't be when my lawyer gets through with you."

"Are you fucking him too?"

"Well, that's not a bad idea. I'll give it some thought."

"You really are one sorry piece of crap, Sugar."

"I guess I've been hanging around you too long, Nick. Shit rubs off, I suppose."

"You'll never get a damn dime out of me, Angie," Dave said, still all hunched over from the pain in his balls.

"I don't plan on getting a dime, Dave," his wife told him. "I plan on getting at least half of everything you have."

"Forget it!"

"Not likely, boy-o. Just remember before you fight my divorce settlement, you guys came into this house and shot it up. One of you murdered that guy in the kitchen and wounded half a dozen others. Keep that in mind."

"And you women were involved in all sorts of dope," Nick said. "And probably crimes against nature as well. And that's just the beginning of the charges that will be filed against you if you get too damn uppity with this thing."

"Crimes against nature!" Sugar yelled. "What the hell are you talking about, you idiot?"

Sandoval smiled. "Use your imagination, baby. I plan to."

"This dead guy just farted!" Honey yelled from the kitchen. "It's gross! And there's another body in the backyard."

"Go get your wife, Morris," Nick said. "Then we'll all go home and talk this thing out. I don't believe anybody is getting a divorce."

"Says you!" his wife taunted him.

"That's right, Sugar. Says me. You've handled enough money from dope deals to involve you up to your cheatin' ass. You wouldn't like prison any more than I would. You all better give that some thought."

"You can't prove that!" Angie yelled.

"You want to bet ten to twenty years in prison?" Nick challenged.

Honey had walked out of the kitchen and was listening. "He's got a point. I don't want to go to prison."

"Shit!" Angie said in disgust. Then she shook her head. "Okay. Let's all settle down and talk about this thing like adults. I have a headache anyway."

"Bad dope?" her husband asked.

"Probably too much dick," Morris said.

Angie ignored both comments.

"What about this house and the bikers?" Honey asked.

"The bikers won't go to the cops," Nick said. "And who gives a shit about the house. Hell, we'll set it on fire and then split."

"We'll drag the body in from the backyard and torch it," Morris said.

"Come on, people," Dave said. "We don't have to torch the place. Just drag the body inside and lock the place up. The bikers won't be back for hours; maybe never. By the time the bodies are discovered, they'll be nothing but rotted crap."

"Ugh!" Angie said. "That is gross."

"With maggots all over them," Morris said.

"Enough already," his wife told him.

"You women get all your clothing," Nick said. "Don't leave nothing behind. Then we'll get gone from here."

"Good idea," Honey said "I am sorta hungry. We'll stop on the way and get a burger."

Morris looked at her and shook his head in disbelief.

"What the hell's your problem?" Honey asked. "I am hungry."

"You just puked five minutes ago!"

"That's why I'm hungry. There's nothing in my stomach."

"Come on, people," Nick said. "Let's get goin' and get the hell out of here."

"Are we all lovey-dovey again?" Angie asked sarcastically.

"Maybe," Dave said. "All depends on when my balls stop hurting."

THIRTY-FOUR

"The Feds are breaking off," Jenny said. "Pulling into the parking lot of that country store we just passed."

John glanced into his rearview. "I see them."

"What's going on?" Don asked on his cell phone.

"We don't know," Jenny told him. "Hang on."

"Maybe we've been made," John said.

"So?" Jenny asked.

"The Feds can kill two birds with one stone, so to speak."

Jenny looked at him, questions in her eyes. Then the questions began to fade. "Oh, you're not serious, John," she said scornfully. "You aren't suggesting our own government would do something like that?"

John smiled his reply.

"You're right, of course," Jenny said. "The Feds made us, called in, and were told to back off; perhaps the muscle would finish us off or we would kill each other. Jesus!"

"It was just a thought, Jenny. Although I can't think of another reason why they would suddenly back off."

"I can't either."

This time it was John's cell phone that rang. Paul on the other end. "The money men and their wives pulled out. You want us to follow them?"

"No. Is the house empty?"

"Far as we can tell. You want us to check it out?"

"No. Get clear of there right now."

"And do what?"

"Head back to motel number three and call us when you're in the rooms."

"Ten-four."

"Jenny, tell Don and Bob to head for motel number three. Check in and stay put. Call us when they get here."

That done, Jenny asked, "Now what do we do?"

"Start a gunfight."

"Oh, boy, Hopalong! You have any idea where this is going to take place?"

"You've got the map. You tell me."

"Hang on.

"About twenty or so miles west of here is absolutely, totally barren," Jenny said after checking the map of that region.

"No towns?"

"Not for thirty-nine miles. There is nothing except a bunch of unpaved roads leading off from the main highway. And the main highway is a secondary road."

"Good. That will work. Tell me where to turn and let's hope the muscle behind us follows."

A few miles further on, Jenny said, "Take a left at the next intersection and keep on driving west."

John made the turn, and a moment later glanced in the rearview and said, "The muscle is right behind us. Those boys are determined."

Jenny said nothing, just reached behind her and grabbed a couple of weapons, laying them on the floorboards. Then she muscled a couple of heavy rucksacks from the backseat and laid them beside the weapons. "Might as well get ready," she explained.

A few miles further on, she asked, "How are w
going to handle this, John?"

"When we get out into the badlands—for lack of
better word—we'll find what looks to be a good spo
pull over, and have at it."

"Simple enough. Nine or ten to two is good odds.

"I thought you'd like it."

"But why did you send the others back to the mo
tel?"

"Too many cooks spoil the soup."

'Thank you. That certainly clears everything up."

"I knew it would."

"About five miles further on take the road to th
left. It's unpaved."

"We've got four-wheel drive; those cars might no
be able to make it."

"We won't have far to go; only about five miles. Th
road looks to be in pretty good shape. And there ar
no private residents near the spot I have picked out.

"Good enough. I trust your judgment."

"What's happenin' here, Largo?" Carlos asked.

"We'll soon find out."

"Hell, they must know we're following them," S
said.

"They know," Largo replied. And he was pretty sur
what those in the SUV were doing: leading them ou
into the country for a showdown.

"I think maybe they're leadin' us out to some de
serted spot for a shoot-out," Sal said. "That's what
think."

"You're probably right," Largo said. "If so, we'll ge
this over with and head on back to the city."

"That suits the hell outta me," Carlos said. "Bu

et's take that blond bitch alive. I want to hump that
ox."

"Yeah, me too," Sal said. "Then we'll kill her. How
bout it, Largo?"

"We'll see how it works out. I don't care."

"She's a prime piece, looks to me."

"Whatever," Largo said. "But if any of you get a
hot at her today, take it. It's gonna be close anyway
ou cut it."

"What do you mean?"

"We don't have that many hours of daylight left.
Maybe two or three at best. Call Mills, Carlos. See if
e's spotted any of Barrone's backup. Still bothers me
vhy that second SUV just dropped out all of a sud-
en."

"And where in the hell is the other SUV of theirs?"
al asked.

"Good question."

Before Carlos could complete the call, John braked
nd pulled off the secondary road, turning onto an
npaved road. He drove for a few hundred yards, then
topped.

"Here we go," Largo said.

"Let's see if I can tuck this vehicle behind that hill
ver there," John said, dropping the SUV into four-
heel drive and rolling out. "I'd hate to have to walk
ut of here."

"This sure is some desolate country," Jenny re-
narked. "And I'm glad we've got water with us."

Both Jenny and John were wearing outdoor clothing
nd lace-up hiking boots. They each had very warm
ip-length coats. When they were parked behind the

hill, they gathered up their equipment and headed up the hill.

"Call Mills," Largo said. "Tell him to come on. This time we're gonna finish this thing."

"What about the other part of Barrone's team?"

"If they're not in sight by now, and they're not 'cause Mills hasn't called, they're not coming. Get them here."

John and Jenny settled in on the crest of the ridge about ten feet apart. Both of them were using Ruger Mini-14s in .223 caliber.

"We got troubles," Largo was informed. He turned to look at Carlos, who was holding his cell phone out to him. Largo didn't bother to ask Carlos what the trouble was. He took the phone and said, "What is it, Mills."

"It just came on the news, Largo. Some sort of shoot-out between local businessmen and the bikers out in the country. Two/three bikers killed and some others wounded."

"What the hell does that have to do with us, Mills?"

"The businessmen were our people."

Largo was silent for a moment. "Sandoval, Curtis and Grayson?"

"That's them."

"The bikers reported the shooting?"

"Naw. A doctor at a local hospital did. The sheriff come right out and one of the bikers let something

ip. Seems the wife of Sandoval is the sheriff's sister.
id you know that?"

Largo ignored that. "Did the sheriff arrest our peo-
le?"

"They're being questioned right now."

"Son of a bitch!"

"I thought you'd better know about this."

"Yeah. Thanks for calling. We'll finish up with Bar-
one soon as you get here and then get gone. Come
n."

"Be there in a few."

Mike was talking to Jenny, informing her of the
reaking situation just as Largo was being told.

"Hang on," Mike said. "Something else in coming
n on the scanner. Tell John about the money men
hile I listen to what's shaking right now."

Jenny told John about the shoot-out, ending with:
You think the muscle will back off now and head
ack to L.A.?"

"I rather doubt it. They were sent here to kill us.
My guess is they'll try to finish the job."

"Okay. Well, then let's make sure they stay right
ere," Jenny said, a mischievous smile curing her lips.

"As in shooting up their vehicles?"

"You read my mind, John."

"Suits me. Tell Mike to keep a close ear on that
canner and keep us informed."

"You don't want them to give us a hand?"

"It would take them an hour to get here. By that
ime I hope we'll be finished and heading back to the
notel for a cold martini and dinner."

"You mind if I have a beer instead?"

"If you insist."

The two of them waited on the ridge for the muscle to start something. And waited.

"What are they waiting on?" Jenny finally asked. "Reinforcements?"

"Probably. The last Caddy dropped back at our turnoff, remember?"

"They want a real odds-in-their-favor, don't they. Six to two isn't good enough for them."

"Well, let's start putting some holes in fancy cars. You ready?"

"Let's do it."

John and Jenny began shooting out tires and punching holes in the hoods of the cars. Both cars were disabled before the goons from L.A. were able to react. But by then it was too late. The tires on one side of each vehicle were flat, and the electrical systems of the cars were out of commission.

"You bastards!" Mabini shouted. "We'll get you for this."

Jenny shouted a long string of profanity right back at him, and John grimaced and then grinned at her vulgarity.

"I'm gonna spread your legs and give you something to remember me by, you bitch!" Carlos yelled.

"I doubt it, you needle dick!" Jenny called back.

"Needle dick!" Carlos exploded. "That does it. I'm gonna kill that bitch right now." He headed out, intending to flank the pair on the ridge.

"See him?" John asked.

"I see him."

"Get back here, Carlos!" Largo yelled.

But Carlos's manhood had been insulted and he was determined to avenge the slur. He didn't get far.

Jenny lined him up in the open sights and squeezed

e trigger. The .223 round hit Carlos in the right leg,
st above the knee, and knocked him down.

"Damn this shooting downhill," Jenny said. "I for-
t to compensate for that."

"Carlos!" Mabini yelled.

"I'm hit! Got me in the leg. But I'm not bleedin'
o bad. Don't try coming over here, boys. Too much
•en ground and that Barrone can shoot."

"That wasn't Barrone that shot you, needle dick,"
nny yelled. "That was me."

Carlos gritted his teeth as the shock of the bullet
ound began to wear off and the first waves of pain
t him.

"Give 'em a taste of lead!" Largo yelled. "Fire."

John and Jenny ducked down as the muscle a hun-
ed yards below them opened fire with automatic
:apons.

"Let's work our way to the sides of this ridge and
turn the fire," John said. "But be careful."

"Yes, sir. I'll sure do that. The same goes for you,
o."

"I'll try."

The goons were not very combat-smart. None of
em were watching their flanks. Jenny and John got
to position and opened fire on the two mob mem-
rs who were exposed just enough for a hit. Two
:nt down. One would never get to see L.A. again in
is life. Mabini took a round in the center of the
rehead, and his lights were turned out before he hit
e rocky ground. Sal took a .223 round in the shoul-
r that spun him around and dropped him to his
.ees.

"This ain't worth a shit, boys!" Largo called. "Sal's
en hit."

"Mabini's dead," Lucas said. "He took one right
the center of his forehead."

"Let's get outta here," Pizarro said.

"How, you dumb bastard?" Largo shouted. "W
don't have no wheels."

"Well . . ." Pizarro hesitated. "We can walk ou
can't we? Jesus, Largo, it's better than gettin' kille
ain't it?"

"We'll back off until Mills gets here," Largo to
his people. "Then we'll decide how we're gonna ha
dle this thing. At my signal, we'll go one at a tin
back up the road a few hundred yards. Zigzag ar
stay low until you reach that big pile of rocks up the
on the right. Everybody understand?"

"What about Sal and Carlos?" Lucas asked.

"They got to stay here and out of sight. We're n
gonna leave them."

"Who goes first?"

"Take off, Lucas. Then you, Pizarro. I'll cover yo
Move!"

"I'm gone," Lucas shouted, and took off runnin

Lucas zigged and zagged and hollered as bulle
howled and whined all around him. He someho
made it through the hail of lead from John and Jenr
and jumped behind the huge mound of rocks. Pizar
jumped up and began running and serpentining. Jol
and Jenny both fired and Pizarro went down, but n
for long. He crawled into a natural depression in th
earth and threw lead back to cover Largo's successf
escape.

"Three down and three got out," Jenny said, sli
ping a full thirty-round magazine into the belly of h
Mini-14. "They're out of range now."

"Except for the second one in that ditch, or wha
ever it is."

"He's hit, but not hard."

"And here comes the third Cadillac," John said. "Three men in it. What do you figure the range is?"

"About five hundred yards."

"And the .308 is in Don's SUV."

"Sure is."

"Well, the light's getting tricky anyway. Even if we had the .308, it would be a damn long shot with factory ammunition."

"I do have a sack full of grenades. If they get too close we can make it real interesting for them."

"Yes, we can."

"So we wait?"

"Yes. We've got food and water and plenty of ammo. And we have the high ground. We may spend a long cold night. But we're secure here. We'll wait it out."

"Ah . . . John?"

"What?"

"I have to pee."

THIRTY-FIVE

"How long have you been seeing these scummy bastards, sis?" Sheriff Morales asked his sister.

"My husband or the bikers?" she fired right back.

Morales stared at her for a moment, and then shook his head and sighed. "My people are out with the state boys and the Feds now, sis. Gathering evidence . . . and believe me, there is plenty to gather. This is no time for jokes."

"I haven't done a thing against the law, brother."

"That's bullshit and you know it. You have one chance and one chance only to stay out of the bucket. And that is to level with me all the way."

Morales's sister sighed heavily. "And if I say nothing?"

"I told you, sis. You'll go to trial. And when you're convicted, and you will be, you'll do hard time in the women's prison."

"I wouldn't like that."

"I told you how to avoid it."

"You can't make me testify against my husband."

"I know that. But you can testify against the others."

She laughed without humor. "Sort of a round-robin, huh, brother? Everybody testifies against everybody else."

"Something like that."

"Sounds messy to me."

"I won't lie to you. It's going to be."

"And that will keep me out of prison?"

"I've talked to the D.A. We can arrange probation
or you women, if you all testify."

"What do the others say?"

"They'll go along. You're the only holdout."

"You were saving me for last, hey?"

"You're like me in one respect, sis. You're hard-
eaded."

"Just in one respect, brother?"

Morales said nothing.

"Mr. Law and Order," she said contemptuously.
Mr. Do Things by the Book. You dumb prick!" she
shed out at him. "Don't you know your own kids
re using the products the bikers are manufacturing
nd bringing in?"

"I know it, sis."

"And you're going to book them?"

"The boy already has been booked."

"You're kidding!"

"Do you see me laughing?"

"You put your own son in this fucking crummy
il?"

"He's legally an adult, sis. Yes, I did."

"You're an asshole, *Sheriff!*"

"I enforce the law. Fairly and equally."

"Hooray for you."

"What's your answer?"

She looked at him. "You really would throw the
ok at me, wouldn't you?"

"Yes, I would."

"Okay, brother. What do you want me to do?"

Morales pushed a legal pad and ballpoint pen to-
ard her. "Write it all out, sis. From the beginning.
on't leave anything out. Take your time."

* * *

"I wonder what they're arguing about," Jenny said after viewing the muscle through long lenses. "They're sure in heated discussion about something."

"Whether to stay or go, probably," John said.

"You think they've heard the news about the mass arrests?"

"I would guess yes. Unless the police have arrested their sources in the various departments."

"They can't leave," Jenny said. "They've got two wounded buddies down there."

"You think they'd stay out of loyalty?"

Jenny shook her head. "No. I think they'd stay for fear their buddies would talk to the police and give them up."

"Then they might be talking about ways to shut their buddies' mouths?"

"That thought did occur to me."

"They can't come back to the base of this ridge to silence their buddies, and we can't get out," John said. "Impasse."

"But they can't afford the time to wait us out," Jenny countered. "Sheriffs Morales and Watson will be looking for us soon . . . if they're not already looking for us."

"Probably."

"I'm getting hungry, John."

"Have a candy bar."

"I'd rather have a cheeseburger and some fries."

"I imagine that's what Don is having about now."

"I hope he has one for me."

"I wonder just how widespread these arrests are?"

"I hope they're statewide," Jenny said. "So we can get the hell out of here and maybe get a nice easy assignment for our next op."

"You long for a nice easy assignment?"

"I long for a nice long hot bath and an icy cold beer."

John dug in his pocket and held out a Snickers bar. "Will you settle for this?"

"I didn't have any choice in the matter," the deputy told Sheriff Jimmi Watson. "The bikers threatened to kill my wife and kids if I didn't feed them information."

"And you believed they'd do it?"

"They showed me pictures of what they'd done to other people, Sheriff. I got so sick I puked down the front of my shirt."

"How do you know they were really the ones who did it?"

"Several of the bikers were in the pictures. Chink, Griz, Pisspot, and some others. I believed them, Sheriff. And you would have too."

"You're going to have to testify in court about this."

"I know it, and I will."

Jimmi pushed a legal pad and a ballpoint pen across the table. "Write it all down. Don't leave anything out. I want lots of names."

The deputy sighed and picked up the pen.

"I want to catch John Barrone and his people," the FBI agent told the ATF agent.

"We don't know where any of them are. They've changed credit cards. Probably using some sort of corporation card."

"I still want to know who gave the orders for us to

break off the chase this afternoon. I'm still pissed about that."

The ATF agent shrugged his shoulders. "My people don't know any more than your people. All we know for sure is that the orders were false."

"I know this much. Sheriffs Morales and Watson are picking up people all over the place, and for the most part we're being left out in the cold, looking stupid."

"All that will change when we find Barrone and his team."

"Depends on what they're doing when we find them," the FBI man said sourly. "That is, if we find them."

"Shit!" the AFT agent swore in frustration.

The FBI agent's cell phone rang and he answered it. "We found Barrone's team, Matt. They're in a motel in Los Alamos," said the man on the phone.

"Stay on top of them," Matt ordered. "I'm on the way."

"What?" the ATF man questioned.

"Barrone's team. They've been located. Come on."

"What the hell are we gonna do about Sal and Carlos?" Mills asked.

"I don't know!" Largo snapped at him. "I already told you that. I don't know."

"We can't just leave them," Reese said.

"Nobody's gonna leave them," Largo said. "For more than one reason," he added.

"Why's that?" Mills asked.

"You want the cops to sweat them, Mills?"

"Sal and Carlos wouldn't say nothin'!" Otwell said

"Don't be too sure about that," Largo told the men "They'd offer them a deal to keep them out of the bucket if they'd roll over on everybody, and then put them in the witness protection program."

"I couldn't stand no more prison," Otwell said with a shudder. "All the time fightin' off them goddamn fags. Ain't nobody sendin' me back to prison."

"Me neither," Lucas said.

"I'm with you guys," Pizarro said. "I ain't going back to prison."

"Then we'd better quicklike decide what we're gonna do about Sal and Carlos," Largo told his men.

"Maybe if we stick around long enough, they'll bleed to death and we won't have to do nothin'," Otwell suggested.

"That is a thought," Lucas said.

"We don't have that much time," Largo said. "We got to do something within the hour and get gone from here."

"What about the cars?" Mills asked.

"If we can ice Barrone and that cunt with him, we'll torch the cars and then cut out," Largo said.

"And if we can't take Barrone and the woman?" Pizarro asked, then spread his hands. "Hey, somebody had to ask it."

Largo cleared his throat and then met the eyes of his men. "We'll kill Carlos and Sal and get the hell gone from here."

"Poor Sal and Carlos," Otwell said woefully as he took off his cowboy hat. "They was good guys."

The teams of federal agents that converged on the motel where John's team was staying had been advised to do so very carefully and to deal with the team members politely. The Feds followed orders and much to their surprise, found no illegal firearms in the rooms or the vehicles of the men and women. They found several hunting rifles in .308 caliber, several Ruger Mini-14s, half a dozen pistols of various makes and models (the team members were all legally licensed to carry), and a lot of ammunition. However, had they checked at a ministorage place on the other side of town, the Feds might well have gone into shock.

"Where is John Barrone?" one of the Feds asked.

"Gone sightseeing," Don informed them. "Said he'd see us in the morning."

"There was a woman with him," another Fed said.

"Is that illegal?" Don asked.

"Let's go," the chief of the federal detail told his people. "We're wasting time here."

"What the hell is going on?" several of his people asked, standing outside the motel on the parking lot.

"I just got the word to back off of Barrone's people. So we're backing off."

"The word an hour ago was to nail Barrone and his team!"

"We have new orders and you just heard them. It's over. Let's go."

Sheriffs Morales and Watson walked into the interview room and looked at three of the men sitting at a long table. Grayson, Sandoval, and Curtis were all sober and had become very belligerent.

Nick Sandoval glared up at his brother-in-law. "You're going to pay through the nose for this, buddy. When my lawyer gets through with you, by God, you're—"

"Shut up, Nick," his attorney told him. "Just keep your mouth closed and let me handle this."

"You ready to talk about this situation?" Jimmi asked the lawyer.

"Possibly," the attorney said.

Morales motioned to a deputy, and the deputy opened the door and waved the county D.A. into the room. The D.A. sat down at the table and opened her briefcase. She smiled at the lawyers representing the three soon-to-be defendants.

Before she could speak, Curtis blurted out, "Don't believe anything that damn wife of mine says. She's a lying bitch."

"Shut up, Dave," his attorney warned him.

"I've already spoken with her attorney," the D.A. said. "And the attorneys representing the other women involved."

"They're all lying bitches!" Sandoval said.

"Shut up, Nick!" his attorney yelled.

"Let's review the charges against you three men," the D.A. said. "Murder, attempted murder, assault with a deadly weapon, kidnapping, the manufacturing and distribution of illegal drugs, torture, extortion, rape . . ." She looked at the lawyers representing the three men. "You really want me to go on? The list is very long."

"I ain't done jack-shit!" Sandoval yelled. "And you can't prove any of those things you just named."

"Let's talk about a deal," the three attorneys said as one.

The D.A smiled. "Oh, let's do that."

THIRTY-SIX

"Sal, Carlos!" Largo yelled. "We're gonna get you out of this mess. Okay?"

"Yeah!" Carlos yelled. "How?"

"We'll give you cover fire; keep Barrone and the cunt pinned down. You run to the two cars. You catch your breath there. Then we'll give you more cover fire while you make it out of range. Okay?"

"Okay, Largo," Carlos. "But I'm hit in the leg. I'm gonna be movin' slow."

"That's okay. We'll give you all the cover you need."

"Sounds good. You ready?"

"Yeah. Soon as you hear us fire, you come on."

"We're sittin' on ready," Sal yelled.

"Go!" Largo yelled, and the muscle opened fire on the ridge.

The range was long, but John and Jenny ducked down and let the lead whine and howl, with most of it coming nowhere close to them.

"Go, boys!" Largo shouted. "Go!"

"We going to let them make it, John?" Jenny asked.

"They're not going to make it, Jenny. I'll bet you a steak dinner on that."

"They're almost halfway home now."

"Gunshot wounds have to be reported by the attending doctor, Jenny. And both those men have lead in them."

"You think—"

She never finished the sentence. Another hard volley of shots came from the L.A. muscle. But none of it reached the ridge. Jenny chanced a quick look over the top. Carlos and Sal were sprawled facedown on the road.

John was lighting one of his rare cigarettes. "What is it, Jenny?"

"So much for loyalty. They're dead."

"We'll see you around, Barrone!" Largo yelled.

"Bet on it!" John yelled back.

The men piled into the one car and pulled out in a shower of rocks and dirt.

"Think we'll see them again, John?"

"Oh, yes. For a certainty. You bring the SUV round, Jenny. I'm going to walk down and take a look at the dead."

"Have fun."

Sal, Carlos, and Mabini were dead. John left them where death had touched them and waited in the roadbed for Jenny.

"Another totally screwed-up operation," Jenny said as John got into the SUV on the passenger side.

"And it's just about over," John added as she headed out.

She glanced at him. "Are you kidding? You're forgetting there are still dozens of bikers to deal with."

"Oh, I haven't forgotten, Jenny. But the dope business, in this part of the state anyway, is in shambles. Vergano is on the run, if he isn't dead. By this time I would imagine Sandoval, Curtis, and Grayson have been named in several indictments. And Sheriff Jimmi Watson has reported back to Control about us."

"You still think she works for Control?"

"Oh, yes. I sure do. Control has law enforcement people on the payroll all over the United States."

"I guess so. Then you think this op is all but wrapped up?"

"Yes, I do."

"What about the dead men we left back there, John?"

"Carrion will take care of them quickly. The cars will be stripped clean in a few days. Nothing left but the shell." John picked up a cell phone and called Don. He listened for a few minutes, then punched the end button.

"What?" Jenny asked.

"The Feds visited the team at the motel. They were very polite and left rather suddenly. None of our people were pulled in for further questioning."

"Interesting. Nothing said about the weapons or explosives?"

"The team stored all that at a ministorage place before checking in."

"So what do we do now?"

"Take a hot bath, get something to eat, and get a good night's sleep."

Every newspaper on the stands the next morning carried the story; every radio and TV newscast put out every detail they could dig up.

"I like this one," Linda said, reading a newspaper headline. "Prominent New Mexico businessmen conduct drunken raid on wives' love nest."

"How about this one?" Don put in. "Heavily armed drunken husbands in a jealous rage attack bikers."

John was sitting in a chair in the suite, relaxing and

working on his second cup of coffee. Room service would be bringing breakfast in a few minutes.

"Where's our next assignment, John?" Paul asked.

"I don't know. Let's finish this one first."

"Jenny was saying you didn't think this one was over," Mike said. "What's left?"

"The hoods from L.A."

"You think they'll still come after us?"

"I do, and they will. And don't forget about forty or so very irritated bikers still on the loose. You can bet they haven't forgotten us."

"Yes, but there are warrants out for all of them," Don said. "They're all running from the law."

"The bikers are survivors," Bob Garrett reminded them all. "Don't ever forget that. And most of them are not nearly as dumb as they look. They're quick and crafty as well as mean. I would suggest we all keep that in mind until we're sure this is over."

"And a lot of them know this country and believe it or not, they have friends all over the place," John said. "People who will hide and protect them. This is not over yet. So stay alert."

A knock on the door interrupted the conversation. "Room service," a man's voice called.

"I'll open the door," Mike said.

"Good," Don said. "I'm hungry. Starving."

"I never knew you when you weren't," Jenny said.

Mike opened the door and got a food cart slammed against him. Two big men came rushing in, guns in their hands.

Mike managed to trip one of the men, who fell against his partner. Paul grabbed the gun out of the hand of the man Mike tripped, while Jenny and Linda tackled the one still standing. Before he could bring his pistol to bear on John, Linda kicked him hard on the knee and he went down. Jenny stomped hard on the back of the man's neck with her foot, and he suddenly went limp on the floor.

"Damn, I think I broke his neck," Jenny said.

Don knelt down and felt for a pulse. He found one, strong and steady. "Nope. He appears to be okay. His breathing is all right. He's just out."

"Anyone recognize either of them?" John asked.

No one did.

Paul jerked the conscious attacker to his feet. "You have anything to say, asshole?"

"Yeah. Fuck you!"

"Quite a conversationalist," Jenny said. "Harvard-educated, I'm sure."

"Fuck you too!" the man said.

"Perhaps Yale," Linda said.

"Get that food cart out of here and down the hall," John ordered. "Our breakfast will be here any moment. Let's get the other jerk on a bed and cover him up." He turned to the second attacker. "You open your mouth while the room service man is here and you'll never see another sunrise. Understood?"

"Yeah."

The breakfast cart was delivered without incident. As soon as the door closed behind the hotel employee, John said, "Let's check the I.D.s of these two, then we'll decide what to do."

"Motorcycle endorsements on both driver's licenses," Linda said after inspecting the wallets of the pair.

"I thought as much. All right. Let's have breakfast and then we'll clear out."

"What the hell are you goin' to do with us?" the biker that Jenny had knocked out asked. He was sitting on the side of the bed, rubbing his sore neck.

"I'm sure we'll think of something," John told him.
Now just sit there and behave and keep your mouth
closed."

A half hour later, the bikers were dumped by the
side of the road outside town.

"If you're smart," John told them, "you'll get the
hell out of here as quickly as possible. If I ever see
either of you again, I'll kill you without hesitation.
Understood?"

"You're just turnin' us loose? That's it?"

"That's it."

"We're gone, Barrone," the other one said. "This
deal is all screwed up around here anyways. But you'll
see us again. Another time, another place."

"Your choice, your funeral," John told him.

Back on the road, John used his cell phone to call
Sheriff Morales. "I just wanted to tell you we'll be
clearing out of your area, Sheriff."

"I can't tell you what a thrill that is," Morales replied.

"Are you about to wrap things up?"

"Are you kidding?" Morales asked. "It'll take us a
month to sort all this crap out."

"Hopefully, the hoods from L.A. will follow us out
of your jurisdiction. I can't tell about the bikers."

"I would ask where you're going, but you'd just tell
me a lie, wouldn't you, Barrone?"

"I don't know where we're going, Sheriff. And that
the truth. Believe it or not."

"I don't. I'm just glad you're leaving."

"Have fun, Sheriff. It's been a pleasure knowing
you."

"Strangely enough, Barrone, I feel the same about
you. But I sincerely hope I never see you again."

John laughed and broke the connection.

Jenny was talking on her cell phone. "John, Do
just spotted the L.A muscle. He gave them the finge
a couple of times and stuck his tongue out at ther
and they're following him. He's leading them int
the country. I've got his route."

"Advise the others and tell Don we're on the way.

"Keep going on this highway," Jenny said. "Ou
turnoff will be to the right in about four miles."

John smiled and reached for his cell phone.

"What now?" Jenny asked.

"I'm going to do this by the book, Jenny. I'm callin
Morales and Watson. You tell Don to lead them int
one of their counties."

"Oh, this is going to please both the sheriffs. Yo
know those hired hoods will be armed with automati
weapons. And I seriously doubt if they have license
for them."

John informed Don what they were doing, and Do
got a good laugh out of it. "Will do, John. See yo
in a little bit."

"Why so generous all of a sudden, John?" Jenn
asked.

"Too many bodies in their counties, Jenny. Let
ease up a bit."

"Sure suits me."

Then John called Morales, and John and Jenny bot
laughed at what Morales said over the speaker phon
"Thanks, John. I'll notify Sheriff Watson and we'
have more cops there than those so-called tough boy
have ever seen. Will you be there to see it?"

"I think not, Sheriff. This is your play. Have fun.'

"I assure you, I will. I'm going to enjoy this."

THIRTY-SEVEN

"We gotta get the hell gone from here, boys," Griz told a gathering of bikers. "And I mean, like right now."

"We ain't got enough vans and trucks to haul all the Hogs, man!" Chink told him.

"Then ride the goddamn things out. Shit! Whatever works. But move!"

"How about the guys who joined us the other day?"

"They got a choice. They can either ride out with us or they're on their own. I don't give a big rat's ass which way that plays. It's save-your-own-ass time now. Goddamn, do I have to explain that, Chink?"

"No." He turned, then paused and looked at Griz. "But I'm stuffin' my saddlebags full of pills."

"Good idea. Tell the others to do the same. We'll ride out of here with a damn fortune in pills. Good thinkin', Chink."

"Where do we link up?" another biker asked.

Griz gave that a few seconds' thought. "There ain't no easy route outta here. We'll head south until we hit the interstate, then cut west. That's the best I can tell you."

"That's good enough. I'll pass the word."

"Be ready to roll in fifteen minutes," Griz said.

"We'll be ready."

"No guns," Griz ordered. "If we're stopped by the cops, let's be legal all the way."

"With five thousand pills in our saddlebags?" Pinhead asked. "That don't make no sense, Griz."

"Suit yourself," Griz replied. "As for me, I ain't carryin' no guns. You do whatever the hell you wanna do."

"I'm packin' some heat," Pinhead said. "Cops ain't takin' me without a fight."

Griz shrugged. "Your funeral."

A few minutes later the bikers were on the road.

A few miles away, the muscle from L.A.—Largo, Lucas, and Pizarro in the Cadillac, Mills, Otwell, and Reese in a rented car—rounded a curve in the road and drove up to a roadblock.

"Good God!" Lucas said. "Look at all the cops."

"Stay cool," Largo said. "They're not looking for us. They don't know who we are. They don't have no reason to stop us."

"Then why do they all have their guns pointed at us?" Pizarro asked.

"I think we're fucked," Lucas announced.

Sheriff Morales and Sheriff Watson strolled up the Caddy. "Hello, boys." Morales grinned at them. "Nice day, isn't it?"

"Sure is, officer," Largo replied. "What's going on here? You folks hunting some desperadoes?"

"No," Jimmi said. "We found them."

"Oh?" Largo said.

Morales waved a piece of paper at Largo. "This is a search warrant, pal. Get out of the car and do so very carefully."

"We're fucked," Lucas repeated.

* * *

"What the hell is all that?" Hook asked, pulling up beside Griz and Chink. The three of them sat their Hogs at the top of the hill and stared at the sight below them.

"There must be five or six hundred motorcycles down there!" Chink said. "All kinds of bikes."

"From Hogs to Hondas and everything you can name that's in between," Griz said. "What the hell is goin' on around here?"

Big Hurt and Hammer rode up and sat and stared. "Jesus," Hammer said. "What is it, a damn convention?"

"I don't know," Griz said. "But whatever it is, I don't like it."

Big Train rode up. "Griz!" he yelled. "You gotta see this. They's three or four hundred bikers blockin' the road."

"I know, Big. You idiot. I can see them right down here."

"Not them, Griz," Big Train said. "Behind us. Come look."

Griz and Chink rode back through the dozens of bikers, some of them in trucks and vans, most of them straddling Hogs. At the end of the column, they sat and stared in disbelief.

"Holy shit!" Griz muttered.

"There's as many back here as there is in front of us," Chink said.

"How do we get through them?" Big Train asked.

"We don't," Griz said softly, his words just audible over the grumbling of his engine.

"What do you mean, we don't?"

"There's about forty of us, Big. Must be eight hundred to a thousand of them. Have you got any idea how we could get through that mob down there?"

Fussbucket walked up. "Some of them folks got guns down there," he announced. "And Pretty Boy was listened to the CB in his van. These roads has been blocked off at both ends. 'Bout a mile or so back, each end."

"Where's the damn cops when you need them?" Griz asked.

"Nowhere around here," Fussbucket said. "Some disc jockey on the radio is flappin' his mouth 'bout the candy riders has had enough of bein' tarred with the same brush as us outlaw riders. They's gonna take the law in their own hands and settle this thing once and for all."

"Settle it how?" Chink asked.

"I don't know."

"Hell," Chink said. "Them's weekend riders down there. Lawyers and store clerks and shit like that. They ain't nothin' we can't handle."

"A thousand of 'em?" Big Train asked. "You been smokin' our own product again, Chink?"

"I'll ask again," Griz said. "Where are the damn cops?"

"They ain't gonna show up," Pretty Boy said, walking up. "Not for about an hour or so. They're diverting traffic away from this area."

"How do you know that?"

"It just come on the radio."

"Shit!" Griz said.

"What are we gonna do, Griz?" Big Train asked.

Griz shook his head. "Damned if I know."

John and Jenny were sitting in a truck stop having a cup of coffee. John had told Don and the others to go on ahead; they would link up down the road. This assignment was over.

"We really didn't do all that much," Jenny said. "We just brought it to a head, that's all."

"Sometimes that's all it takes."

Jenny toyed with her coffee cup for a moment. "You know, John, it's going to come to a head in this entire country one of these days."

"I won't argue that. But when it does, let's just make damn sure we're on the right side."

"We already are."

"Oh?" Then he smiled. "The *right* side. Cute, Jenny. Very cute."

THIRTY-EIGHT

"Them damn candy-assed bikers is movin' toward us, Griz!" Pretty boy said. "What the hell are we gonna do?"

"Run," Griz said. "Run for your lives." With that said, Griz left his Hog in the middle of the road and took off on foot, heading for the hills. Chink was right behind him, and about fifty civilian bikers were chasing them, several of them armed with long cattle prods.

The outlaw bikers were outnumbered about thirty to one. Most did not offer any resistance. When approached by the mob of mostly baseball-bat-wielding and law-abiding bikers, they shook their heads and put their hands in the air. Those who did try to fight were quickly beaten into submission.

A mile away, both east and west, state police rerouted traffic onto alternative routes and did their best to hide their smiles.

"Whoooa! Shit!" Chink hollered as the man behind him touched him on the butt with the cattle prod. Chink jumped about a foot into the air and when he touched down on earth, really started pickin' 'em up and puttin' 'em down.

The man behind Griz poked him in the butt with

a cattle prod and hit the juice. *"Wow! Oh, shit!"* Griz yelled.

"Run, Griz!" Chink yelled.

"I am runnin'," Griz hollered. "Fast as I can!"

Griz was hit again by the cattle prod.

"Goddamn!" he yelled, and jumped. "I give up!" he hollered, sliding to a stop. "I've had it. No more of this."

Chink continued running. The man behind him poked him again with the cattle prod. *"Whooo!"* Chink squalled.

More concerned with the pain in his butt than his direction of travel, Chink ran into a tree and knocked himself goofy. He was trussed up with rope, hands and feet, and dumped unceremoniously and nearly unconscious beside Griz.

Griz sat on the ground and cussed.

Minutes later, the state police moved in, rounding up what remained of the outlaw bikers and the fracas was over as quickly as it began. The civilian bikers went home; the outlaw bikers were taken to jail.

Jenny answered the cell phone, listened for a moment, then laid the phone aside. "We have our next assignment, sort of."

"Sort of?"

"Control said to head for southern California. Said to call in when we reached Los Angeles."

"We don't get a vacation?" John asked with a smile.

"I guess not. John?"

"Yes, Jenny?"

"Stop at the next gas station, will you?"

John sighed.

William W. Johnstone
The *Mountain Man* Series

The Wingman Series
By Mack Maloney

__#1 **Wingman**	0-7860-0310-3	$4.99US/$6.50CAN
__#2 **The Circle War**	0-7860-0346-4	$4.99US/$6.50CAN
__#3 **The Lucifer Crusade**	0-7860-0388-X	$4.99US/$6.50CAN
__#4 **Thunder in the East**	0-7860-0428-2	$4.99US/$6.50CAN
__#5 **The Twisted Cross**	0-7860-0467-3	$4.99US/$6.50CAN
__#6 **The Final Storm**	0-7860-0505-X	$4.99US/$6.50CAN
__#7 **Freedom Express**	0-7860-0548-3	$4.99US/$6.50CAN
__#8 **Skyfire**	0-7860-0605-6	$4.99US/$6.50CAN
__#9 **Return from the Inferno**	0-7860-0645-5	$4.99US/$6.50CAN
__#12 **Target: Point Zero**	0-7860-0299-9	$4.99US/$6.50CAN
__#13 **Death Orbit**	0-7860-0357-X	$4.99US/$6.50CAN
__#15 **Return of the Sky Ghost**	0-7860-0510-6	$4.99US/$6.50CAN

Call toll free **1-888-345-BOOK** to order by phone or use this coupon to order by mail.

Name _____

Address _____

City _____ State _____ Zip _____

Please send me the books I have checked above.

I am enclosing	$_____
Plus postage and handling*	$_____
Sales tax (in New York and Tennessee only)	$_____
Total amount enclosed	$_____

*Add $2.50 for the first book and $.50 for each additional book.
Send check or Money order (no cash or CODs) to:
Kensington Publishing Corp., 850 Third Avenue, New York, NY 10022
Prices and Numbers subject to change without notice.
All orders subject to availability.
Check out our website at **www.kensingtonbooks.com**